Thou Shalt Not

Thou Shalt Not

by

Anne Gumley

Order this book online at www.trafford.com
or email orders@trafford.com

Most Trafford titles are also available at major online book retailers.

Printed in the United States of America.

ISBN: 978-1-4269-4319-5 (sc)
ISBN: 978-1-4269-4320-1 (hc)
ISBN: 978-1-4269-4321-8 (e)

Library of Congress Control Number: 2010913508

*Our mission is to efficiently provide the world's finest, most comprehensive book publishing
service, enabling every author to experience success. To find out how to publish your
book, your way, and have it available worldwide, visit us online at www.trafford.com*

Trafford rev. 09/29/2010

 www.trafford.com

North America & international
toll-free: 1 888 232 4444 (USA & Canada)
phone: 250 383 6864 ♦ fax: 812 355 4082

For Phillip

Chapter 1

'Are you sure you are all right Mam?' Gina's anxious voice floated up the narrow staircase. She stood poised, one foot on the bottom step ready to sprint up the rest if needed. She waited patiently for an answer, her knuckles whitening as her hand clutched the stair rail.

'Mam,' she yelled louder, this time irritation beginning to creep into her voice. She glanced at her wristwatch, the hands indicating ten minutes to ten. Tears welled up in her eyes. It wasn't fair, nothing ever worked out like she dreamed it would. Couldn't God be on her side just for once, tonight of all nights?

A shaft of light from the top of the stairs sent a ribbon of gold along the dingy wallpaper of the stairwell. A door creaked, and then the echo of worn floorboards sounded under an unsteady movement followed by a slurred voice.

'For God's sake girl, leave me alone.'

The sound of bedsprings and a clink of glass followed.

A sense of relief flooded through Gina. She drew in a deep breath and exhaled slowly. Her mam would be out for the count soon: snoring her head off before awakening with a disabling headache and vomiting up the contents of her evening's binge.

By that time, Gina knew she wouldn't be missed. She grabbed her thin anorak that was balancing precariously on top of a variety of coats slung over an equally precarious wooden peg. Pulling the front door of the cottage quietly to behind her so her mam wouldn't hear her leaving, she made her way along the paved path to the broken gate. This she didn't have to open or shut for it had stood half open not moving one way or the other for as long as she could remember.

She had locked the front door behind her, the feel of the cold key in her pocket giving her a sense of control for the first time in her life. Tonight she wasn't going to find a locked door awaiting her and the inevitable long hours she would have to spend curled up in the old shed at the back of the house. At this very moment her father would be miles away, driving the big transport lorry up the M6 to Scotland. A momentary vision of the lorry overturned with ambulances flashing lights arriving at the scene brought a faint smile to her pale face, but then quickly changed into one of utter determination. Her step quickened, the night's darkness was closing in. Overhead the cry of a kestrel was heard. Gina looked up and watched the dark shadow circling before pouncing on its prey. She shuddered, the feeling of vulnerability possessing her frail body.

Suddenly her foot felt a slight impact. She'd caught the toe of her shoe on a stone that had worked loose from the pavement. Stopping by a lamp and examining the damage, she cringed. The leather of her shoe showed a long well defined grey scrape.

Gina's mind began to tumble out wild excuses she would have to make up for the mishap. The familiar hard knot gripped her stomach as she foresaw the inevitable consequences that would surely follow. At that moment she would have heartily welcomed the shouting and beating that usually transpired. It was the other thing that she so greatly feared. It always began in silence, a type of stillness that would hang in the air as if the whole world has ceased to be, apart from the rhythmic ticking of the clock pounding out each second.

Her father would then break the atmosphere by a stepping forward, often followed by a weak protest from her mam that always seemed to fade away into thin air. A thick calloused hand would swing her around in the direction of the stairs whilst a finger would be poked continuously into her back pushing her forward until she reached the door of her bedroom.

Sometimes she would have difficulty turning the cold brass handle: then his head would bend against her neck as his finger closed over hers. She could feel the excited rising and falling of his chest and the stale air from the half opened mouth; the rub of hardness against her buttocks, then the rapid push onto her bed.

Only once had her mam come to her aid. Gina had been about six at the time and didn't know what was happening until her father's cuddling had grown violent and hurtful. Then she had screamed and screamed as her tortured body was being abused. Gasping for breath under his heavy weight, she'd glimpsed her mam's ashen face standing in the doorway. Then the next moment hands and curses began raining down in fury upon her father's back before his weight shifted.

Next, blood had poured through the fingers from her mam's broken nose and splattered over her pillow. She remained curled up into a foetal position, pulling the blood stained pillow over her head in a vain attempt to hide her naked body and shame.

Her mam had changed from that day on, and for the next seven years there had been a distance between them. Gina suffering from shame and guilt, while her mam made the gin bottle her constant companion. Occasionally, but very briefly, Gina thought she saw pity in her mam's eyes but it always vanished before any approach could be made.

The physical beatings that produced bruises had stopped the day she told her parents that a local social worker had talked to her. Fear had swept over her father's face and her mam looked nervous and agitated, to be followed by relief only when she said she'd told the social worker she was fine. What Gina hadn't stated was that she was terrified of her classmates calling her a whore or tart like her father said she was. She'd tried so hard not to appear as a temptress or harlot. It was something bad she had to hide.

The sound of a car approaching brought Gina's mind back to the present. The car passed, its dipped headlights picking out the structure of the old stone wall that flanked the churchyard on the opposite side of the road. There was no pavement on that side, nor had there ever been one. In fact there was never likely to be one unless the only pub in the village was pulled down.

Gina was approaching the parking lot entrance of the Horseshoe Inn, which was adjacent to the pavement. She stopped to allow a couple of cars to drive through. The door at the side of the pub was open; the warm yellow glow playing over the faces of a couple of locals shouting their goodbyes.

She pulled up her hood, looked one way then the other before crossing the road, having no wish to be seen. Walking as close to the church wall as possible, she could smell the lichen that had spread over the centuries-old stones. Sometimes ivy would touch her face. She pulled her hood down further, her eyes searching for the opening in the high wall.

With a sigh she stopped at the almost hidden entrance. Turning into it she started to climb the four uneven stone slabs that led to the north side of the church. In the daylight she would have been able to look down on the road and pub quite clearly for the churchyard was on higher ground. As it was, only the thin light of the pub's lantern by the parking lot could be seen and a few pinpoints of light from the windows of the cottages further afield.

The path ahead of her was covered by a grey hazy mantle of mist with various shapes of gravestones appearing on both sides beside her. Gina stopped, her heart was now beating fast and her legs felt weak. Normally she would never have had the courage to enter the churchyard at night, not even through the front gates. Above could be seen the dark square of the Gelsby church tower that thrust its tall spire to the heavens, spiking the watery moon as it broke through the clouds.

'Just keep to the path,' Gina told herself; her strength and courage coming from the hope of the help to come. She would brave anything to be normal and not feel so guilty all the time. Under her feet some very old gravestones had been laid flat to form the path. Here and there moss had taken hold, leaving parts of the path quite slippery. The Grenville's canopied tomb reared out of the mist, the stone figures it covered beneath lying silent in their vigil, as they had for over five hundred years.

Gina kept her eyes trained ahead looking for the old yew tree that she knew straddled the pathway. A tree so old it predated Edward the Third's Act of Parliament that required all churchyards to be planted with yews to provide wood for the bows of medieval archers. In truth this particular tree's function had its origin further back in time; more to the pagan belief of the planting of yew trees to keep away evil spirits. But none of this mattered to Gina whose interest in history proved nil. Her only interest in the tree tonight was the person she would be meeting under it. At last the giant leaning trunk of the old yew came into view. It had long since split itself almost in half and was propped up by a man-made structure to form an archway, the branches still producing thick foliage.

From the centre of the archway a figure stepped forward. Gina's relief stopped short of any utterance, as a hand was put to the figure's mouth in a gesture of silence; then a finger curled towards her beckoning her forward.

No words were spoken as the two walked single file towards the north wall of the church. The leader halted before a heavily studded Norman door in the wall of the church and an iron key was inserted into the lock. Gina stood hypnotised by the shadows on the gargoyles that were carved either side of the weather beaten archway. The key turned and the door swung open. It groaned and creaked with the movement.

Inside it was pitch black as the door closed behind them. Gina felt the first twinge of real panic. She could smell the cold dampness of age; visions of being encased in a tomb flooded her imagination. The fear gradually subsided for within seconds there was the tiny glow from a lighted match, which increased as it lit a candle.

It took a while for Gina to get her bearings. She'd only ever entered the church from the great west door and that had been with the school. She usually sat right at the back and was always very glad when the service was over. No matter how hard she prayed, the God they talked of never helped her, even though she'd prayed until her knees were hurting and sore.

As her companion moved so did the only light present, revealing rough stone walls, the facing one having black vestments hanging from it. The glow remained steady for a while. A table stood by the door; hymnbooks were piled on top, a pencil with a string attached hung down, its point dangling against the table leg.

Cautiously she followed the movement of her companion, catching a glimpse of another wall. This one had been plastered and adorned with red, gold and brown lettering, chipping off in places. It looked like old writing but she didn't have time to read for a soft voice commanded her to sit down. The only thing she could see was a stool.

She sat.

'You know you are a daughter of Eve, don't you.' A thin voice asked.

Gina looked at the face that was in half shadow bearing down over her. It was no longer kind and understanding but hard and stiff.

'Who is Eve?' For a quick second Gina thought she was about to gain knowledge that she was adopted. She straightened her back, unsure to where this line of questioning was going

'Eve…the temptress of Adam.' The voice sounding irritated as if it wished to get the moment over.

'Oh yes, of course I know about Adam and Eve,' Gina couldn't stop her own voice rising. She hoped she wasn't in for one of her friend's religious speeches. Some of it was nice enough but sometimes it made her feel worse than ever.

'You can be cleansed you know,' the lips on the zealous face moving as the candle flickered.

'Cleansed of what?' Gina didn't much like the tone this conversation was taking; and what about those promises of a new life and a new home.

'Cleansed of sin'!

Gina blushed and hung her head.

'What do I have to do?' At that moment shivering had taken an involuntary hold over her legs. It was getting colder and her anorak was so thin.

'Confess!' Now there was a sense of urgency in the tone of her interrogator's voice.

'Confess what?' Gina was finding it hard to speak as her throat became dry and tight with mounting apprehension and anxiety.

'Confess you have tempted your own father to lie with you.' The pitch grew stronger and threatening. 'Make clean your vile ways, before coming before Almighty God.' Gina stared into darkness as the standing figure moved. Bile rose in her stomach bringing with it an acid taste. She didn't understand what was happening or what was expected of her. She was so cold and her whole body was shaking now. She would say anything to get outside again. She didn't want to be here any longer. This was not the way she had been led to believe that help would be forthcoming. Terrified now, all the things her father said about her came tumbling out.

'Yes, yes, I'm all those things my father calls me. It's my fault not his. I was born a slut.' A sob broke out that she couldn't contain. It came out suddenly at that moment. That is what she now believed. Best get it over she thought, and then she could be saved. Her interrogator moved quickly and as the light moved too, it left a dark void.

Something rough touched Gina's forehead; she felt it graze against her cold skin, but her hands were not quick enough to stop it tightening around her throat. It cut into her flesh taking away her breath and leaving a pounding in her ears. Her head felt as if it would explode. Then everything was falling away; her whole being sliding into oblivion, all sense of herself falling into blackness.

The figure that stood behind Gina's slumped body let a feeling of exhilaration sweep through throbbing veins, before lifting the deadweight and carrying it to the door.

Nothing was left to chance. Every carefully planned detail was checked and rechecked before closing the door and stepping outside.

The gargoyles maintained one more secret in cold silence, as they had done for centuries, and an owl hooted in the distance.

The mist had thickened. Villagers had long closed their windows against the damp night air and most were asleep. Once the pubs had closed and the last programs on TV watched, there was little else to do in Gelsby.

Gina's mother tossed and turned; too fragile to get up and too weary to bother whether her daughter was safely in bed.

One other lay awake that night, savouring the emotions that would have proved too disturbing for the average person.

Chapter 2

The same morning sunlight that dappled the Gelsby village green, played hide and seek through the canopy of trees in the neighbouring town park. In the park itself a game of bowls was in progress as Ernest Heath strolled along the narrow path that skirted the local bowling club. The sudden movement of a rolling bowl caught his attention as it travelled towards him, missing the jack by a yard or so before it stopped.

Ernest slowed his usual measured pace and stopped to watch the game; subconsciously taking up the stance that gave clues to his profession. Legs spaced apart; hands clasped behind an erect back gave odds to either the military or the police force. Both assumptions would have been correct, although the first was nothing more than two years of compulsory National Service spent in the army. Most of the credit had to be given to the police force that moulded him into becoming the man he was; from an insecure young constable to Detective Inspector of the Cheshire Force.

Now in his sixties, Ernest still cut a fine figure that could be attested to by the furtive glances that came his way from the ladies bowling team. Although his hair was thinning and receding a little, what remained was steel grey and wavy giving it body. Thick dark eyebrows sheltered brooding eyes that gave little information away to what he was thinking. Half an inch over six feet with wide shoulders and a chest to match left the impression of an unstoppable individual that had intimidated many a villain over the years. If nearer to him, the ladies of the bowling team would have been more wary, as a permanent scowl was not offering any invites. Yet those that were allowed in were often rewarded by a wide and genuine smile; tipped slightly to the left and showing a set of teeth that defied the lack of calcium during his childhood war years.

Ernest watched as the next bowl arced towards the jack, colliding with the two opponent's bowls, knocking them both out of the way and into the gutter. Memories of games of marbles in the schoolyard floated through his mind.

Moving on, he followed the path around the back of the clubhouse to where the river flowed as it cut through the park from the west side of the town. The path stretched out before him, river on one side flanked by iron railings to keep any one from falling in the often-flooded water, and the park on the other. Here and there a seat was placed with a brass plaque honouring some long forgotten donor.

Ernest's hands remained clasped behind him, a shade too tightly gripped perhaps, but it stopped him from reaching into his pocket to retrieve the packet of cigarettes he was trying to ignore. There was hardly anyone around, apart from a young mother pushing a stroller; in it a wide-eyed youngster trailing a bucket and spade over the side making a rattling sound. Ernest heard the mother say she'd throw the damned things into the river if he didn't stop. He grinned at her as he passed, but received only an indifferent look in return.

On one of the seats a hippie lay fast asleep; his long hair flowing over his knapsack, both badly needing a wash. At his feet lay a crunched up Coca-Cola tin. Ernest bent down and placed the offending tin in the trash bin. He met no one else, and even the birds seemed to have lost their usual twittering. A slight breeze picked up, rustling the long grass by the river. A water hen called, then again the quietness.

'It's very quiet for…' Ernest pondered, then panicked momentarily when he couldn't remember whether it was Tuesday or Wednesday, before the memory of buying fresh eggs from the milkman caused him to relax. Fresh eggs could only be bought on Wednesday. This lack of knowing what day of the week it was had happened before, the trouble being he had no reference now that he was retired. For some people the week started or ended with going to church or work. Ernest had no desire for the first, remembering his difficult years attending a church school. He was always singled out for not memorising his Catechism or the other doctrines that were rammed down his throat. He wasn't about to attend church just to begin a week. As for work, he was resigned now to the fact he no longer had an office or a position.

Ernest sighed as he sat down on a seat that looked as lonely as he was. He leaned back stretching out his arms and legs before crossing his ankles. Good resolutions fading, he dug deep into his jacket pocket pulling out a battered cigarette packet. A slightly bent cigarette was slipped between his lips for a full two minutes before a lighter was produced and clicked into life. Drawing on the damaged cigarette and inhaling proved difficult between bouts of coughing. He quickly reduced the cigarette to a stub end that was dispatched to the ground only to end up under his well-polished size twelve shoe.

Ernest leaned forward, cupping his head between his large hands and staring blankly at the river through the black railings.

'How the hell had he come to this?' He felt more depressed than ever. He thought of Jean who had been dead now for a decade. Ernest wondered for a moment what it would have been like to have had children, but didn't dwell on it. What he had never known he couldn't visualize, having no model on which to gauge parenthood. He had always set his worth by his work, which had been paramount throughout in his career. In fact he was rather grateful Jean never asked too much of him. He had his work, she had her committees and it worked well. To be honest he had been content. The marriage worked in its own way and no one could say he didn't give her all the best attention and care during her years struggling with breast cancer.

He tried to recall Jean's face but couldn't, and that bothered him. He missed her presence, especially when he came home to an empty house. Gazing ahead with a blank look, Ernest next tried to bring up the faces of his parents. Not that he missed them, for there had never been any love coming his way from that quarter. All Ernest could visualize was a hand coming down on him, which was attached to a blurred figure. He remembered the pain, but mostly the hunger, his stomach always felt empty.

He never knew his real mother. She died of tuberculosis when he was two. He liked to believe she loved him, but still there was no face. In fact he'd never seen a photo of her. His stepmother had seen to that by burning any she found.

Only one face came clearly to mind as it had done for as long as he remembered. Given he was no more than five when he first met Rita, it was almost a lifetime. Although Rita was now in her sixties like him, the image of her was a mixture of all she had ever been. She was the only person that made him feel special. During their school years she had not seen him as a troublemaker but rather as a hero, being the best fighter in the school. A smile hovered over Ernest's face as he remembered the way she'd brought him fish and chips out of her pocket money when he had been so hungry. The best meal he'd ever had. Ernest let himself indulge in the memory of their first date and the first kiss until the pain took over; the mind recalling her desire to go to Canada, leaving him vulnerable without any address to write to.

Work and his dedication to promotion saved him. Jean gave him stability and a home. Even after her death he still had his work, but yet he couldn't forget his childhood sweetheart.

Ernest pulled out the cigarette packet, took out the last cigarette, crumpled the packet and aimed at a nearby wire litter basket. He'd lost none of his skills, the empty packet falling into the basket; dead centre. Sitting back and uncrossing his legs, he took a long deep drag letting the smoke out slowly after holding it for a second in his lungs. A coughing bout shook his chest and he vowed to wait until after his dinner before he smoked the next one. He wouldn't of course; his daily self-indulgence was a tot of whisky before dinner, with a cigarette as part of that routine while watching the news.

A sparrow flew by, leaving a patch of white at his feet. He stared at it, and then went back to evaluating the past, his eyes growing more broody.

Rita's face was as clear as crystal to him now. He recalled the shock he'd had seeing her back in England after forty years. It was only last year he'd attended the sherry party at the Mill House. He'd known the Mill House was owned by Rita's uncle and her aunt, but he'd never thought Rita would be there. The recognition was instant for both of them despite the intervening years. Ernest shifted his position, his emotions raw at the memory.

During those perfect weeks in each others' company, Rita never said why she'd left for Canada all those years before and he'd not pushed for an answer, although his instinct told him Rita held a secret she wasn't willing to share. He remembered her waiting patiently in his car whilst investigating the discovery of a skeleton in an old quarry. The skeleton turned out to be an American soldier from WWII. He wasn't too interested at the time, but records had to be checked anyway in case the Yank's immediate family were still alive. It proved to be difficult as the identity discs of the serviceman were missing.

It was during dinner afterwards that Rita had hinted at her coming back to England permanently. That was one of the highlights of his life.

Ernest rolled his head around his stiff neck, feeling tension as he recalled the promise of a happy future. But it all went terribly wrong. Nothing could have prepared him for what had subsequently happened.

Rita was staying with her aunt to give her cousin a rest from his alcoholic mother before she returned to Canada. Then out of the blue, Ernest was called to a crime scene and was horrified to find it was where Rita was staying. He remembered every detail of that tragic day, namely because he'd gone over it so many times in detail; always finding the facts and his intuition were at war with each other

The memory of finding Rita's aunt lying dead at the bottom of the stairs with Rita sitting quietly by the fire was still ingrained in his memory.

Then the horrific realisation that the woman he loved had had a complete mental breakdown. He had taken the hand she held out to him and stayed with her while they took her to a psychiatric hospital and for once in his life he was totally confused.

The inquest found Digoxin in the body but not enough to kill her and couldn't return a verdict on whether the body had fallen or was pushed down the stairs

The awful truth was that Rita took Digoxin for her irregular heartbeat, but because of her mental breakdown she couldn't defend herself.

A full investigation revealed a more sinister case. Evidence of her aunt's involvement with the person whose skeleton was found in the quarry came to light. Letters indicated the father of her son was the Yank who had disappeared. Another surprise was discovered in the overgrown garden. It was the body of her aunt's husband Frank who had also disappeared many years ago.

But the question still remained. How had Rita's aunt died? Was it an accident or suicide? Ernest couldn't bring himself to consider the possibility that Rita had anything to do with her aunt's death. He remembered finding a bottle of Digoxin tablets with Rita's name on it and its lid off in the dining room. 'How had Digoxin got into the dead women's body'? That was the question that haunted him.

The need for a resolution remained buried in the soil of his fertile imagination and only Rita in her right mind could give him the answer he required.

Ernest was aware of the leaden feeling at the bottom of his stomach. It didn't take a doctor to tell him he was depressed and needed to pull himself out of it.

Never one to believe in pills for moods Ernest looked to himself. He knew he had to do something to change his lifestyle and he wasn't about to give up on Rita. He still had his dreams.

But for the present, he had to put these thoughts behind him, and think seriously of where he would end up living. The house he'd lived in for most of his adult life belonged to the constabulary and time was running out, as some other police family would need it.

Ernest stood up; pushed back on his heels to take out the stiffness that seemed to creep in his legs these days. Then with a purposeful stride he closed the distance from the river to the main gates of the park. He knew where he was heading, for he did it a couple of times every week.

Chapter 3

Cupping her hands around the mug filled with hot tea, Detective Sergeant Lisa Pharies allowed the warmth to seep through her fingers. Her hands were always cold no matter what the weather.

'Cold hands, warm heart,' her mother used to say. Lisa winced at the memory. It was a long time since she had heard her mother's voice. She bent her head, sipping the sweet liquid, her gaze blank as she remembered her life before her mother's stroke. Shifting her position to uncross her legs, Lisa's elbow caught the edge of a small pile of papers on her desk. She watched fascinated as the pen that lay atop rolled back and forth before finding the momentum to leave the paper pile and fall on the floor. She bent down awkwardly to retrieve it with her one free hand.

'Morning Pharies.' A familiar voice brought her up quickly, sending slops of tea flying over the desk.

'Oh hell,' Lisa exclaimed, frantically looking around for something to use as a cloth. The owner of the voice that had caused the chain of events grimaced, then proceeded to pick up the pieces of paper from the soaked desk top, waving each slightly to allow the liquid to drain off. Any ardent observer of human behaviour may have noticed that each piece of paper was quickly scanned before being discarded as being of little interest.

'God, Ernest, why do you always creep up on me like that?' Lisa moaned, her frustration showing whilst wiping up the spills with the only thing she could find; her handkerchief.

'Nothing of interest'! Ernest pulled a chair away from its place by the wall, placing it down in front of Lisa's desk before sitting down.

It didn't seem to bother Ernest that all his working life he had sat as the interviewer and not as the interviewee. In truth, whether the position of his seating arrangement was behind the desk or not, he still gave the impression he remained the one in charge. After a lifetime of police investigations it was impossible to just switch off and potter around the garden. For one thing he hadn't much of a garden and for another, he didn't like gardening. To his mind everything about gardening took far too long to achieve results and couldn't be forced along by pitting one's determination against it. So Ernest like any true homing pigeon often found his way to the police station.

P.C. Buzzard, the desk sergeant, popped his balding head around the door.

'Morning Gov; didn't see you come in.'

Lisa shook her head as though it was not such a surprise, as Jack Buzzard's head was more often than not bent over some cheap paperback. What he got out of those silly romances baffled her. Surely at his age he was long past any titillation of that sort.

'Cuppa?' P.C. Buzzard asked the question like he always did, then as always didn't wait for the answer. Instead he shuffled off to the tiny kitchen at the rear of the police station.

Ernest watched him go with a slight affectionate smile on his face. He'd known Jack a long time and knew more about him than most. It was far too late in his career for Jack to 'come out of the cupboard,' as everyone called it these days. Old Jack would die of shame if he thought anyone knew.

Lisa gave a sharp little cough denoting to those who knew her that someone wasn't paying attention. Ernest looked up and caught her two steely blue eyes focussed on him.

'Well,' she said, as if a conversation had already been exchanged and she was awaiting her companion's input. Ernest looked puzzled for a moment, and then remembering the drift of an earlier conversation, he leaned forward placing a pair of very big hands downwards on her desk, the fingers tapping out an indistinguishable rhythm.

'I've thought about it Lisa, truly I have.'

'And,' Lisa leaned forward, their eyes locking.

Ernest moved back dragging his hands back across the desk with him. He always found Lisa's eyes disconcerting when they had that penetrating look about them. In fact, every thing about Lisa's appearance left him a little bewildered. The policewomen he'd known in the past were bigger somehow, or at least looked bigger and certainly stronger. Lisa had the height. In fact she could look most men in the eyes. It was her frailty that unsettled him, slim to the point of thin with pale nondescript hair that lay wispy and fine. Ernest in all honesty couldn't call her pretty, or even outgoing in nature. He really didn't know why they seemed to get on so well, but they did and had done so since the newly appointed female detective had been placed under Ernest's care.

For moment softness entered Lisa's eyes and her voice took on a gentler edge. She no longer had to call him "Gov", but old habits die hard like with Jack.

'Gov, it's a police house you are in. They are not going to let you stay there forever.'

Ernest didn't need reminding, he'd already had a couple of notifications that the house was needed. It wasn't that he couldn't afford to buy a house. He had money put away, as both he and his wife had been careful and, since her death, he'd spent even less on himself.

'It's a nice house Ernest, nothing needs doing and the garden is manageable,' Lisa added, knowing of his aversion to gardening. 'It's an excellent price, you won't do better.' Lisa's voice took on a persuading tone.

The house, or rather cottage she was referring to, was in the same row in which she lived with her invalid mother. It had just come on the market and both knew it wouldn't be for much longer as rural cottages were being snapped up.

The village of Gelsby once thought of as being out in the country lay now within sight and sound of the main road. The ancient church of St. Anne's dominated the village by its elevated position. Its solid stone structure looking down on the cottages built around a village green.

It was a picturesque village and the cottages seldom came on the market. Springtime always brought sightseers from miles around just to view the hundreds of daffodils that had been planted on the green. The yellow carpet would have inspired any would be poet and often brought to mind Wordsworth's tribute to the daffodils dancing and fluttering in the breeze.

No new housing estates blotted the landscape. The surrounding land had traditionally always been agricultural and still was. . The ancient manor house was now just another farm with little of note to distinguish it from its neighbours. Only history buffs would have recognized the origins of Glebe Farm, the word 'glebe' pertaining to some of the money from the farm's produce funding part of the parson's salary hundreds of years ago.

Local names could still be traced back for centuries like the name Pharies.

Lisa's family had lived in the same cottage for four generations. Lisa, still unmarried, had lived at number seven all her life and, following the death of her father and her mother's stroke, it was there she would probably die. Years ago she'd thought it possible she might walk down the aisle dressed in white on the arm of some nice young man. But no such nice young man had come along and that vision had now faded to an acceptance of her present lot. Her future was now looking after her infirm mother until she died and then becoming just an old maid still living in the same house.

'What's your problem then?' Lisa asked Ernest bluntly, for she was never one to sidestep on an issue.

Ernest shrugged his shoulders and looked down at his hands. He was quite honest with himself and he really didn't know why he couldn't make a decision. He'd seen the 'For Sale' sign on the cottage and it was really all he needed. It had two bedrooms, although he was not sure who would ever need the second one, unless... It was always at this point that Ernest got a mind block.

Lisa sensed something from his past was barging in.

'Rita would like it. Quiet, away from the town,' and as an afterthought she added, 'and she'd just love the daffs in the spring.'

A few moments passed as they looked at each other, not quite knowing whether to hold back or move forward on the subject of Rita.

'How is she?'

There was real concern in Lisa's voice. She hadn't been on the force when the investigation into the discovery of an American's skeleton in the town had been going on, but had quickly learned of Ernest's personal involvement in the case.

It was probably the understanding coming from each loving someone who couldn't communicate with them that had brought Ernest and Lisa together despite the difference in their ages. If Lisa could have remembered her father, she would have liked him to be like this elderly detective now before her, and Ernest would have been more than happy with a daughter like Lisa; someone whose mind was equally quick at assessing any situation.

'About the same,' replied Ernest scratching his ear; a habit he always had when feeling useless.

The phone rang startling them both and for a few seconds Lisa stared at the instrument. Ernest nodded his head at it, his ears opening themselves up to any information that might be of interest. However he wasn't ready for the change in Lisa's face. Her eyes widened and a slow flush crept over her face as she stretched out her arm for the pen, at the same time indicating to Ernest the need for paper.

'Where?' She asked the question sharply down the phone then listened, tucking the mouthpiece under her chin and writing with her free hand.

'St. Anne's?' There was a question but more indicating a need for confirmation.

'I'll be there in twenty minutes.' She slammed the phone down, picked up the paper and was already pulling on her coat before noticing Ernest's puzzled frown.

'A girl has been found in St. Anne's churchyard,' then she added, 'strangled.'

Before the impact of what she'd said hit Ernest, she was through the door shouting orders at P.C. Buzzard.

Ernest sat down after circling the desk, perhaps by habit. Sitting in his old chair he began to experience the buzz again he had in the old days.

He looked over the desk, hoping to find a clue, anything to get the wheels of his mind turning. Nothing. The notes Lisa had jotted down were gone and there were no imprints on the paper beneath he'd already looked carefully over.

He felt like a child not invited to a party.

Chapter 4

There was nobody at the desk when Ernest stepped through the door of the Estate Agent's office in the main street.

Sandra, whose job it was to be there had nipped across the road to purchase fresh milk. No matter how poorly the job paid her, she was not going to put up with powdered milk in her coffee.

She had her pride; no farmer's daughter would stoop so low as to do that. Good old-fashioned homo milk for her or none at all. There had been times when she was more than tempted to tell the Pakistani that ran the convenience store about real milk, the sort that comes warm and creamy straight from the cow. She didn't of course because she could barely understand his broken English and he; her unforgiving Cheshire accent.

So Ernest stood alone in a perfectly square room, the front side mostly glass with display windows and door. To one side of the room stood an overly large desk, probably bought in an auction room by the owner at a low price and an easel with an equally oversized board displaying computer printouts of house sales.

His eyes rested on a door in the wall, the sign giving the occupant's name and profession.

S. Gupta
Estate Agent

'Indian,' nothing went unnoticed by Ernest even though he was retired; he couldn't just switch off a lifetime's practice. He was tempted to knock but instead walked out of the building, then turning around re-entered giving a swing to the door that set off the ding-dong of chimes again, producing more dings and dongs than necessary to activate the hearing apparatus of anyone that might come to his assistance.

Waiting for any signs of life, Ernest glanced at the name sign again wondering if the 'S' stood for a man's name or a woman's.

He hoped that the Estate Agent would turn out to be a male. The world seemed to be changing far too quickly for him. Wherever he went these days he was faced with a female. His new bank manager had turned out young enough to be his daughter. Quick as lightening with his investments and accounts, he found it difficult to keep up with her. He'd got used to it but it took some time. His lawyer he had accepted too, although he didn't understand a word she was saying sometimes but everything seemed to be in order with his legal affairs. But he did have trouble when his old doctor retired and a pretty female confronted him the day of his medical. He had never felt so embarrassed in all his life when she asked him to cough and squeezed the parts of him that were rarely seen. Ernest was no male chauvinist, he being one of the first to recognise the significant contributions made by the female members of the Police Force. But tradition dies hard and he was too old to change his ways overnight.

Ernest jumped as the shop door swung open creating another racket from the chimes. A character straight from a comic book entered carrying a bottle of milk sporting a gold top. The hair surrounding the face of about eighteen was bright red with gel set spikes that were tipped with green. Long chain-linked earrings dangled on her shoulders catching the fluff from a short-waisted pink angora sweater.

Ernest had to look twice at her eyelids and mouth, the make up giving her a look of a Halloween trick-or-treater, for they were carefully painted with thick black crayon.

He didn't get any further in seeing what the bottom half looked like, for she'd rounded the desk, sat down, turned on the computer and was typing some keys at a speed he'd never witnessed before. After a full four minutes she turned to give him her full attention.

'Yes.' The words snapped out of the black embellished slit that was her mouth.

Ernest's eyebrows lowered, a familiar annoyance creeping over him. He hated it when someone gave an answer before asking a question. He swallowed hard, and then bent down a little so his hands spread out on the top of her desk; his arms stretched and tensed holding his body stiff.

'I'm here to ask the questions.' He glared at her.

She ignored him and began tapping the keyboard again. He could have been a pesky fly for all she cared.

'Young lady,' he began.

She stopped typing and looked up.

'Sandra Greenfield,' she stated then added 'Miss'.

Ernest's shoulders tensed. He didn't really want to be here. He felt pushed into a corner and didn't want to leave the police house, but he had to. Yet another reminder had been given him that very morning.

'Well Miss Sandra Greenfield.' He stood up. 'I want some information about a cottage for sale at Gelsby.'

'Miss Gupta will be back in a moment.' She eyed him up and down. 'If…. you should care to wait,' she said sarcastically placing emphasis on the "if". Then suddenly taking pity on him added, 'there's a listing of the cottage on the board.'

Ernest looked over the listings crushed together and straining under a drawing pin. As he attempted to lift the paper underneath, the drawing pin fell out and four or five papers floated to the floor. He bent down to pick them up; his rear end turned upwards, and while in this position, was immediately confronted by another pair of legs. It was the shoes he saw first. Thin strips of black leather wrapped around dainty feet moulded into three-inch platform soles. Slim dusky coloured ankles led to perfectly sculptured calves and knees. Then rounded smooth carves ending abruptly with a line of black leather.

Ernest jumped up, his face burning. Even in her platform-soled shoes, Ernest had to look down on a slim dark-haired woman of

Indian extraction; her sense of dress indicating a European flavour and her black leather suit looking very chic and modern.

'He's come about the cottage at Gelsby,' Sandra piped up her eyes never leaving the computer screen.

'Follow me.' The words came out in clipped but well-spoken English. Ernest guessed an expensive boarding school.

She led him through the door into a small room, small but comfortably furnished. He found himself filling a soft leather chair, wondering if the same material had been ordered for both her skirt and chair.

'Mortgage or cash.' she asked abruptly, seating herself down to face him.

'Cash I guess,' he certainly couldn't afford a mortgage out of his pension, but wasn't lacking in a tidy bank balance, aided by his late wife's money she'd inherited from her family.

'How much is the cottage?' He thought it a reasonable question under the circumstances. She told him and he winced, but even then he knew it was a fair price.

'It's empty, the owner died and the family want to get rid.' The Estate Agent rapped the point of her pen on the figure listed before her.

'How long must I wait to move in?' Another reasonable question he thought.

'Today if you want to,' she paused before continuing, 'rent it until the finances are done.'

'You mean its okay to live in it right away.' Ernest felt some of his lost energy returning. The thought of just getting on with it and not worrying about the move appealed to him.

It was there and then that Ernest really decided to buy. It seemed ridiculous later, making that decision without seeing or having an inspection done and all those other things that had to be attended to.

'I'll go and see it then,' Ernest took the key she offered and, as he neared the door, turned with an afterthought; 'by the way, what's your Christian name?'

A genuine laugh escaped her throat.

'I wouldn't call it a Christian name. You see I'm Hindu. But for your interest, its Santosha,' then smiling added, 'It means contentment.'

Somehow he was glad he'd asked. Although not a superstitious man, he felt it a good omen.

Driving through the busy traffic fed from the motorway, Ernest turned off into the road that led to Gelsby village.

As soon as he sighted the village sign he checked his watch. Twenty minutes, it was always good to know how long it took to get to places.

Turning again he took the left side of the village green and saw a FOR SALE sign sticking out like a sore thumb from the row of cottages. Ernest slowed down, and then saw a sign he was not expecting; it read NO PARKING quite plainly. He looked over at the other side of the triangular shaped village green and saw the same sign repeated again. The small space where he could have parked outside the church was lined with police cars.

Most problems have reasonable solutions. This had always been Ernest's motto and so far that philosophy hadn't failed him. Even Rita's problem would be solved one day he was sure. Ernest quickly assimilated his present situation and, knowing Lisa had a car she must park it somewhere close by. If his hunch was correct, there would be parking spaces behind the cottages.

As he was also interested in what was going on around the church, he followed the road around very slowly before finding an entry to the back with enough room in each garden to park a car. The gardens at the front may have been small but there was more than enough land at the rear to park. It didn't surprise Ernest. He remembered the chicken runs at the back of the smallest houses during the war. Fortunately a number eleven was painted on a post or he may have been faced with yet another problem.

Parking his car, Ernest strolled around to the front again taking his time and was a little disappointed there were none of his old police colleagues he could stop and past the time of day with. He opened the wrought iron gate of the cottage and stopped to inhale the fragrance of a yellow rose, whose branches threatened to snare his jacket.

Next door a curtain moved slightly in the window. Turning the key, the door swung open, creaking a little on its hinges. The smell that wafted towards the open door was pleasant, there was a hint of lavender, which brought to mind the sachets that his gran filled and hung among the clothes in her wardrobe. One of the happier memories of his childhood and there were not that many to chose from.

There was no doubt the cottage was small and seemed much smaller than the council cum police house he was used to. But nevertheless it had a certain cosiness to it, and reminded him that after his wife's death, he usually only used one armchair anyhow.

The curtains had been left hanging, a nice sunny colour with roses on them. He ran his hand along the oak mantle atop the brick fireplace and visualised the brass candle sticks he'd once brought at an auction standing at each end, with Gran's old clock in the middle.

Ernest poked his head around the kitchen noting money had been spent not to long ago on modernisation. That would save a bit he thought.

The stairs were steep and creaked under a sisal type of carpeting. No looking over a railed banister for there was none, only walls on either side with white-washed over plaster swirls that had once been popular in the older homes.

Both bedrooms were curtained with the same material as downstairs. Something darted across the room. Ernest caught the sight of a small mouse disappearing into a hole in the skirting board. He didn't mind. Catching mice was no problem to him. He had been a champ at it in the damp house he was brought up in as a child.

Having sized up which bedroom was most likely to harbour his bedroom suite, he wondered how he'd missed seeing the bathroom. It certainly wasn't upstairs.

His eyes gathered into a frown until he remembered spotting a small extension on the back of the house. Going downstairs again, there was a door from the kitchen that took him down a little passageway to a fully equipped bathroom.

'Very posh'! Ernest had never seen a bathroom suite in pink before. Well he could get used to it he mused, admitting to the excellent tile work.

Coming back into the kitchen he leaned across the kitchen sink looking out into the garden. It wasn't too big, especially as the stony drive had taken a lot away, but he could see it had all once been cared for. There was a rockery at the bottom where everything seemed to be blooming including the weeds. For a moment he let his imagination take over and visualised Rita sitting there in a deck chair.

Chapter 5

Ernest's temperament was not known for patience when his mind was firmly made up in the direction he wanted to go, although at the opposite end of the scale no one could measure up to his dogged determination for answers when he wasn't sure.

Now that he'd signed the rent agreement for the cottage until the final sale could be completed, Ernest couldn't be bothered with any hanging around. His mind was already ticking away at those little things that make a place one's own; shelves to put up, hooks to screw in and lights to fix.

A few days later, a large van appeared outside number eleven with many an eye watching the unloading. A couple of young kiddies, not quite school age, stood by the ramp intent on each item being lifted down hoping some child's bike or toy might be forthcoming.

The day brought out more than the usual passers-by and neighbours and it couldn't be attributed to the sun, as it remained firmly hidden behind grey skies. Gardens suddenly appeared in need of weeding and windows cleaned; their curiosity always directed at the unloading activities and, more to the point, what the new owner of the cottage looked like.

Ernest didn't seem to mind the growing interest for during his working life he'd grown used to people's interest at the scene of any investigation, the police cars and the recent activity around the church however now being forgotten for a while, as the attention was on a dreadful modern wardrobe that was totally out of keeping with the cottage's size and vintage. Curiosity grew as to whether it would go up the narrow stairs or not. There was a lot of head shaking and those all-knowing looks from the 'I-told-you-so' group, as the wardrobe was returned to the pavement by two harassed looking removal men. Two hours later with the unloading complete, the van had gone taking with it the offending wardrobe.

Ernest flopped gratefully into the familiar contours of his favourite armchair. His mouth felt like sandpaper, sore from giving directions and dry from lack of liquid refreshment. He did think of putting the kettle on, but couldn't remember which box it came in.

Somewhere between the sounds from the back door swinging to and fro and his aching back, he fell asleep. Four hours passed, his exhaustion was so great that Ernest slept like a log

Awakening came abruptly, his eyes flashing open. Someone was moving around in the kitchen

Footsteps. He closed his eyes, listening and assessing every sound.

Now someone was standing over him.

Ernest sprang up and a splash of hot liquid hit his trousers. 'Christ.'

He pulled the material of his trousers away from his legs, giving a silent thanks to the name he'd invoked for leaving his crown jewels safe.

'Oh hell,' Lisa stood before him, a saucer with an overturned cup shaking violently in her hands. Ernest waved her away indicting that he was all right.

'Get us another cuppa love,' he said seeing how shaken she was. As she left hurriedly for the kitchen he shouted after her.

'How did you find the bleeding kettle anyway?' It was something he just needed to know.

'Brought my own electric kettle and some cups,' the answer floated back above the noise from the hissing kettle.

Satisfied there was no mystery surrounding his lack of unpacking, Ernest decided his pants didn't warrant a change, and pushed the wet tea-stained hankie deep into his pocket.

Lisa came back with a fresh cup, this time on a tray which she laid carefully on the stone hearth. Ernest wondered which box the tray had come out of.

'So what's new?' asked Ernest, casually stirring his tea and watching a whirlpool appear on the surface. He didn't look up at her, but waited patiently for her answer, knowing she didn't like being questioned unless she had something positive to give.

'New?' Lisa raised her innocent eyes and gazed at a small balding spot on top of her companion's head.

'The girl,' Ernest forced himself not to let her eyes meet his as she was now staring directly at him. 'The girl who was found in the churchyard: Any clues?'

'Not many,' said Lisa.

There was a long silence.

'There must be some?' He couldn't contain the feeling of irritation that was growing inside him. He shifted his position hoping to ease the feeling.

'Very little,' Lisa rose and began to walk around the room, picking up a Royal Doulton figurine that Ernest had brought in his car, not trusting the removers.

Lisa placed it on the mantelpiece, stepping back to look at it. Then moving it to the oak windowsill, she adjusted the curtains around it. Lisa had a slight obsession with tidiness and liked a place for everything. It was like her mind; odd pieces that she couldn't find a place for annoyed her. She knew she had skirted around Ernest's enquiries but it was because she was unsure of any clear answer. When she was ready she would maybe share what she had, although not yet.

'Do you want help to get this place in order?' asked Lisa.

Ernest knew he wasn't going to get anywhere with his questioning, then was taken by surprise when suddenly, out of the blue, Lisa blurted out 'there was no evidence of sexual interference.'

Lisa started to unwrap the newspapers around some plates, wondering why she had come out with that statement.

'Virgin was she?' Ernest asked quietly not wanting to shut down the now open line of communication.

'No, she'd had sex, but she didn't appear to have a boy friend in the village.'

'One off?' the inquiry slipped out as smooth as syrup. 'A bit young though, wasn't she?' Ernest had always had a hard time with the ages of the sexually experienced youth.

'Seems she kept herself to herself; didn't have any friends to speak of?' Lisa was looking at the maker's name on the underside of a plate. It always gave her a clue to the care she needed to take in handling pottery.

'One off then?' he asked again.

Lisa raised her shoulders but didn't answer.

'Parents?' he asked tearing at a difficult-to-remove tape from a box. He opened it and pulled out a book. Turning it on its side he read, 'Gulliver's Travels by Jonathon Swift.'

Momentarily Ernest had a flash back of walking around the churchyard of Banbury Church. He and his wife had being fascinated by the fact Jonathon Swift had taken the name of Gulliver from one of the old gravestones there; his wife, he recalled, looking pretty in a blue dress. Ernest put down the book and reached for another.

Lisa volunteered no more information

'Best let it go for now,' he thought to himself. After all he had so much to do, and then there was Rita. He had meant to phone the hospital the night before.

He felt a pang of guilt as Rita's face flashed into his mind. Yet he had to be honest that since he had made the decision to move, he wasn't brooding on what could have been. Instead he now had a positive goal, one that would involve Rita and the cottage.

Ernest set about filling the shelves of his bookcase with books, but taking Lisa's advice about discarding the ones he'd never read again, he put them back into a box she'd already marked JUMBLE SALE.

What Jumble Sale? Ernest hadn't a clue, but he was quite willing to be guided by Lisa. He missed a woman's hand in the home making.

It was late afternoon before Lisa finally left and Ernest began to feel the first pangs of hunger. Opening the fridge door he stared dolefully at the only edible thing, a cheese and macaroni casserole looking rather flat and doughy, with signs of burning at the edges. Although it was nice of Lisa to bring it, he really didn't fancy it. Banging the fridge door closed, Ernest picked up his jacket from the back of a chair, patted the left pocket, ensuring his wallet was there and made for the front door.

The stroll around to the Horseshoe Inn was what he needed. He liked to stretch his legs and breathe the fresh air ever since he was a constable on the beat.

Stepping through the red tiled doorway, he made straight for the bar. The room was no different from any English country pub. Low beamed ceilings sporting an array of brass and pewter, black and white walls adorned with horse brasses and old prints of the village.

He leaned against the highly polished bar, watching the publican pulling draught beer from the pumps that had scenes of fox hunting painted on the handles. Waiting patiently, one foot on the brass foot rail fixed around the bar, Ernest turned and surveyed the occupants in the room.

One old man in a corner was talking to a young chap holding a pad and pencil in his hand. He was writing furiously while his informant sipped happily on the large whisky that had obviously been bought for him.

There were a couple of farmers, who were easily identified by their red cheeks and traces of cow dung mixed with straw dried around the heels of their boots.

Over by the window a young couple sat, obviously just passing through, their camera pushed against a basket of chips on the table.

'Quiet evening'! Ernest ventured; turning back and addressing the publican.

The publican glanced up. Thick set with a sort of rugged good looks, spoiled a little by an eyelid that tended to droop.

'The police and reporters have homes too.' The accent was local. 'Hear you've just moved into old Goodall's place. What's your drink?'

'Draught bitter'! Ernest replied, looking over the menu written in chalk on a blackboard; before adding 'and steak and kidney pie with a large helping of chips.'

The publican popped his head through a serving hatch and yelled the order.

Ernest savoured his drink, awaiting the next question, which he knew would be forthcoming.

'What brings you here?'

'Oh, just the need to retire; somewhere quiet.' Ernest looked down at his drink adding nonchalantly, 'Hear you've had a murder?'

Gerry Platt sighed, shook his head and leaned heavily over the bar towards him.

'Nice young thing,' he stated. 'Goes--,' then quickly amending his sentence, 'rather went to school with our cleaner's kid. Butter wouldn't melt in her mouth and she wouldn't hurt a fly that one; too timid.'

Ernest pushed his glass forward and told Gerry to pull one for himself.

It wasn't long before the two farmers joined them and were freely offering their opinions also. Deep in conversation about village life and gossip, time passed quickly. With his stomach full and his liquid requirements satiated, Ernest had learned quite a lot for a new guy on the block and by the time he was ready to leave the Horseshoe Inn, his inquisitive nature had been more than well exercised.

Everyone seemed to hold the same opinion of the murdered girl. Quiet and not many friends to speak of, she didn't belong to any group or club, with an alcoholic mother and an overly strict father. The last bit of information volunteered by Sharon, the barmaid, who looked as if she'd have benefited from a strict father herself with her overly flirting manner and suggestive clothing.

Mulling over the information, Ernest crossed the road and wound his way through the parked cars that almost blocked the entrance to the church. He stood for a while reading the inscription on the gate

'Good morning Inspector.' A lanky man in black leather jacket slid from behind the other side of the church entrance, his camera equipment dangling across his chest.

'Might have guessed'! Ernest raised his eyes towards the sky and took a deep breath, giving the man a fixed smile. He had had many encounters with this reporter in the past.

'Geoff. Leigh. I need not ask what brings you here.'

'Maybe I should be asking what brings you Inspector.' He purred for once like he'd got the upper hand; then added, 'seeing as since you are now retired.'

Ernest gave a hint of a smile and moved toward the gate making Geoff step aside.

'Just visiting my Granny's grave,' he said respectfully, leaving the reporter staring at his back.

The flagged path led up to the main doors of the church but Ernest stepped aside picking his way through the oldest of gravestones. Curiosity made him stand and read the inscription on several ones dating from the fifteenth century.

Ahead his eye caught sight of the familiar yellow tape forming a square around what looked like a fallen yew tree, but on closer observation he saw the tree was split in two and propped up. 'How the English hold onto the past,' he thought, slightly amused.

A group of forensics and police personnel were arguing with some sightseers that had managed to climb over the church wall. Ernest caught sight of P.C. Tattersal, arms flapping in desperation, trying to keep some ardent reporters away.

Ernest quickened his step anxious not to be recognized. In two minutes he would be around the back of the church and out of sight, but to his surprise came face-to-face with another young constable that obviously had needed to find somewhere quick to relieve himself. The policeman recognised Ernest. Not quite knowing whether retired cops could join the investigation or not, he said the only thing he could think of.

'Sir'!

'Carry on Constable,' murmured Ernest and walked briskly away and out of sight among the gravestones, stopping occasionally to read an inscription on the top of a tomb. He was standing bent over by one when a voice brought him up sharply.

'Who are you?' The voice appeared to come from nowhere.

Startled, Ernest looked around. A figure popped up from behind a half broken oblong tomb. It leaped over the grass to confront Ernest, its back bent from a lump between the shoulders, the legs a little bowed and too small for the lumbering body. The head appeared large and the mouth gaping allowing spittle to dribble out. The eyes were wary, black and shaded by brows that almost met in the middle.

The apparition didn't wait for an answer; instead it gave its own identity.

'I'm Kane,' he pointed to himself. 'I'm in charge around here.'

For a second Ernest thought he'd come face to face with a madman, but after quickly taking in the dirty clothes, and the spade he dragged along, he guessed Kane, or whatever his name was, looked after the graveyard.

'Good job you make of it too.' Ernest smiled and held out his hand. 'I'm Ernest Heath, I've just moved into a cottage here.'

The mouth opened into a grin showing brown uneven teeth.

'Them's weavers cottages.' Kane placed his finger against his nose and tapped.

He pointed to the church. 'I lives there,' he said.

'Really,' replied Ernest for once feeling out of his depth. The man called Kane half turned to go; then looked over his shoulder, his face muscles twitching.

'Bad thing happened here. It's bad, bad.' He babbled away dragging his spade behind and still muttering.

Ernest, staring after him for a while, shook himself and felt in his pockets for his cigarettes. Satisfied they were there; he rounded the church and made for home by a side gate.

All in all it had proved to be a very productive day, if not a little alarming.

Chapter 6

Feeling refreshed after sleeping soundly all night, Ernest gave a long yawn and stretched. The mattress groaned under his weight and a pair of large feet slipped out at the bottom of the bed. Raising one leg up so the bed covers slipped down it, he examined his long toenails, wondering where the nail clippers were, or if indeed he had any.

A shaft of sunlight slipped through a crack in the drawn curtains and warmed his face. It was the first night in years he had actually slept right through. After his wife had died he'd often awoke in the early hours staring into the darkness, sometimes wondering if there was any truth in the departed reappearing in some astral form. This was usually followed by him getting up; making a cup of tea and spending the remaining hours sitting in his armchair; going over whatever investigation he had been dealing with at the time.

He eased himself out of bed, did a few bends and arm swings that constituted his exercise and put on a dressing gown before going downstairs to the kitchen.

Suddenly it dawned on him he'd done no grocery shopping, the only food in the house was Lisa's creation that he didn't fancy at all, and a half carton of milk that had been left standing on the table overnight. He pulled at the waxed cardboard making a funnel and tilted it into his mouth. It tasted off. Sighing, he wiped his mouth on his sleeve, and then spit out the bits of fluff his tongue had picked up.

There was nothing else to do but find the nearest supermarket. Gelsby didn't even have a corner shop, so there wasn't much of a choice.

After dressing and a quick shave, Ernest's car slipped into the morning traffic on the main road. He leaned slightly forward, eyes searching for any sign of a mall along the way.

He saw one. Breaking heavily, he turned sharply ignoring the horn blasts from several cars following him. He had been in too many police chases to be intimidated by those sorts of sound, but still had to restrain himself from raising a finger.

The mall looked new, bigger and more colourful than most and the parking lot huge. He found a place to park as near to the mall's entrance as possible, pulled out a cart from an unyielding line, found the hastily scribbled grocery note in his pocket and went in.

Ernest gazed around him, not sure where to start. This mall not only sold groceries but also included a section for all sorts of electrical appliances, books and even clothes. After walking up and down the aisles and being confused by all the choices, Ernest realised the walk around the mall, if done daily, could be cheaper than a health club. He sighed; the eggs and bacon must be at least two aisles apart from each other. There was such a variety of food to choose from, that he ignored his list and put into his trolley anything that stimulated his fancy.

He picked up a box of dairy milk chocolates by the cash-out. The young cashier gave him a becoming smile.

'For your wife?' she said.

Ernest's face didn't give a thing away as he replied 'No my dear, they are for my old granny'.

The girl stared at him, her mind ticking over to comprehend whether or not it possible for a man his age to have a grandmother still alive. She decided he was being sarcastic, but wasn't going to stoop to his level.

'Have a nice day,' she chipped in, in a monotone voice.

Ernest smiled to himself. It was a Canadian saying Rita often used. It didn't take long for cultures to merge these days what with holidays aboard and shared TV programmes.

Driving back to Gelsby he took a side road, bringing him around the back of the village. He slowed down until he had pinpointed a cottage with the curtains closed and a police car parked outside. He was in no doubt that the murdered girl had lived there. He drove slowly towards the church, passing the side entrance in the wall across from the Horseshoe Inn and wondered if anyone had seen the young girl on the night of the murder without realising it. Sometimes memories of that fateful night would only come later, especially after a few drinks had been downed.

He was tempted to walk around the churchyard again, but thought he'd have a better chance of knowing what was going on by visiting Lisa. She'd be at home now. Saturday was important to her. He'd already found that out. Time with her mother was necessary, as the woman whom Lisa hired during the week wasn't around at the weekends. Funnily enough Ernest had never gleaned too much about Lisa's personal life, just that her mother was an invalid after having a stroke. Lisa could be quite secretive when she wanted to.

He popped into his cottage to drop off the groceries and put them away, after which he picked up the chocolates and set off on his errand on foot. Number seven was one of the four semi-detached cottages that had been given a facial at some period, for they were the only ones that sported a rather small, but never-the-less proper, bay window, together with a porch built over the door. In height they were taller than the rest of the cottages that flanked the village green. The largest house was the black and white one built closest to the church; having once been two cottages now converted into one.

Ernest pushed open the iron gate of number seven, took about six good paces and was facing a shiny brass lions-head knocker on the front door. The tiny overgrown patch of garden was covered with bright yellow dandelions growing around a struggling rhododendron bush devoid of any blossom.

Just about to reach for the knocker, the door was opened and Lisa appeared.

'Saw you coming,' she said, glancing over to the bay window on her left.

Ernest stared at her with interest. He'd never seen her in jeans before. She looked nice, the slim black tee shirt giving length to her body and showing she possessed a good figure. The hair that usually was pulled back under a pink elastic band framed her face, making her look younger and vulnerable. He pushed the box of chocolates towards her

'Thanks for helping,' was all he could think of.

'My pleasure,' Lisa held the door open wider.

He stepped into the hallway and stood awkwardly for a moment, before being gently guided to a room at the back of the cottage.

'Mum has her bed in the front room,' volunteered Lisa as if she had to explain the pokey room Ernest found himself in.

He nodded.

'And this is my mother.' Lisa stood beside a well-worn armchair that cradled a bent figure. Ernest moved forward ready to hold out his hand, then placed it behind him when he realised the occupant of the chair was asleep.

'She nods off,' Lisa smiled and tucked the knitted shawl around her mother's shoulders affectionately, 'I'll put the kettle on,' she added, not quite sure what to do with her visitor.

She left him sitting across from the old lady staring into the flickering flames of a modern gas fire. The air held a slight smell of urine and peppermint. He looked around noting a folded wheelchair, and another chair that looked like an old-fashioned commode.

'Well,' he thought, 'everyone has to pee.'

'Alright in there,' Lisa's voice called. Something fell and rolled.

'Dam,' he heard, before answering he was just fine. He looked at her mother. He'd seen stroke victims before, strong healthy people reduced to half an existence. He hoped to God it didn't happen to him. There couldn't be that many years between them; her mother and him.

Off guard, he caught two steely blue eyes watching him. Ernest gave a start, not knowing quite what to say and was relieved by Lisa's entrance. Putting the tea tray down, she picked up the present of chocolates and gently placed them on her mother's knee, then took her mother's good hand giving it a pat.

'Mother, this is Detective Inspector Heath.'

Ernest straightened his back in response to his old title. Lisa went on, 'now he's retired and living almost next door.'

Emily Pharies' face remained blank, but there was a little nod of acknowledgement and her good hand lifted.

Lisa hadn't done yet. Picking up a photo album lying on the side table, she replaced it with the box of chocolates.

'Ernest,' she beckoned him over, 'Mother would like to show her family to you.'

For a second Ernest felt bewildered then quickly understood. The photo album was her mother's way of communicating, so he stood by the side of her chair and bent over while Emily's hand moved the pages.

There were black and white photos of a man and woman and child ranging from the nineteen thirties to the seventies. Now and then Emily's finger would be placed on one and she would turn her eyes to Lisa.

'That's Mum and Dad and me,'

'She's pretty.' Ernest was pointing to a young woman dressed in a floral summer frock and holding a child. Emily placed two of her fingers on it and gently moved them over the photo. Ernest guessed she was remembering when she was young and healthy.

'Tea,' offered Lisa, beginning to pour.

Ernest returned to his seat and began watching Lisa gently holding a cup with a spout to her mother's lips. He'd no idea this was Lisa's life, and what sort of a life was it for a young woman. He felt a new admiration for her, mingled with a great sense of pity.

'She's slipped off again.' Lisa smiled and put the cup down. Emily breathed heavily as she slept.

Lisa pulled up a stool to sit by the fire. To an outsider it would have appeared a contented scene.

The clock ticked away its seconds, neither spoke.

'Any new developments'; Ernest broke the silence. Lisa sipped her tea looking up at him over her teacup.

'Not much, Forensics found nothing, apart from a speck of wax on her coat.'

Ernest's ears pricked up. 'Wax'!

'Oh for Christ's sake,' Lisa chuckled. 'We are always having power failures. We had one only last week, so you must remember to buy candles like everyone else.'

Ernest's face reddened. Best change the subject he thought.

'Who's Kane?' he asked.

Lisa turned the gas flame down a bit. Her legs were getting hot.

'He looks after the graveyard and is a general dogs-body around the church, why do you ask?'

'Just curious.'

Ernest went on to tell her about his meeting with him.

Lisa laughed. 'Scares the living shit out of you doesn't he, but he's quite harmless. Rachel, that's our rector's sister, hired him a few years ago. She's a kind and compassionate person. Even lets him live in the old priest chamber.'

'The what'! Ernest was getting interested.

'Above the south porch there is a room that visiting clergy and monks would use centuries past' she explained. 'Bit of a change from the comforts they enjoy nowadays, our rector's got a lovely stereo I'd die for.'

'So he lives there.' Ernest sat back pondering on Kane's life. 'Bit morbid isn't it, living surrounded by dead people.'

Lisa sniffed.

Ernest thought Lisa would have said something like… 'having quiet neighbours,' but she didn't. Instead she stood up.

Placing her cup down with a heavy hand, she turned to face him; her body posture indicating her profession.

'If you're thinking what I think you're thinking, just forget it. We have already checked Kane's whereabouts at the time of the death.'

'And'! Ernest would not give in once he'd got a bone to chew on, and she knew it.

'He was watching TV at the vicarage, Rachael feeds him there often and lets him stay on and see a programme or two.'

'Did he tell you what he saw?' Ernest blushed. He knew he'd gone too far.

Lisa coughed sharply.

'Yes, he knew what was on,' and catching her breath she added, 'are you suggesting our clergy's family lie?'

His blush became crimson, and he tried to change the subject.

'Nice touch giving your mum those chocolates I brought for you.' He laughed, trying to lighten the conversation.

'Oh,' she said, looking him straight in the eye. 'I thought you had brought them for her.'

Ernest knew he was beaten and tried another tack, hoping to pre-empt her.

'What time is church tomorrow?'

'The eight am Holy Communion is a short service, ten am long and Evensong is at six thirty pm. It is written on the church board. Our own rector won't be taking them though, as he is convalescing after a minor heart attack.'

She stopped short looking at him quizzically.

'Are you thinking of going?' She looked at him in disbelief.

Ernest raised his eyebrows, signalling he was none committal on the subject of his churchgoing.

'We are expecting a young curate anytime soon, Rachael certainly could do with help looking after her brother and everything else.'

He'd let her talk away and was now realising he was quickly getting himself into a situation of having to attend church. By being evasive on the subject, his only way out now was to find an excuse to leave and head back home. She walked to the front door with him. 'Maybe see you at church,' she said, giving him another long quizzical look.

'Maybe I'll just wait until the new curate comes,' he replied, moving quickly through the door.

Lisa watched him go. She smiled. It was always like playing a game of chess with him, it kept her on her toes. But what was really going on in his mind? What had he thought about that she hadn't? Those thoughts stayed with her for the rest of the day.

Chapter 7

The rain started during the night and didn't give any signs of easing off in the morning. It poured down continuously producing a curtain of water that obscured the bottom of the garden with its fury. Heavy drops hit the rusty corrugated roof of the small garden shed pounding out a rhythmic drone. Rapid waterfalls formed as the eves troughs overflowed.

There was still no sign of a break in the weather by lunchtime. Ernest stared moodily through the window and began to feel the first signs of claustrophobia. All at once the walls seemed to press in and the greyness became overwhelming.

He went back to his chair and glanced around for something to arrest his attention, he needed to switch his line of thought away from the weather. Yesterday's newspaper lay forlornly on the floor half opened. Ernest picked it up remembering he'd fallen asleep last night before finishing with it.

Flattening the paper out across his knee he carefully folded back the pages already read, then ran his finger and thumb along the middle to form a sharp crease. Turning it over, the page's headlines caught his attention.

GELSBY GIRL FOUND MURDERED.

The whole page gave an account of the finding of the body. A vivid description of the girl was given along with her parent's remarks made during the press interviews, together with a few words from the police. The rest of the article was made up of the history of the church and the last murder committed there in the eighteenth century, when a body had been found cut to pieces and thrown into a local stream.

Ernest read it thoroughly, and then re-read details of the recent murder again. He felt quite depressed as he read his successor's name. How quickly someone takes one's place, he thought dolefully. He pushed the paper down the side of the chair seat and stood up. Stretching and yawning, he gazed around the room.

'Rain or no rain, the Horseshoe do a good lunch,' he mumbled to himself and instantly felt more cheerful. Five minutes later he had donned his oversized mackintosh, and was lifting a large black umbrella from its perch by the side of the monk's bench.

As he opened the door, a sharp blast of damp air blew back at him. Rather than getting soaked by opening the brolly outside, he opened it inside and faced the deluge by using it as a shield. By the time he'd reached the pub, he could feel his shoes squelching against his socks and wished he'd put on his Wellington boots.

Depositing the dripping brolly and mac in the entrance, he opened the door to the bar. It was packed, and with the fire blazing, a whiff of steamy dampness hung in the air. A group of locals jostled for the attention of reporters, holding out their pint mugs in the hope they got filled for any other titbits of local information. Ernest had seen it all before.

One or two heads did turn in curiosity, mostly from the older regulars who were always probing for details about any newcomer to the village.

A man raised a glass; Ernest nodded wondering who it was, or whether it was just customary. He pushed his way past the tables to the space at the bar. Someone on his right had had more than his fill. He put his arm around Ernest's shoulder and laughed; his breath thick and heavy.

'Bring my buddy here a drink landlord,' he shouted then collapsed back on his stool, his face turning a distinct shade of purple.

'Home time John,' the publican called and to Ernest's surprise, the said John grinned and sauntered out after saluting.

'Hope he's not driving,' stated Ernest.

'Nay man, he lives but two minutes away. Harmless as cats' piss;___ right Sharon'!

He glanced at the barmaid who affirmed it with a laugh.

Ernest couldn't help staring at the barmaid. She was certainly well endowed and made no effort to hide the fact. The mini she wore was as high as minis go and the neckline of the sweater as low as they went. Thick blonde hair curled around a heavily made up face. Certainly an asset to the place decided Ernest noting the landlord himself was also not immune to her looks by his habit of touching her at every opportunity.

The reporters were starting to leave, followed by the freeloaders, leaving the place quieter and more relaxed.

'Another?' the publican gestured to Ernest who had emptied his glass whilst swishing down the remnants of a slice of blue Stilton cheese, bread and a pickle.

Ernest slid his glass along the counter and moved further down the bar, where the publican had begun to wipe glasses. Slipping onto a stool, Ernest eased into conversation.

'Hear you had a blackout in the village last week,' he uttered, as he helped himself to a handful of bar nuts.

'Did we? I cannot keep count anymore,' came back the reply, as the publican blew on another glass before polishing it.

A tall man pushed his way up to the bar and slapped it with the flat of his hand, before calling out 'Whisky.' The publican pushed a double whisky at the man, avoiding looking straight at him and said.

'On me Stan'!

The man called Stan tipped it back, ordered a bottle of gin and walked out.

Ernest was aware all eyes were following the man and, as he left them, the room was filled with a general buzz as tongues started to wag

'Here's yours' the publican said; handing Ernest a pint of ale. 'Sorry about him getting served first. Must be in bad shape after what happened to his girl.'

Ernest frowned, but it quickly cleared as a full understanding of the situation became apparent.

'The murdered girl's father'!

'Aye, and their only one,' the landlord nodded and began to clean and polish more glasses again; the customers unlikely to need more fill-ups and no new ones had come in. 'Guess the gin was for Muriel.'

'Muriel?' Ernest queried.

'Muriel's his wife. Can't say Stan's the friendliest person at the best of times, he's not the easiest of blokes, but I have to say he's got his hands full, what with his missus and now after what's happened to his daughter.' The publican shook his head then changed the subject.

'Our Lisa says you are an ex-cop,' he half smiled at Ernest, not sure what kind of chap he was dealing with. There were those that were sticklers for closing times and such and those that turn a blind to such minor infractions, retired or not.

The publican started to smile as he caught the fleeting glimpse of Ernest's confusion.

'Don't mean she's mine, just a figure of speech; known Lisa forever it seems,' he indicated a fill-up.

Ernest nodded.

'Wouldn't mind being a little closer though,' he winked, certain that Ernest understood the connotation that all men like a bit of skirt.

Ernest let it go.

'About the recent power cut here, do you get them often?'

'Often enough'!

The publican, insisting he be addressed as Gerry, pulled himself a pint in the hope of finding out more about his new customer but sensing the direction in the conversation, so far going the other way.

'Everyone keeps a supply of candles as there's no shop hereabouts,' he said, adding, 'be a long night if they were ever without.' Gerry wasn't about to say he'd managed very well without them though, his wife being away and the barmaid having to stay over because it was too dark for her to walk home one night. Instead he said,

'Reckon it's harder at Stan's house. He won't have a candle in the house since the time his wife knocked one over when she was drunk and nearly set fire to the place.'

Ernest was now considering a third pint since it might take that to keep the conversation going.

'What do they do for light then?'

'Sit in the dark I suppose, probably by the fire if he's home. Otherwise I guess she'd go to bed, as he's usually supping with us when not on the road.' Ernest remembered reading the girl's father was a long distance lorry driver.

Ernest opened his mouth to ask a further question but was stopped by a tap on his shoulder.

'Ernest; is that you?'

He knew the voice. He spun around to see Lisa with a slender neatly dressed man at her side. He didn't have to guess who the man was, having seen his photo on the cover of the police gazette___ Detective Inspector, Alan Edgeworth; forty-one, educated at Manchester University. Ernest remembered everything about his successor.

Ernest set his fixed smile and lifted himself down from his stool. Lisa knew that smile. She coughed and cleared her throat.

'Sir, this is my old Gov.' as soon as she'd said it, she reddened. Ernest looked right through her. No one would have guessed she'd touched a sensitive nerve.

Her companion called for a round of drinks after the handshaking was over.

'It's bloody awful out there,' said Lisa, pushing back a wet piece of hair that had fallen over one eye.

'Drinks on me,' Edgeworth said pulling out his wallet, whilst frowning at Lisa's choice of words.

Ernest ordered a whisky. He wasn't paying.

'Rain stopped play.' Edgeworth nodded in the direction of the church and Ernest thought bloody right it had. If they hadn't found anything already, whatever clues were left would be washed away by this time.

Silence followed.

Lisa looked uncomfortable, and kept trying to make conversation that wasn't about police investigations or retirement.

'What school did you go to?' Detective Edgeworth asked, obviously hoping they might have something in common, although noting Ernest's un-ironed shirt, doubted it very much.

'Boys Secondary Modern,' Ernest stated looking proud, as if he'd attended some private school or other.

'Don't know it,' replied Detective Edgeworth, his brow creasing as if he should have.

'Before your time I guess,' injected Ernest, 'how about you?'

'Manchester University, '87.'

Silence again.

Lisa shifted and coughed, looking at her watch.

Her boss followed her example, glancing at his own rather expensive looking one, before stating.

'Well some of us have to keep the law and order.' He stood up and offered his hand to Ernest.

'Damned right,' said Ernest, still smiling as he shook the limp hand whilst thinking, 'it won't be because of you.'

Lisa said she had to pick something up and would follow him later in her own car. She glared at Ernest, who was now leaning back against the bar, legs crossed and looking totally relaxed. Edgeworth made for the side door, stepping aside at the last minute to allow a young man in.

Ernest and Lisa made for a table by the fire and ordered coffee. She hadn't intended to do this but there was something about the stranger that had just come in that stirred an interest in her. He wasn't anything out of the ordinary but his eyes had crinkles at the corners as though he laughed a lot and had a soft sensitive mouth. Almost an inch or two taller than herself; his body was slim; not from working out, but a natural slimness that denoted energy being constantly put to the test. He was taking off his wet anorak, revealing a woollen polo neck sweater and faded jeans beneath.

Their eyes met for a brief moment, she looked away, blushing slightly and played with her coffee spoon.

Ernest watched amazed, this was a Lisa he didn't know. She appeared confused. Taking in the situation quickly, he took action and stood up. Beckoning the stranger over, he offered the young man a vacant seat at the table.

'Let me buy you a drink,' he said in a voice taking no argument. 'You look frozen.'

Lisa sat like a statue, her eyes glued to her glass, making no move to finish her day's work at the station.

'That's very much appreciated, thank you kindly.' The young man took out a grubby handkerchief and began drying his face before sitting down.

Ernest put the young man's accent down to either Cheshire or Lancashire, before deciding on Cheshire.

'Live in the village?' the guest enquired, pulling at his polo neck sweater as he warmed up.

'Yes,' Lisa and Ernest said together in chorus.

The three of them spent a good hour chatting about all manner of things until Ernest gently reminded Lisa she was still working. She threw him a look spiced with pure hated and picked up her bag. Her facial features changed, softening as she turned to the third party at the table.

'Sorry I really have to go, I'm still on duty.' She hesitated, not daring to ask a name she realised he hadn't given.

'A nurse?' he lifted his eyebrows.

'No no; not a nurse.' She wished desperately she had been, when she saw his face looking surprised at her response.

'Detective Lisa Pharies,' she stated, her shoulders stiffening.

'Well it's truly a pleasure to meet such a pretty policewoman.'

By now Lisa's face was like a beetroot. Rooted to the spot, she stood there awaiting their companion to tell them more about himself. He got the message quickly.

'I'm Robin Ashton,' just thought I'd get my courage up with a drink before starting my new job.'

'And what is that?' enquired Ernest.

'I'm the new curate at St. Anne's.'

It was difficult to know who was the most surprised, but Lisa had already made definite plans to attend Sunday's service before she left the Horseshoe.

Chapter 8

It was still raining when Ernest set off to visit Rita. Although the hospital was only fifteen miles away it seemed like double that distance. The traffic on the regular roads had increased since people had already started to commute to the city.

Ernest had purposely kept off the new Manchester motorway because he always had trouble recognizing the right intersection to take. It always came up too quickly and he was never in the right lane.

However today he wished he'd taken it for every Tom Dick and Harry seemed to be behind and in front of him. His windscreen wipers were going full-tilt to deal with the rain and car spray. A traffic roundabout was coming up and he started to manoeuvre into the outside lane only to be cut off by a large lorry.

Ernest cursed, shook his fist and circled the roundabout again. This time slipping into the lane he needed, thankfully leaving all the traffic behind. This road was far quieter although the bends in it took all his concentration. The scenery around became more hilly and windswept, as the trees became sparser and the landscape gave way to moorland. A low grey mantle of mist rolled over the ground, broken here and there by stone walls. Huge boulders stood out above the mist like guardians of the moors as they had done so for centuries; and more than likely for many centuries to come.

Ernest thought of Wuthering Heights. He'd never been to Yorkshire but guessed the moors of the Bronte sisters looked very much akin to this.

A rabbit ran in front of him, he braked heavily straining his body against the safety strap. Stopping, he turned off the engine, the animal turned, looked at him briefly before disappearing into the gorse.

Ernest reached into his pocket. He needed a cigarette as his nerves were on edge. It wasn't only the rabbit that made him feel the way he did. It was the thought of seeing Rita and the guilt from not visiting her for such a long time.

Leaning back he took a deep drag of the weed and as he exhaled, he watched the smoke curl against the damp windscreen.

Thoughts cruised around in his brain. What would he talk about to Rita?

He needed something to bring a smile to her face, something they could both laugh at.

He inhaled again; it seemed to do the trick as he remembered Lisa's cooking. Keep it light he told himself, no need to mention the ongoing police investigations.

Having decided on the topic of conversation, he pressed the cigarette stub firmly into the ashtray and restarted the engine, and proceeded to drive for a further three miles.

Ahead a large black and white sign loomed up.

WEST MOORE PSYCHIATRIC HOSPITAL

No one could remember when the last letter on the word 'Moore' first appeared. Whether it was a spelling mistake by the sign writer, or just an acknowledgement of some benefactor with that name, was not known. In fact to the locals, the 'West' part of the hospital's name was often dropped totally and it simply became known as 'The Moore', confusing to say the least for many a hiker asking for directions.

Ernest slowed down, and turning, he drove up the long black tarmac drive that glistened silver in places with the reflection of the sun that was now breaking through the cloud cover. The drive was lined with dwarf rhododendron bushes; dwarfed not from a type of species but from the prevailing wind that swept off the moor.

He considered lighting up another cigarette and just relaxing for a few moments after parking the car. The temptation was great, for the sight of the grey Victorian building in front of him was depressing. So many of these old institutions had long out lived their raison d'être and newer facilities were often desperately needed.

Ernest pulled out the cigarette packet from his pocket, held it for a moment and then placed it back into the glove compartment, slamming it shut. Rita's face drifted into his mind as he leaned back, his head pressed against the headrest. She didn't like the smell of tobacco and it might already be too strong, as he'd just finished one. Turning awkwardly to pull his mackintosh from the back seat, he got out of the car. A cold wind mingled with rain slapped his face. He turned up the collar of his raincoat.

Once inside the building, the stillness of the moorland faded away. All the activity associated with hospitals at once became apparent. The smell of cooking and disinfectant hung around. The receptionist at the desk was an oriental, but whether Chinese or Japanese, Ernest could never quite tell the difference, but reasoned they too must see all Europeans in the same way.

He gave his name, and whom he wanted to see. The man thumbed lazily through a large, much used register, trailing a finger down a page till his finger stopped.

'Ah,' he said.

Ernest's heart began to race and pulsated in his ears.

'Ah,' the receptionist repeated like a doctor after examining a patient. 'The Nursing Officer wants to see any visitors of Rita Goodwin.'

He picked up an intercom, signalling at the same time to a woman pushing a tea trolley, indicating he wanted a cup.

Then remembering Ernest was still waiting for further information, he pointed further down the passage to a counter behind which was the Nursing Officer he was to see.

Ernest walked down the tiled floor; the thumping in his ears seemed to be getting louder.

The Nursing Officer was tiny, but her girth more than made up for it, the buttons on her uniform straining against her overburdened chest. A round fresh face beamed at him.

'You must be the Policeman who brought her in,' she was eyeing him over like he was a potential suitor before adding, 'never forget a face.'

'Retired,' he murmured, unwilling to meet her direct stare that he found disconcerting. He glanced at the floor saying weakly, 'just plain Mr Heath now'.

'Well Mr Heath.' She emphasised the mister, 'we are more than pleased to tell you that the therapy Rita has undergone has been very successful. She appears to know who she is and what happened to her.'

The Nursing Officer sat back as if awaiting acclaim, but Ernest suddenly felt extremely angry. No one had let him know about her recovery and she must have wondered why she hadn't been visited for so long. For a brief moment, he wanted to both cry and laugh, but all he did was gaze at her. Realising no congratulations of the hospital's achievements were forthcoming, she reverted to her job in hand.

'Go easy with her, and no questioning her. Just listen, she's still extremely delicate and we want no relapses.' She smiled dimpling her face and, waving her hand said, 'go on then, off you go to the patient's lounge upstairs.'

Ernest bounded up the stairs to the second floor. There was no way he was going to wait among the wheelchairs and trolleys assembled at the elevator. His mind was in turmoil wondering what her reaction would be on seeing him. Slowing his step, Ernest found the entrance to the lounge and peered cautiously in.

He saw Rita right away; she was sitting by the window. He noticed she was slimmer than she used to be and her hair was tinged with grey. She was gazing down onto the tarmac drive Ernest had just driven up on. He wondered if she'd seen him already or whether she did it daily, hoping one day he'd come.

He stood at the entrance to the room, oblivious to the other patients scattered around. Memories flooded his mind. He'd known her all his life from a child to maturity and the same feelings for her had never left him. He simply loved her.

She turned as if a sense stronger than normal, was telling her he was there. Their eyes locked and tears formed on both their faces as he crossed the room. He took hold of her small hands and caressed her fingers.

'I'm sorry darling, for not coming sooner', he said; his body bending towards her as she lifted her hand and moved a strand of hair away from his forehead.

'It's all right Ernest, you needn't be afraid anymore.'

Ernest knew she'd hit at the very core of his unwanted absence from her. He'd been so afraid of losing the woman he long remembered.

'Charlie has left for Canada,' she said with a little laugh, she was always good at changing the mood. Charlie was the son of her aunt whose death had been the cause of her breakdown.

'He left that awful wife of his, and he's gone on a much needed holiday with that nice young lady from the garage.' She sat back and watched Ernest's face.

Ernest looked at her questioningly.

'You are not thinking of going back to Canada?' He panicked for a moment.

'No,' she said firmly. 'I don't need to run away again.' She looked thoughtful for a moment, and then took his hand.

'Ernest, I don't believe I could have given Aunt Ada my tablets, it's against my nature to be careless with medicines.'

It took his breath away for a second as he hadn't been prepared for any sort of reference to the death of Rita's aunt and was not sure how to handle it. Don't push her, the nursing officer had advised.

'I'm sure you didn't darling.' He was quick to keep things low key.

He changed the subject; going on to tell her about his new cottage, the village and how he was hoping she would come soon to stay, hinting with facial gestures that the stay could be permanent. He was careful not to make any reference to the goings on at the church, hoping it would likely be all tied up before Rita came.

He told her about the mass of daffodils on the village green and about Lisa's cooking and her invalid mother.

Rita nodded in sympathy at the last reference.

'It's not easy looking after anyone like that,' she said, drawing on her own nursing experience of the elderly.

Ernest wasn't sure he wanted to carry on with this line of conversation and was relieved to hear a voice behind him.

'Hello.' A girl of about fifteen had slipped up behind Rita and began stroking her hair.

'Hello my dear.' Rita pulled the hand off her head and patted it. The girl moved away.

Ernest must have looked a little uncomfortable, for Rita was quick to follow up with an explanation.

'Raped by her uncle for years, poor girl,' she looked sadly after the figure moving away from her, 'and nobody did anything about it until she slashed her wrists.'

Ernest gave a long slow whistle just as a bell rang indicating it was time for the visitors to leave. Rita and Ernest looked at one another.

'I'll be back my love,' he said giving her a hug. 'Just get well and think about those daffodils.'

Rita smiled; a smile that tugged at Ernest's heartstrings and brought a newfound energy to his body.

'Can I phone you?' he said.

She nodded.

Suddenly Ernest found himself very, very hungry and as he walked to the parking lot all he could think of was a meal of fish and chips.

Later, as he sat in his car parked in a little used lane, eating a steaming packet of fish and chips and a large carton of mussy peas, he recalled every moment of the time he'd spent with Rita that day. The coffee steamed through the hole in the lid of the plastic cup, warming the side of his leg; his gaze remaining unfocussed through the fogged up windows of the car as he ate.

Then Ernest's hand stopped: a chip halfway to his mouth. Something was forming in his mind.

'Was the murdered girl in the village an abused child?'

The thought lingered for a short period while other thoughts nearer to him personally, wrestled with a different set of possibilities.

Had Ada taken Digoxin tablets by mistake for other pills?

He sighed; what did it matter now. No use putting Rita through her nightmare again. But he did recall her saying to him, 'I couldn't have, it's not my nature.'

Ernest had to agree. Licking his fingers and screwing up the chip papers and wrappings, he dropped them to the car floor and drove off.

Chapter 9

Not being the tidiest of men and still mentally preparing himself for having someone to stay, Ernest let Lisa persuade him to borrow her cleaning lady.

Now Jeanne was busy wielding an assortment of cleaning materials and utensils. The bathroom reeked of disinfectant and the kitchen floor tiles looked dangerously shiny.

Ernest clung to his chair and newspaper as long as he could, but a sharp poke against his legs broke his resolve. He lifted them whilst she ran the sweeper underneath, and as he moved his newspaper fell to the floor, which Jeanne immediately snatched up and folded neatly before placing it back on his knee. He settled back with a sigh, half listening to her chatter.

'Lisa should find herself a young man,' she was saying.

Ernest gave up on the newspaper and, never one to ignore gossip, gave her his full attention.

'Nice,' she said, picking up a Doulton figurine in the window, while sweeping underneath it with a feather duster.

'Yes; my wife's.'

'Married long then?'

'Long,' he pondered over the years past, 'yes, quite long.'

'Good husbands are hard to come by these days.' There was a hint of sadness in her voice, then began to relate to Ernest the goings-on in the village.

'Just look at that hussy in the Horseshoe,' her voice tinged with a streak of viciousness. 'They've been at it for months. Everyone knows apart from the poor bugger of a wife. They're always the last to know, aren't they?'

Ernest didn't know whether to say yes or no, but in the end opted for just a raised eyebrow. He took it she was referring to the publican's wife.

'What about Stanley Breasley?' he enquired innocently. 'Must be no plain sailing there, having an alcoholic wife.'

Jeanne stopped dusting for a brief second, and then let out a long drawn out sigh.

'She was always a timid little thing, wouldn't say boo to a goose, and he's not adverse at speaking his mind.'

'Quick with his fists is he?'

Jeanne looked at him searchingly, not sure how to answer. It didn't do to gossip too much to strangers, and in her opinion Ernest was still an outsider.

Ernest knew when he had reached the end of the line, but couldn't help one more try.

'I saw him buy a bottle of booze to take home, a bit silly if his wife likes her drink, isn't it?'

'No one knows what goes on behind locked doors, but God or the Devil will find out in the end,' she replied; now rearranging the mantelpiece. 'Brings booze back from Scotland on his trips there too.' She chattered on about the lorry he drove and what an eyesore it was when parked on occasions in front of the church.

'The rector had to tell him more than once over it.' She was now going on and on with little input from Ernest, who was by now looking out of the window, hardly listening. The rain had stopped and a splash of blue was appearing to separate the grey cloud cover. He needed to walk; walk and think.

Placing some money on the kitchen table, and telling Jeanne to put his key on the nail inside the garden shed, he took off with Jeanne's parting words still ringing in his ears.

'Lisa wants you around for dinner six-thirty sharp.'

Ernest walked steadily for an hour or so, enjoying the fresh air as it cleared out his nose and chest of the fumes from Jeanne's polish and bleach. There were not many people around and few cars passed. It was a working day and the village was quiet. There were a number of paths and gated farm lanes, all seemed well used and took off over the fields. Ernest climbed a stile, went a few yards into a field before deciding it was far too muddy.

His mind swung between thoughts of the past with Rita, to why the murdered girl had gone to the graveyard alone. Who was she meeting? Whoever it was, not even the ever-watchful gossips in the village had any idea. He turned his step back home again.

The key was hanging in the garden shed when he arrived back. On stepping into the cottage, Ernest knew he'd done the right thing in taking Lisa's advice about having Jeanne. Everywhere he looked, there was order. She had found a place for everything, a problem Ernest constantly battled with.

He picked up a note on the spotless kitchen table.

"Lisa's 6:30 sharp."

Ernest smiled. Jeanne was wasted. She would have made a first-class hospital matron in the old days, where they ruled with disinfectant and carbolic soaps to uncompromising schedules.

Ten minutes later found him still searching for a bottle of wine to take to Lisa's. He eventually found six, neatly lined up under the kitchen sink. So much for Jeanne's opinion on drink, he thought, then spent another five minutes looking for his waste bin that now had found a home by the back door, scrubbed to perfection with a white plastic bag draped inside.

Opening one of the bottles, he took a large glass of wine into the other room; picking up the day's newspaper that must have come while he was out.

The paper had another photo of the church; this time showing the huge yew tree where the body was found. A smaller photo was underneath of Detective Inspector Edgeworth with some details of the on-going investigation taking place, along with a summary of his educational credentials.

Ernest sipped his wine as his eyes roamed over the black type. Edgeworth's investigation it seemed was proceeding on the basis that Gina's killer was an outsider, probably from Manchester, and on drugs. He was speculating that Gina was tempted into the churchyard with some story or other and things had gotten out of hand.

Ernest felt his hackles rising and threw the paper down in disgust. He couldn't see her going off with a stranger that no one in the village knew. Gerry Platt himself had said she was a timid girl. He needed another drink.

Six-thirty came and went while Ernest snored, his head back against his armchair and mouth wide open.

The phone rang.

Struggling to find his way back to the living room and nearly falling over his shoes, he picked up the phone.

'Get your butt over here this minute.' Lisa shouted, before slamming the phone down with a bang.

'Oh God,' Ernest ruffled his thinning hair and looked over at the clock.

It was now 7:00 p.m., a few minutes later Ernest presented himself at number seven looking very sheepish.

Lisa never mentioned the phone call, she just ushered him in, and pointing to one of the two chairs at the table, then went into the kitchen.

Two blue eyes watched him from beside the fire. Ernest nodded to Emily and was about to say something, when Lisa came in holding a huge dish filled with what looked like stew. Disappearing again into the kitchen, this time she brought back a wicker basket filled with rather burnt garlic bread. Not bothering to let him help himself, Lisa filled the large bowl placed before him.

'Lamb stew,' she announced.

He wondered if she'd told him, in case he couldn't guess. The lamb taste was hardly perceptible, being overwhelmed as it was by the many vegetables and thick beef gravy browning.

The apple pie proved good though. He'd bought the same at the supermarket, but had never had it with lumpy custard.

The meal was eaten in almost silence, apart from a curt remark or too. But by the time the first wine bottle was emptied, Lisa was beginning to mellow.

Ernest cleared the table and opened another bottle, while she hand-fed her mother

Lisa's bluntness had softened and before long they were discussing the on-going investigation as though he'd never retired. Ernest, never liking paper work, had always worked alongside his team, unlike his successor who hardly ever left his office according to Lisa.

Ernest waited for the right moment to catch her off-guard.

'Lisa, have you considered incest?'

Lisa shot up from her chair and stared at him, part of her ready to deny such a thought, the other part remembering that Ernest hadn't moved up the ranks for nothing.

'Are there any uncles or close relatives of the girl around?' he asked, glancing across at her mother as he sensed her watching him. He was waiting for Lisa's answer, but was already weighing up the possibility that Emily might have more to tell about the Breasley family if only she could speak. He couldn't explain it, just a strong feeling.

'It's a thought.' Lisa was saying, her forehead showing lines of surprise. 'I'll enquire, but whatever made you come up with that?'

Ernest confessed he had no evidence at all and, although he had mentioned uncles, he was really thinking of Stan and why he continued to ply his alcoholic wife with drink, instead of denying her like most husbands would. Why hadn't he got help from the AA?

'Best recheck his alibi, I guess,' Ernest advised, but before letting the matter go he needed to know one last thing.

"Did they do any test on the type of wax found on her sleeve?"

'Edgeworth thought it wasn't necessary.' She got no further as the bell on the front door rang. They looked at each other quizzically. Lisa stretched her shoulders and went to find out who it was. Ernest could hear voices, followed by Lisa's loud laugh and footsteps coming down the hallway.

Robin Aston, the young curate stood in the doorway, the same overly large polo-necked sweater and, to Ernest's amazement, blue jeans with holes in the knees.

'Thought I'd do my rounds.' He acknowledged Ernest and moved over to Emily. 'So Mrs Pharies how are you today?' He bent over her; obviously not quite sure what to do next, for Emily was staring at him as if she'd seen a ghost; saliva dribbling down one side of her mouth.

'Mother.'! Lisa stepped forward, not quite sure of her mother's reaction either. 'This is our curate, the Reverend Aston, come to help out at the church.'

'Call me Robin,' smiled Robin.

Not a sign of any acknowledgement was forthcoming, and Lisa did the only thing she knew best to help her communicate. She placed the album on her mother's knee and opened the book. Without any warning, Emily lifted her good hand and closing the book, laid her palm across it.

Lisa looked puzzled and embarrassed.

Ernest took control and offered Robin a seat.

'So Robin, where are you from?' He liked to find out whether his guess on dialects was right.

'Don't know originally, I am adopted.' Robin answered truthfully. 'Lived in Lichfield all my life, but my Dad did come from Cheshire.

'So you knew who your father was,' said Ernest.

'Oh no,' laughed Robin. 'Sorry I meant my adopted father's family. Never knew my real parents.

'Golly,' said Lisa: maternal feelings, long pushed down, now surfaced. Emily was making little choking sounds. Lisa got her a drink of water, still looking a little concerned about her mother's unusual behaviour.

'I think she's tired,' she said a little forlornly. It was obvious to Ernest that Lisa didn't want to part with her guest, or guests as the case may be, so quickly.

Robin sprang to his feet.

'Just thought I'd meet the parishioners, and I have a few more to meet on my travels.'

Ernest mumbled his thanks and said it was time he went also. The two men walked back towards Ernest's cottage.

'She's a remarkable woman,' said Robin. Ernest agreed and, as he opened the door, he couldn't help wondering which woman Robin was talking about. He placed his bet on Lisa.

Chapter 10

A peel of bells rang out from the church tower summoning the faithful of the parish to worship. It's clanging was so loud it could be heard for miles around, but that was the intention for St. Anne's was the mother church for all the surrounding parishes.

Ernest patted his jacket pocket, checking for the feel of his wallet. He glanced in the mirror over the mantelpiece, smoothing back his hair with one hand. A few strands still refused to lie down; he spat on his hand and smoothed the offending piece.

Satisfied with the result, he was ready, at least on the outside, but the inner scars left from the many humiliations suffered during his childhood tightened his stomach. He tried to counteract these feelings by thinking of deliberately knocking over a pile of hymnbooks stacked at the back of the church and watch what would happen this time around, but then abandoned the thought as just being childish. Instead he reminded himself it was just like being on an investigation. He was going to mix with the villagers and keep his ears open.

Ernest couldn't stand an unsolved mystery. It was like doing a crossword puzzle, all it took was the right word to fill in the blanks. It was the focus that counted and often it would be some oddball clue that sent one off on the right track. He had convinced himself that interpreting clues was just a hobby now, something that he could think about while unable to sleep at night. Retired or not, he just couldn't tune out his enquiring mind and a notebook on his bedside table was filled with scribbled questions ending with large question marks.

Ready now to face one of his biggest lifetime hurdles, Ernest stepped outside into the crisp morning air. It was mingled with the perfume from the daffodils now tinged with a slight decay. Many of the blooms had finished their moment of glory and were fading among the grass and weeds. A while longer and the green would be mowed and ready for the Maypole festivities.

Cars began parking outside the cottages, the 'no parking' signs ignored, as the only parking space outside the church was already full. There was no-one willing to enforce the law, as on a Sunday it was God's law that took precedence in the village. He guessed the church would be full this morning. It is amazing what curiosity will do, he thought cynically.

'Ernest wait,' the call coming from behind him. It was Lisa panting from her exertion from pushing her mother's wheelchair.

Ernest did what most chivalrous men would do in similar circumstances. He pushed Lisa aside and took over the manoeuvring of the heavy chair over the cracked and bumpy pavement. Emily looked up at him, her blue eyes grateful. He patted her hand and tucked the blanket closer to her. Lisa caught him looking sideways at her with a silly grin on his face.

'What?' she snapped, her cheeks as red as the lipstick she wore. Ernest had never seen her wearing any make-up before.

'Oh nothing,' he said blandly. 'You look nice.'

Lisa coughed.

Ernest chuckled to himself. There was more to the change in Lisa than meets the eye, he guessed, as he tipped the chair wheels up to leave the pavement. Pulling the weight up the church steps was no mean feat. An outsider standing around, observing them would have thought they were a family and pitied the burden placed on husband and daughter.

As they entered the great oak door of the church, Lisa glanced towards the last pew indicating where the wheelchair could be parked in the aisle near the wall. A long red carpet graced the aisle leading up to a heavily carved wooden rood screen, separating the nave from the sanctuary. A magnificent stained glass window adorned most of the east wall behind the high altar, the roof above elaborately carved with gilt inlays. Great stone pillars supporting arches gave visual separation to the sanctuary from the Lady Chapel and the vestry on either side.

Ernest, never one to find churches appealing, was captivated by the splendour of it, the building still dominating the small village it served. It was like walking back in time.

He kneeled down clasping his hands together and to any observer looked like he was praying. He wasn't. It had been many a year since he prayed; he'd given up on that at the age of eleven, God answering none of his pleas. His ears had often been left stinging as a child after being dragged by the vicar to the front of his class.

Half turning, he glanced at Lisa and guessed she too was praying without conviction and in reality only going through the motions. He knew her thoughts only too well on the topic of religion for they had often had long conversations whilst on surveillance in the car.

He felt guilty. What hypocrites Lisa and he were, she was there because of her mother and he had his own objectives, Lisa's case being the better of the two, at least there was some good intent behind her motivation.

His own views had been hardened during his childhood by the treatment he received from an overzealous vicar at his church school. Lisa, on the other hand had come to the conclusion that all religious doctrines were the result of man's need to understand his own suffering with a dash of politics and power. Her dad used to say that the hardest of men in the wartime turned to God when terrified. "A drowning man will cling to any straw," was his saying.

It wasn't that she was a total unbeliever, but her intellect made her question that period in history of The Great Teacher's lifetime. The Romans occupied His country and His own belief system was that the end of the world would be coming soon. As far as Lisa was concerned, He was telling everyone to perfect themselves if they wanted to gain a place in heaven; not to put Him up as part of a

Trinity, who had created this universe and all living creatures in seven days. Anyway no one knew about evolution then.

'Give me freedom any day,' she would say. 'Nature doesn't fret and fume about who is right or wrong. Nothing is black or white, and yet nature and the natural order survive. Give me a compassionate person any day.'

'So why the hell do you attend church every Sunday?' Ernest had asked a little sarcastically and bewildered.

'Mother,' she stated, as if there was no more to be said on the matter. It was on that day that Ernest understood one of the meanings of compassion.

The organ music brought an end to his daydreaming, as the congregation stood up. The new curate was making his debut. The procession moved past, the huge silver cross held high by the cross bearer. Robin followed looking every bit like a rector; his vestments flowing rhythmically as he moved towards the rood screen. Then just as he turned to face the congregation; there was a faint ripple of whispers within the hallowed walls. Beneath his flowing robes two large bare feet could be seen protruding from a pair of very open sandals.

Ernest smiled. He was beginning to enjoy himself, hymns were being sung that he well remembered singing as a boy. His voice rang out loud and clear, initiating odd looks from Lisa.

The usual chanting and repeating of prayers brought everyone's attention closer to the sermon. Robin, on mounting the pulpit, ran his fingers around his dog collar saying

'It's jolly hot under this dress.'

There was a stunned silence, followed by a twitter from the younger parishioners in the congregation. Ernest nudged Lisa. She gave him a dirty look.

Robin then asked the congregation to sit and just listen to the silence around them. Every one sat up straight and stiff not sure if they were doing it right or not. the organist looked confused as if somehow she'd missed a cue.

'Just listen to all the small sounds around you, let your minds empty of the grievances and hurts you bring with you. Close your eyes and just be an empty vessel,' he encouraged.

All Ernest could hear was an uncomfortable shuffling and coughing that each tried to suppress.

Robin went on to talk about the importance of silence and although Ernest got quite drawn in by the idea he was still aware that the expectations of the congregation had not been filled. Nothing was preached forcefully about Paul or Jesus, the power of love in the world or even hell-fire. There was nothing to create an emotional response to their being the faithful followers of Christ. Just silence.

Lisa's eyes never left the curate's face. He held her attention like a moth to a candle.

Ernest had long told himself he would forgo communion, kneeling alone with his eyes half shut he could see all he wanted to.

Being at the back of the church he had a good view, even if it was the back view of the communicants for most of the time. However their returning to their pews after communion gave him the opportunity of exploring them a little more.

The first to go up for communion were a man and woman, she held the man's arm as if giving him strength to walk and kneel before the altar.

Ernest was taken by surprise as they turned to walk back for the man wore a dog collar. The woman, raising her head to help him, was striking looking with classical features; her black hair pulled back from her face and twisted into a bun. Ernest quickly assessed her age to be somewhere in the forties; he was rarely wrong. She wasn't looking too happy, and Ernest guessed it was the innovative way the service had been conducted.

'So that is the Rev. Richards and his sister, the village Samaritan,' he mused. 'How an earth had she remained single?

'Why then?' He followed her with his eyes to her seat. He perished the thought she may have other preferences. Surely not in her position, somehow he felt disgusted with himself for even allowing the thought to linger. Devotion to God was the only thing he could come up. What a waste.

He watched as Lisa took communion with her mother. Lisa stared in defiance of any comments by Ernest as she pushed the wheelchair back.

The last one to take the cup was Kane, probably arranged that way. Ernest felt instant admiration for Robin as he consumed the remainder of the wine.

'What a job,' he thought

At last they were outside waiting in line to shake the curate's hand.

Robin grinned at him.

'They say it only takes the first step.' He let Ernest ponder on his meaning before turning his attention to Lisa. Ernest blushed slightly realising Lisa must have told him he wasn't a churchgoer.

Ernest leaned against the church wall, dying for a cigarette. Someone approached him and said,

'Sorry I haven't been to welcome you, it has been a busy time preparing for him.' She nodded towards Robin, a look of disappointment clearly showing in her face.

The woman he had admired in church was even prettier than he had first thought; her eyes big and brown that seemed to pull one into their depths. The introductions over, they chatted for a few moments, before she was called away. Ernest suddenly felt glad he'd come. He still enjoyed the attention of beautiful women no matter what age, although Rita was the only one that made him feel whole. The rector's sister was certainly an asset to the village, and now he had a name. Rachael Richards.

He saw Kane plucking out a large weed that had grown on a nearby grave. Something fell out of Kane's pocket as he walked off, holding the large weed before him like as offending devil.

Ernest strolled over and picked up a folded leaflet. It was part of the TV Times. He thumbed through it as he waited for Kane to come back.

There was a black ballpoint ring around a film that had been shown at ten p.m. a week ago. Ernest never forgot a date; times maybe, but not dates whenever a murder had been committed, and the date and time on the paper seemed interesting.

He waved it to Kane, who was coming back wiping his hand down his best Sunday trousers.

Kane grinned as he reached out, pulling the paper to his breast and rocking it like a baby.

Ernest didn't quite know why he asked the next question, maybe from habit.

'Do you mark all the TV films you want to see?'

Kane stared at him, looked down at the marked paper and looked around, his large head moving from side to side. He spotted Rachael and made for her. Ernest watched the two of them. Rachael was patting Kane's arm and saying something to him. He looked less agitated.

She certainly had a way with him, he thought admiringly and was feeling sorry he'd frightened the boy. Why though, he didn't know?

As Lisa was still chatting with Robin, Ernest suggested he took Emily home. He took charge of the wheelchair, holding his hand out for the house key to number seven.

He was surprised how light Emily was as he lifted her out of the wheelchair and into her armchair. He slipped into the chair opposite.

They didn't need to speak, he knew she had accepted him and he also knew he was giving something of a normal life back to Lisa, even if it was just for a short while.

'Funny,' he mused, looking at the now sleeping figure. 'She's only my age. I should be grateful I'm healthy.' With that thought came a little apprehension at pushing at the powers that be. I should be more conscious of what I eat, thinking of all the packets of chips and chocolate bars he seemed have an obsession with lately.

He and Rita deserved time together. God couldn't be so cruel to deny them that. Looking at Emily lying there, he was as near to praying as he had ever been.

An hour later Lisa came bounding in, apologising for the length of time she'd taken outside the church, her eyes shone and she chattered ten to the dozen.

'Enjoyed church then?' Ernest couldn't help himself.

She glared at him then suggested a drink a little stronger than tea and didn't wait for an answer. The single malt whisky went down very nicely, especially as she had once told him she only kept it for special occasions.

Then, quite out-of-the-blue Lisa said.

'I took another look at Gina's family. No other males other her father were investigated and his alibi checked out. He was on the road to Scotland.' She took another sip from her glass.

'Had a word with Ducky'! Ducky was Lisa's pet name for Dr Duckworth who did most of the autopsies.

'And,' added Ernest; now giving her his full attention.

'No sperm found.'

He sat back, trying to hold his tongue.

'But,' continued Lisa, not sure whether what she was about to say was relevant information or not. 'Ducky seems to think she's been at it for sometime, maybe a good year or even more.'

She looked at him to see how he took the information.

'Well now...' he uttered. But to himself he was thinking she's either a randy little bugger or someone had been having his bloody way with her for years. He dismissed the former. Whoever he'd talked to, there was never any evidence of any boy or sexual interest on her part. It was the opposite in fact. Shy, introverted, Gina didn't sound like a nymphomaniac to him.

'Look nearer home' his instincts kept telling him, and if Edgeworth is worth his salt he would be already onto it, but somehow Ernest doubted it.

Chapter 11

Rachael poured out a cup of freshly brewed coffee and took it over to the kitchen table. Even though the tabletop was the old scrubbed top type, Rachael placed a mat under the hot drink and sat down.

She slid along the polished bench picking up a pile of papers that lay at the far end of the long table and slid back to her original position. She stared blankly at the papers, finding it hard to concentrate. There were too many things she felt compelled to do. She'd tried to cut down on charities and organisations that could do without her, but it was difficult. Anything in God's name was difficult to ignore for Rachael and it seemed God's need was never ending and quite exhausting.

She tried to add up the money for the Mothers Union, as the treasurer was on holiday in Spain, but her eyes ached. She made a mental note to herself to make an appointment with the optician. Her reading glasses were becoming of little use in her ability to see small writing.

A note pad lay under the vicarage keys with jottings of people Rachael was to visit during the week. The writing was large and hastily written. Rachael moved the keys and frowned at a new name. For a moment she was mystified. It wasn't anyone she could bring to mind at that moment, but then recalled the rather distinguished looking gentleman who had attended church with Lisa.

She'd written down Ernest Heath ending with a rather large question mark; the mark a way of telling herself to learn more about the person. In that way she could always be of some help.

Suddenly she felt weary and a little sick, the coffee didn't seem that appealing any more. She got up and pouring it down the sink filled the cup with cold water. The coldness hit her stomach having a calming effect. Rachael was aware she was overdoing things and was probably run down.

She sighed, and looked through the large modern kitchen window that overlooked the south side of the graveyard and a small coppice of oak trees. It was one of just two rooms in the house in keeping with the times, the rest belonging to the sixteenth century. The churchwardens, realising that the rectory needed to be updated, had generously dipped into the coffers and a large up-to-date kitchen had been added on, taking away a large portion of the garden and leaving the churchyard much closer.

A bedroom with an en-suite bathroom had been added later over the kitchen. As neither John nor Rachael had ever claimed it for their own use; it had become a room for guests. The other rooms remained Tudor in every aspect, although another bathroom had been plumbed in with difficulty in the smallest room upstairs.

The phone rang, but before Rachael could put her cup down, it rang off.

Reminiscing again, she gazed into space. If only John's health would improve. She had prayed nightly for some small miracle to happen. God would listen she assured herself because she had been a faithful Christian and had never questioned His will, doing all she could to be without sin and worthy of His grace.

Dr. Farley had told her that John's chances of recovery were good only last week.

'Give him time' he had said. 'It's a shock for a man of his age to suffer a heart attack and you have to have patience.'

Rachael looked over at the cross on the wall with Christ's figure hanging on it. 'He suffered horribly' she thought compassionately. 'My suffering is nothing, compared to John's health, perhaps we are both being tested,' she sighed and all at once felt better. She needed to be challenged, it proved her love for God and she would not be found lacking. Rachael took a deep breath and forced herself to concentrate on the jobs at hand.

She must visit Gina's mother again and take her some of her homemade lemon cheese tarts she liked. Stan Breasley was not as abrasive following his daughter's death. He now seemed less eager to leave his wife alone, so at least that was a good sign for their future relationship. Sometimes it took a tragedy for people to accept their responsibilities in marriage. Rachael smiled to herself, warming to the thought that something good could well come out of something bad.

Still she must keep her eye on other lost souls and those in need of the Lord's guidance. She would pop around to Lisa's mother and spend a little quality time with her. Perhaps show more interest in her old photo album. Poor woman, it must be hard not to be able to communicate. Lisa was a nice young woman and it couldn't be easy for her to sacrifice her life in that way.

Yet nothing mattered to Rachael as much as seeing her brother living to his full potential as a rector to God's people. Alone she understood his need to be the very best in his chosen vocation and her own sacrifice was given freely. It had not been easy growing up under a dominating father. Their mother, having died in their early years, hardly figured at all in their childhood memories. They only had each other to rely on to understand their deepest thoughts.

The front door opened and a man's voice could be heard in the hallway.

'Any tea going?'

Rachael jumped up startled. Robin stood in the doorway, the morning post in his hands. Rachael's eyes travelled the full length of him, instantly bringing tension to her shoulders. The same threadbare jeans he'd worn all week, a faded and somewhat stained sweatshirt with a seam that needed stitching and the same toeless sandals. The only redeeming feature was his clean-shaven face that beamed with enthusiasm and the rather large silver cross hanging from a leather thong around his neck.

Rachael stiffened; she was having trouble being charitable about Robin Ashton. John's new assistant had taken them both by surprise when he gave his first sermon, or rather the lack of it. She had seen the disturbed looks on the parishioner's faces as they sat in silence for fifteen minutes.

Now confronting Robin, Rachael wasn't able to keep her tongue in her mouth when it came to Robin's dress code. She stood up facing him with a cold look

'What on earth were you thinking of coming to church in sandals instead of socks and decent shoes, where was your reverence to God in God's house?

'Jesus wore sandals'. He'd looked at her with laughter in his eyes. She felt belittled and looked away smarting from his arrogance.

Rachael turned her back towards him and busied herself preparing a tray for tea. Robin watched her, wondering why he felt so uncomfortable in her presence. On paper it seemed the ideal placement, a country church and reasonably young rector. What was wrong? Underneath he really knew the answer. The fact was John and Rachael still leaned towards the old school of thought and had not moved with the more progressive church of today.

Robin stared at Rachael's slim shapely figure, her dark hair tied into a ponytail. It didn't seem right that she hadn't a family of her own instead of devoting her life to her brother. It might have helped to bring her into a more realistic approach to the way the new generation looked at the doctrine of the church.

He opened the biscuit tin by his side and helped himself to a ginger one. Rachael gave him a swift glance of annoyance. In defiance he chomped nosily on the biscuit as he sat on the edge of the table, daggling his long legs and nibbling at the remainder.

'John was telling me about your childhood,' he said, more for something to say than anything else. A cup rattled dangerously as it was set down suddenly on its saucer. Rachael's body stiffened again, her voice wavered a little, then sharpened.

'Did he,' she said abruptly, busying herself with placing spoons on the saucers, although no one took sugar. 'There's not much to tell. Ours was quite an ordinary upbringing.'

Robin sensed Rachael didn't want to continue in that vane, so took another tack.

'He says he's feeling much better and might give communion on Sunday.'

It was as if the world had taken a quick spin and stopped on a bright sunny day. Rachael turned, her face beaming. Her beautifully designed features and the softness of her liquid eyes momentarily captivated Robin in surprise. It was like being confronted by a totally different person.

'Did he indeed,' she asked eagerly, waiting to hear the confirmation over again.

'Indeed he did,' and then not being able to help himself added; 'I guess he's almost ready to give a sermon.'

'Oh ye of little faith;' Rachael said to herself as her heart leapt, as that passage from the bible suddenly came to her. On an impulse born of renewed energy, she found herself speaking generously.

'Leave your washing by your bedroom door. I'll do it and do a little mending for you also.' She said it almost in one breath, keeping her eyes lowered onto the tray that she handed to him.

Robin felt he wanted to touch her hand, tell her he knew she was tired and thank her for what he knew was a kindness. Instead he gave a raucous smile and said:

'You might be sorry you offered.' He hummed a tune as he carried the tray to John's office.

John sat at his dark oak desk, his head half buried in his hands re-reading what he had written. It had seemed good at the time. Now that he'd read it again it appeared dull and uninspired; his writing reflecting how he felt. He wasn't up to banging the pulpit to make a point or raise his voice to command attention like he normally did.

Now somewhere deep within him he wanted to express the peace of God's presence. The truth being that Robin's sermon had kindled something inside. The sermon had affected him differently from his sister. Something he'd felt when young, long before father took to scrutinising his writings and leaving him feeling he could never come up to his standards.

John looked up as Robin came in. He pushed away his writing with his arm making room for the tray.

'You do it,' he said flatly. Robin nodded and began pouring out the tea.

Apart from the underlying feeling of being an outsider with new ideas, Robin actually liked the village. Gelsby suited him well enough; plenty of walks to indulge in his bird watching hobby. He loved the old rectory with its low-beamed ceiling and open fireplaces. He liked John, though he guessed he would never really know him for he seemed to harbour a much older and more fundamental mind.

Rachael too was an enigma. A beautiful woman with so much compassion, yet she held herself tightly, frightened now to step outside the box she'd made for herself.

John was saying something about forgiveness. Robin coughed and gave him attention.

'Do you believe God forgives all sin?' John asked, his gaze flitting to the window where the soft rays of sunlight hit the stone mullioned and leaded panes.

'Yes.' Robin had always been clear on that point.

John smiled, showing his perfect teeth. 'Would you think forgiveness came quicker if one showed by effort they were truly sorry?' He waited for the answer sipping his lukewarm tea.

Robin thought for a moment, wondering where the conversation was leading, and then answered slowly and with conviction.

'I believe God forgives all sins if the sinner repents and I'm certain any effort to show repentance will be known to God.'

'That's my belief too Robin, would you write a sermon on it?'

So that was what it was all about, mused Robin, thankful no great confession was about to take place. He could tell Rachael that

John was very much an inspiration for the sermon yet not quite up to giving it himself. He was glad he had something nice to tell her, he'd liked the way she smiled when something pleased her.

John was talking again; he seemed relaxed and anxious to get back into his role as rector of the parish.

'I thought it might be a nice gesture to have that new gentleman around one evening and maybe Lisa. They appear to know one another, work I think it was, ex policeman or something. Maybe you can ask Rachael to arrange something.'

Robin said he would, although thought he'd better approach Rachael cautiously first. She didn't look as if she was ready to take on too much more, although the thought of helping Lisa stirred pleasant feelings and he would welcome any excuse to talk to her again. Spending a whole evening in Lisa's company would certainly be nice.

John then came up with something quite unexpected.

'Robin how's your Latin?'

Taken by surprise at the question, Robin pondered on his abilities before answering,

'Average I guess, not brilliant but I can usually manage to get the gist of it.' He looked at John with a questioning frown before asking. 'Why?'

'Just asking,' replied John with a faraway look in his eyes.

Chapter 12

Sharon came out of the ladies toilet, her face paler than usual even under the layers of make-up. The heavy black mascara on her left eye was smudged. Her bright red lips glistened with what appeared to be some of the contents of her stomach.

She'd been sick, the nausea still rising from her stomach. This was the third time this week and Sharon had already decided the sickness was not from something she'd eaten. Gerry's face came to mind and she felt sick again, this time from anxiety. He'd have to be told. Sharon had told herself that fact many times during the day but it wasn't so easy with Donna hovering around and with her weird looks and all.

Sharon struggled to give herself the appearance of normality. She touched her hair giving an extra bounce to the curls and pulled down the front of her top to give more view to her cleavage. Whatever she did she mustn't let him lose interest, not now when she needed all the support she could get. Not for a moment did the landlord's wife figure in her mind. Gerry was always eager to let her know his marriage wasn't satisfying, and by his ardent lovemaking she believed him.

Taking a deep breath she pushed open the door at the side of the bar, Gerry glanced up at her as he pulled a draught for a customer, then he beckoned with a slight movement of his head that someone needed serving at the other end of the bar. She pushed past him, the smell of the ale churning her stomach.

Sharon recognised the customer as the new tenant in the village and a friend of Lisa Pharies. She'd served him before. He was leaning on the bar, his elbows bent with his head cupped in his hands. He looked deep in thought.

'Usual?' Sharon asked, never one to forget a local's drink.

Ernest jumped, his elbows slipping and scattering a dish of peanuts. He blushed and tried to scoop them up scattering even more on the floor.

'Don't worry.' Sharon moved the dish with the remaining nuts automatically as if it happened regularly.

'Sorry,' he spluttered feeling clumsy. Then, momentarily surprising himself, he ordered a large whisky.

Sharon stared at him, then at the clock located over the spirit bottles. The little hand was getting close to closing time and hoped he wasn't going to linger over his drink.

Holding the amber liquid in his hand, Ernest lifted it to the light, stared at it for a moment and then tipped his head back drinking a good half in one gulp.

Opening his mouth he inhaled deeply letting the warmth travel through his body. It felt good and he could feel his anxiety lessening. His stomach had been fluttering since he had made the decision to bring Rita back to his cottage for a couple of days.

He let his gaze wander around the pub; glass held high in his hand and now and then taking small sips from it. The fire was dying, the red-hot embers glowing, causing the horse-brasses to sparkle with bright reflections of light. It all appeared homely and peaceful.

Only a couple of locals remained, it was a working day and the out-of-towners had already taken to the road. The nook by the fireplace looked cosy and intimate. Rita would like that he thought, recalling the last time they raised their glasses to a new beginning together.

'Give it time,' he reminded himself. 'Just give it time.'

Finishing the remainder of the whisky he called goodnight to the landlord and taking a quick look at the clock he left the Horseshoe.

'Time please.' The last call having been made, Gerry shouted to his wife, 'how about a cuppa Donna,' before pushing himself closer to Sharon's back more than necessary as he slid past her to the till. Sharon gave his roving hand a playful tap out of habit, then sidled alongside him.

'I need to see you alone Gerry,' she whispered as she started counting out the notes whilst he emptied out the remaining coins on the bar.

'Not now Shar,' he moved slightly away from her, his eyes straying nervously to the side door.

'When then___?' Sharon couldn't keep the irritation and disappointment out of her voice. Gerry looked down at the bulging invitation of her breasts struggling within their restraints. Feeling his desire growing, he threw all caution to the wind.

'Meet me by the style after you've left. I'll say the lamp outside needs attention or something.'

Satisfied she'd got her way, Sharon's nausea seemed to lessen. She'd tell him and they would plan their future. His wife's place in all this never entered her head; divorce was no big deal these days. Her own Mum and Dad had already had a couple of partners and she'd turned out all right hadn't she.

Sharon refused the tea offered after the days taking was done and said she was tired. Donna didn't urge her to stay.

Gerry mentioned someone had told him the light on the gate was flickering and he'd just take a look. Donna nodded, understanding the need for light on that part of the road and said she was off to bed.

Outside Gerry walked a little way past the lamp and a couple of yards around the corner to the old wooden style tucked between a high hawthorn hedge and a stone wall. Occasionally a local would use it to take a short cut across a field to the school lane but at that time of night it was rarely used.

Gerry caught the outline of Sharon's figure in the darkness, the moon and stars veiled by cloud cover. He dare not stay too long, but in his eagerness for satisfaction hurried his step. Nothing was said as they climbed the style, almost falling into the hawthorn hedge in their attempt at rushed lovemaking. They were oblivious to the lone walker who for whatever reason had decided to take the path across the field from the opposite direction.

The walker stopped, it was impossible to see who was struggling by the style. Staying close to the hedge and creeping nearer to see what was taking place.

The watcher froze for a moment, then moved closer like a large cat stalking its prey, each movement so quiet and deliberate, all senses alert to every movement.

Oblivious to anyone around, Sharon was convinced she still had the power over her lover and pushed him away.

'I'm pregnant,' she stated firmly pulling her skirt down which hardly meant anything at all owing to its short length.

'What.' Gerry struggled with his zip, eager now to be gone. 'For God's sake don't say things like that.'

Sharon put her arms around his neck and whispered in his ear.

'But it's true my darling,' she tried to nibble his ear only to be pushed roughly away.

'What the hell are you saying?' His voice had risen and the observer could now identify him bringing a shiver of anticipation as to who the woman might be.

Gerry was still speaking, his speech angry and condemning. Birth pills were mentioned bringing out a sarcastic laugh from his companion.

'I told you I hadn't any when you were so eager to get me into your wife's bed.' The woman's voice was raised and emotional, leaving no doubt as to who she was.

'What are you going to do?' Sharon waited, her whole life seemed to be crumbling before her and even in the half-light there was no mistaking the look of complete horror on Gerry's face.

'It's not mine; don't throw that one on me.' He pushed her away, the thorns on the hedge scraping her face. 'I always knew you were a tart, just look at the way you dress, egging men on.' His attitude had changed; taking on a moral tone and no longer led by his primitive desires. 'Couldn't get your panties down fast enough,' he sneered, 'well you won't trap me.'

Sharon felt terribly sick again. She was no longer in charge, normally getting the attention of men just by offering the forbidden fruits. She was condemned, made to feel like an insect of no concern. Suddenly angry, she reared up lashing out with her long fingernails leaving a long scratch down Gerry's cheek. His hand went up, feeling the oozing blood as he pushed past her making for the style. Sharon gave one scream and bent down sobbing and curling up in a foetal position.

That's how the observer found her. Helping her up, Sharon leaned gratefully on the arm of her comforter. They crossed the dew-laden field, using it as a short cut to the old school lane that was near to Sharon's home.

Sharon sniffled and sobbed as she stumbled along. She waited for her companion to say something but nothing was forthcoming, which to Sharon meant condemnation.

The clouds lifted letting a pale moon give an eerie light. A crafty look stole over Sharon's face. She silently counted days since her last period and Donna had been away at her sister's over that time. Sharon wasn't going to be anyone's victim and revenge would be sweet.

'I was raped,' she said simply. Her companion stopped short, facing the stone wall as if turning her back on the lie.

'He raped me.' Sharon blurted out again more forcibly and with real conviction this time adding; 'when his wife was away, and now I'm pregnant.

There was a movement as her companion turned and Sharon caught the fanatical burning in the eyes that seemed to search her very soul.

'How many more lies Sharon?' The questioner sounded weary.

'I'm not lying.' Sharon was now ready to defend herself against the village if needs be.

'You should ask God's forgiveness, not add lies to your behaviour.'

Sharon stared in disbelief at the figure before her. What right had any one to talk to her like that?

'Now look here, I....' she got no further. She heard a quick intake of breath as something was raised over her head, then the distinct sound of cracking and a second of intense pain, before falling lifeless to the ground. Only the moon witnessed the stones from the wall being lifted and thrown on top of the still form.

In the front bedroom of the Horseshoe Inn Donna lay awake. She fancied she heard the back door slam to and awaited Gerry's footsteps on the stairwell. Minutes passed; a clink of glass. Donna knew that Gerry was helping himself to liquor which rather surprised her, for although Gerry was many things he never abused the position he held by drinking solo. A warm feeling cruised through her thin body as another thought reared up, but as time passed she turned over once again feeling empty and disappointed. Sleep came begrudgingly whilst downstairs Gerry stared into the now cold embers and poured himself another drink, emptying the bottle.

Chapter 13

Number eleven was as neat as a new pin. The lemon scent from the furniture polish filled the air mingling with other cleaning agents. Jeanne had left the kitchen window open to invite fresher air, permitting the distant sound of an approaching police car siren to drift through.

Subconsciously Ernest recognised its wail although his mind was somewhere else. If he had been more attentive he'd have guessed it would be some traffic infraction or an accident. But today his concentration was focussed on Rita's visit. He'd waited a long time for this day, and he wanted it perfect.

Rita liked cleanliness and order, as most nurses do. The one thing Ernest always admired about her was her ability to make a home inviting; a thing Ernest lacked as a child. His former wife was by no means considered a nurturer. Although she had been good housewife, clean and tidy, she'd lacked the homeliness about her that Rita had. Ernest however was not being perfectly honest with this comparison. In truth it was only an assumption, for he'd never been inside any home of Rita's. The ideal of his childhood sweetheart was more based on his own needs, but over the decades it had stuck and for some uncanny reason he would have been proved perfectly correct.

Ernest closed the kitchen window. A draft had blown over a small cactus plant spilling the soil. It was quickly potted again and the sink cleaned. No need to upset Jeanne by leaving bits of dirt scattered around.

With nothing else to do, he opened the fridge door and surveyed the stacked shelves; the amount of food well beyond even his needs but Ernest wanted variety and had overdone his usual conservative grocery list.

He glanced at the large kitchen clock; then checked his watch. They both tallied exactly with Big Ben on the BBC news, another obsession he'd acquired in the police force.

Too early to leave to pick up Rita, he sat on a chair at the kitchen table and stared into space. He'd thought of leaving right away and picking up something to eat at one of the transport cafes along the way, but his stomach felt more like throwing up any food rather than keeping it down. The anxiety over having Rita to stay was a new experience for the normally self-controlled Ernest and it felt as though his body didn't belong to him anymore. So many questions ran through him, although this time they came rushing from his heart and not his head.

Another police siren wailed; louder this time although the window was shut. Ernest flinched. He expected to hear it followed by the sound of an ambulance and he didn't have to wait long, the blare of the latter confirming that someone needed medical attention urgently. Somebody's day shattered he thought, recalling the many tragedies he'd witnessed over the years.

For a while he debated the speed of traffic and the narrowness of the country roads, a difficult on-going issue to address in England with all its history. Again the sound of sirens, they seemed to be behind him, but there was only the field there, and beyond that a school. Ernest froze for a second and hoped it wasn't a child.

Agitated by the lack of not knowing what was going on and acknowledging he had more important things to think of, he got up abruptly and gathered up the things he needed for his journey to pick up Rita. The back door was locked and he started his car.

Instead of heading north and investigating whatever was happening, Ernest turned south and made for the motorway. His life had now changed, he reminded himself.

The third transport café along the way found him eating a large plate of eggs, bacon and chips, two coffees and toast. His appetite now returned having started on his journey to see Rita. He sat in his car in the café parking ground afterwards and smoked two cigarettes, deliberately blowing the smoke through the open window. He sniffed the remaining air and searched in the glove compartment for the tin of air spray he'd picked up with his shopping. It wasn't there, only his mobile and another packet of cigarettes.

For a second he thought of phoning Lisa on his mobile, just to pass the time of day. He half convinced himself he should. His large hand had actually picked up the mobile before he recognized another one of his obsessions, by wanting to know what was going on with as many details as possible.

Instead he locked the mobile in his glove compartment and glanced at this watch; at the same time hoping he hadn't put the clean air spray in the fridge. His stomach churned, the chips weren't sitting too well.

Back in Gelsby, Sharon's body had been found by a couple of school children. Fortunately it was only a foot with a shoe on it that they had seen under a pile of stones. At first the teacher thought the stone wall that edged the lane frequently used by the pupils at the school had fallen over on some unfortunate child.

The foot protruding from under the stones wore a black nylon stocking. Tensed up with adrenaline and horror, the teacher was more than relieved he didn't have to face some grief stricken parent. He noticed with interest the two ladders that showed a glimpse of white flesh, but couldn't think why that seemed important. Then coming out of shock he did the most practical thing of looking for the head of the body.

The blonde hair sticking out of the rubble gave the position away and, as he pulled at the stones, he'd forgot about the two lads who had fetched him. The blonde curls under the stones were dyed dark red with blood. Another stone removed and the resemblance of a face appeared.

A shriek coming from behind reminded him of the presence of the two lads. The boy's faces were white, their eyes in shock round and glazed. 'Oh God,' thought Dennis Brent, the maths teacher, the whole school will now have to be counselled. He had a strong aversion to modern day counselling techniques and firmly believed children were much more resilient than psychologists proclaimed. He'd been to counselling himself when his marriage broke down only to find later the said psychologist had been married twice and was at the time dating an eighteen-year-old.

He shouted to the boys to fetch the Headmaster; tell him to stop pupils entering the lane, and to send for the police at once. He also warned them not to talk to any other children. Gratefully the boys left to do his bidding.

The boys stammered out their horrific details to a stunned headmaster, whose first response was to pour himself a medicinal whisky while still in their presence; the spirit being kept in his locked desk drawer for emergencies. This was one emergency however he would never have envisioned.

Later, after he'd given a detailed statement to a very efficient policewoman, the headmaster poured out yet another stiff whisky. Later he joined Dennis in an extra tot, after all it was his school and no doubt he would be in the limelight with photos and reporters. Listening to Dennis with one ear, he was already planning his piece about the school and its impeccable reputation under his headship. His record for pupils ending up at universities was renowned. Unfortunately Detective Sergeant Lisa Pharies was not interested in interviewing him at all and he had to leave the stage to his maths teacher.

Lisa was also out-of-sorts this morning as she felt Detective Inspector Edgeworth was again stepping on her patch. Not that he didn't have every right; but he did have a habit of making everyone else in the police station wonder why they were even there. He seemed to go over everything they did, then come to his own conclusions without asking for their opinions.

Lisa tucked a strand of loose hair behind her ear. She felt tired. Everything seemed to be hotting up, and all of it on her patch. Then there was that niggling feeling she was going to need help with her mother. Jeanne was not so available anymore, she seemed to be spending more time at her job cleaning the church and now she was helping out Ernest. Lisa knew she shouldn't feel resentful, but she did. Feelings were beginning to arise she had never entertained in the past, like resentment and the need for freedom to do her own thing; a place where she could entertain. Within all these fleeting feelings, Robin's face kept coming to mind.

Oblivious to the happening that had brought a sleepy Gelsby to life once more, Ernest drove towards the West Moore Hospital to pick up Rita.

He stopped off at a superstore before heading along the country roads. On the back seat of his sedan now lay a bunch of roses; the ones forced by some greenhouse that appeared dehydrated never really uncurling from the bud stage, and a new can of air spray.

He felt nervous like he did when he married Jean, the underlining thought being 'was he making the right decision?' However the moment he saw Rita waiting for him in the lounge, he knew he had made the right one.

He had to check the tears that seemed to want to spring to his eyes and the lump in his throat made his voice tremble a little.

'Are you ready?' was all he could muster.

She looked so nice; her now grey hair still curled as it always did, the blue eyes tinged with black sparkled with happiness. She had lost weight and looked like she did at nineteen, slim and displaying her well-shaped legs in heeled shoes. A small bag stood by her side; Ernest wondered how long she had been ready waiting for him to come.

Her voice rang out at seeing him. It was clear with a newfound confidence.

'You have to sign that.' She pointed to the man behind the reception desk. It was the same Oriental guy who Ernest had seen before; he took a guess at him being Chinese, but then wavered with uncertainty.

Ernest signed the release form where indicated with great pleasure using his more flamboyant signature, and even plucked up courage to ask the receptionist where he came from.

The man looked at him curiously before replying 'Bradford,' in a thick Yorkshire accent. Ernest blushed and hurriedly picked up Rita's bag with one hand and her arm with the other.

Neither spoke as they got into the car, Ernest could see Rita was struggling with her own feelings. She sat stiffly in the front seat of the car and then remembered the safety belt. Ernest handed her the flowers. Lifting them up to her face, she didn't smell them but gently stroked the buds against her cheeks.

'Lets go home,' Ernest said starting the car. Rita looked at him, smiled and nodded.

'Tell me about the cottage,' she said after a time of reflective silence looking out of the car window. He described the cottage to the smallest detail even to the mouse he'd never managed to catch. Rita knew the village from her childhood days but never had been in the old cottages that that gave village the charm it was noted for.

'Some of them were old weavers cottages weren't they?' she asked. Ernest remembered Kane telling him the same thing. Rita went on, obviously interested in the history of the place.

'I remember our teacher telling us some of the cottages had a room upstairs with a loom and they wove materials for the local merchants.'

Ernest glanced at her, wondering how she had retained the information. They had after all shared the same classroom and teacher. She was always the smart one.

She went on to tell him a lot more about Gelsby than he knew and he was beginning to think he'd been a little more than lucky finding a cottage there. He in turn told her of Lisa and her attraction to the new curate, making her laugh. He took care not to mention the murder.

At last they arrived, rain had just started and it got them running from the car to the back door laughing whilst Ernest fiddled with the key. Soon the fire was lit and after a quick inspection of the cottage, they opened a bottle of red wine.

'Just one,' said Rita, but she settled down with another as Ernest started to prepare dinner, which consisted of a frozen shepherd's pie, peaches and ice cream.

It was good, Ernest was quite amazed and went back to find the package label for another time. Rita said she would really enjoy getting breakfast for them both.

'Are you sure?' Ernest looked away as he asked, not wanting her to see any doubt in his face.

She touched his arm gently. 'I'm fine Ernest, really I am.'

Just at that moment the phone rang. Ernest ignored it, till Rita looked at him questioningly. He shrugged, gave a sigh and went through to the hallway.

'Ernest Heath speaking,' he said. It had taken him a while to relieve himself of his police title but, like Rita, he had an aversion to hearing just hello whenever he phoned someone.

'It's Lisa,' her breath sounded as if she had been running. It was high and quick with small gasps. Immediately Ernest wondered if her mother was all right and asked after her anxiously.

'Your mother ok Lisa?'

'Yes, yes Mum's all right.' Lisa sounded relieved now she'd heard his voice.

'Ernest we have another homicide,' there was a short break before she continued breathlessly,' 'the barmaid from the Horseshoe Inn has been found with her head bashed in.'

Ernest felt momentarily ill, the very last thing he needed was for Rita to be in the area of a recent murder investigation but, true to his former professionalism, he had to know as much as was forthcoming.

'You are talking about the brassy blonde bombshell aren't you?' he asked, remembering the provocative barmaid the landlord couldn't keep his eyes off.

'That's her Ernest, she was found in the lane the kids use to get to school, covered under a pile of stones from the stone wall. The post-mortem hasn't been done yet but there's no way the wall could have fell on her, she was definitely hit before being covered up.'

So that's what the sirens were all about reflected Ernest, then quickly realised Lisa must need something for her to tell him all this so quickly and he half guessed what it was.

'What about Jeanne?' He was never far off the mark.

'She's busy,' Lisa sounded desperate. Please Ernest, I'm at my wits end and Edgeworth's chomping at the bit.'

Once in a while when Ernest feels trapped and there is only one solution for him; to get it over as quickly as possible.

'What time?' he said in a resigned voice.

'Only for a couple of hours tomorrow, two till four.' Lisa's breathing was getting back to normal. 'Rachael can cover after that until I'm home.' Ernest was just about to place the phone down when he heard her cough, 'and by the way, bring Rita around. I'll leave some biscuits and cake out.'

'Ok, but promise not to mention what's going on in the village,' he replied.

Ernest stood for a while looking at the replaced phone, women seemed to organize him without him knowing 'til it was all too late. He really didn't need this.

Over a cup of tea Ernest quietly mentioned an emergency that had come up and how Lisa needed someone to sit with her mother. Rita responded right away, a brightness showing in her eyes.

'Oh Ernest, you have to help,' then, wondering how he might react, added casually

'I can come too, can't I?'

He nodded and patted her hand. There was no way he was going to leave her on her own, and besides the village would be no place to stroll around with all these police activities going on. Best keep Rita indoors or take her for a run out in the car he decided.

Deep down a sense of foreboding overcame him.

Chapter 14

Ernest awoke to the rattle of crockery and the kettle's steamy whistle. Hands folded behind his head, he lay perfectly still almost afraid any movement would dissolve the feeling of contentment that was cruising through his body. When happiness comes to someone late in life it is a gift to be savoured.

His sense of hearing, now tuned in to Rita's presence downstairs, caught the low humming of:

"I'll be with you in apple blossom time."

He sang the words silently to himself and let the memories of past golden moments come alive.

'Ernest.' Rita's voice broke his reminiscing. Realizing she must be standing at the bottom of the stairs, he sat up abruptly.

'Breakfast Ernest?' her voice was loud and clear expressing the old confidence he remembered. It had been a long time since he felt so contented.

Entering the kitchen, the morning sun was streaming in through the small window. Rita had not been skimpy; the bacon rashers alongside two eggs and a piece of fried bread. He offered to do the washing up. Rita refused, but smiling handed him the tea towel. Everything done, they stood for a moment looking through the window at the little garden with its promise of colour once the flower buds opened.

'Shall we go for a walk Ernest?' she turned and looked at him thoughtfully before stating 'we could go and have a look at the old church.'

Ernest froze and was at once faced with a dilemma; he rubbed his forehead as he felt his face reddening.

'I was going to suggest a drive to Rudyard Lake and have a spot of lunch before going to Lisa's.' He felt himself stuttering as his words fell over themselves. He had to do something to get her away from the police and media invasion that would be flooding the village.

Thankfully Rita gave him a delighted grin and nodded enthusiastically.

'Great, I'd really like that, and I'm really looking forward to meeting Lisa and her mother.'

The church clock was striking nine as they backed the car out making for a morning out on the moors. Only Ernest was aware of the local activity with groups of villagers deep in conversation, one or two taking a moment from their gossip to look in their direction and presumably, he thought, to muse on whether or not his lady friend had stayed the night. He was thankful to be leaving Gelsby and have the time to concentrate on his companion.

Every moment they were together, Ernest was aware of the transformation that had taken place within Rita. There was nothing of the woman he'd watched being admitted into care the year before. Here beside him the old Rita, full of confidence vital and witty, was living again. Time passed quickly, the drive and lunch proving very relaxing and he could have stayed much longer.

Rita was looking at her watch.

'We need to get back, remember you promised not to be late,' she reminded him.

Still the capable nurse he thought, letting her lead him to the car.

When they were back on the road he wished his vehicle could sprout a pair of wings and whisk them away to some faraway land.

Arriving back in good time, they strolled around to number seven. Ernest's finger was just about to push Lisa's front door bell when a screech of tires made him turn. An old green sports car had pulled up by the curb side. Geoff Leigh, the reporter leaned out of the open car window.

'Wish I was a fly on the wall,' he grinned, then adjusting his 'Press' sign on the windscreen he took off, screeching his tyres in the process.

Rita blushed.

'What was that all about?' she enquired, her eyes following the quickly disappearing vehicle.

Ernest shrugged his shoulders, wishing his heart rate would slow down.

'Just another nosey reporter that used to hassle the police; guess he still remembers me.' He laughed, 'reckon he thinks Lisa and I still discuss investigations together.' Having said that, he hoped Rita would understand he had retired totally and had no further interest in crime.

She looked at him sideways, giving him the benefit of the doubt, but she knew her Ernest. The police force was the only family he'd ever known and his mind far too trained in ferreting out every detail of any crime. What Ernest didn't know was that she still hoped he hadn't changed and would eventually unravel her own mystery of those hours before her breakdown. Rita would be willing to face any consequences. She had lived too long in the shadows of falsehood and innuendo from that dreadful day. These fleeting thoughts passed quickly and by the time the doorbell had been pressed and the door opened, Rita was fully in the present moment.

She liked Lisa Pharies at first sight and visa versa. There existed an open acceptance between them that only the intuitions of the female species comprehend. Ernest stood back, he felt a little uncomfortable not understanding that a relationship could be formed so quickly as they chatted away like old friends.

Lisa ushered them into the back room where Emily sat in her usual place by the fire. Straight away Rita went over to her touching her gently on her paralysed arm.

Emily reacted by placing her good hand over Rita's. A more sensitive person would have recognised the affinity between them.

Rita's training made her always the caregiver whilst Emily saw her own age group; someone who understood life's changes with the passage of time. While modern thought warns of any co-dependency as harmful, it leaves out the unhappiness of isolation by being too independent. It is nature's way to be loved and loving in return. At that moment Ernest found himself yearning for something he could not quite identify. It was in truth his own early separation from his mother's love, but he didn't recognise it and so it remained as just a feeling.

Lisa was anxious to get away. She was also adrift in her own thoughts and an anxious feeling prevailed when she thought of Edgeworth, at the same time wishing it was Ernest that she was working for. She glanced at him. He looked solid, approachable and reliable, and her tummy knotted as she thought of having to spend the rest of her day with Detective Inspector Edgeworth.

'Press on girl,' she told herself and gave a tiny smirk. It was going to be one of those days.

Sensing Lisa's tension, Ernest walked over to her. Putting his arm around her shoulder, he walked with her into the hall.

'Don't worry so much; Emily will be fine. Rita will be interested in all her old photos,' and mistaking her nervousness as an anxiety for her mother, he added, 'if all else fails we will talk about the war.'

Lisa gave him a dirty look.

'Lisa,' Ernest's manner was now becoming serious, as he helped her on with her coat.

'I know,' she answered, bringing her voice down. 'I'll not say a word about the homicides whilst Rita's here.'

'What about Rachael?' He helped her with a tangled coat sleeve.

Lisa turned and looked at the man she'd got used to covering all the angles. A faint smile played across her face.

'Warned her too,' she answered giving him an affectionate hug remembering how good it had been working for him and wished the old days were back again.

Ernest stood for a moment in the small hallway after the front door was closed behind her. His mind was struggling to become focussed and one-pointed, a position he was always more comfortable with. He was determined to put his time with Rita first, yet there remained a nagging frustration of not knowing what was going on near the school. The nearest he could come to terms with it, was that Lisa owed him one and he meant to collect.

Having resolved his momentary conflict he joined the ladies. They were sitting close together with the photograph album open on Emily's lap. In fact the two of them appeared so comfortable he almost thought of excusing himself to pick up the paper. He quickly perished the thought however; realising details of the latest murder victim would be splashed all over the front page.

Instead he read Cheshire Life and even scanned the adverts for something to do. After a while he had to admit to himself he was not cut out for idling his time away. He got up and stood behind Emily as she shared her precious album with Rita.

They were looking at photographs of Emily and her family years back. Again Ernest watched as Emily tapped a certain picture with two fingers and then pointing to herself. He recalled the same actions he'd seen previously, but was then distracted as someone entered the room.

The person had entered the room so quietly nobody had heard the backdoor being opened. Ernest caught a slight waft of lavender perfume under his nose. It was Rachael standing beside him. She smiled at him, then put her hand on Emily's shoulder and, giving it a squeeze, leaned over to join in looking at the old photographs.

Emily was pointing again to one that looked like her many years ago, slightly stroking it. Then just as she had done earlier, she again tapped the photograph with two fingers.

Rita was chatting about how pretty she was but Emily was looking hard at her, her two fingers never leaving the page.

All at once Ernest was aware of Rachael stiffening; as she bent further to take a better look. She looked pale as the light caught her face, her hand clasping the back of Emily's chair, her fingers quickly becoming white with the strength of her grip. For a moment he thought she might faint.

'Are you alright Rachael?' he asked, his voice full of concern.

Rita looked up from her perch on the stool by Emily, her face registered puzzlement. No one had introduced her to this very attractive woman that seemed to bring out the gallant in Ernest.

Rachael straightened up, her composure re-established and pinkness seeping back into her cheeks, blushing slightly.

'It's nothing really, I've been rushing around.'

Ernest made a beeline for a vacant chair, carrying it over to her. Rachael smiled, her dark eyes showing her appreciation.

'You should at least introduce me to your guest.' She had appraised Rita in one quick glance as her eyes travelling back to Ernest.

Rita picked up quickly on the guest bit, as if she was some odd relative instead of being all-important in Ernest's life. Rachael was a very attractive woman with youth on her side. Momentarily Rita felt threatened, a feeling quite new to her and leaving her with some discomfort she couldn't quite address.

'I'll make a pot of tea,' she said and made for the small kitchen, aware that Ernest's eyes were following her. In the kitchen she stood tensely waiting for the kettle to boil.

'A watched kettle never boils,' she mused. How like her mum she had become, the first sign of stress and on went the kettle.

Suddenly two arms wrapped around her, and a head nestled by her neck.

'Want any help my love?' Ernest's voice whispered in her ear.

It was like a flood of warm caressing water flushing out her insecurity. She melted against him, and then laughed.

'Thanks Ernest. Lay the tray on the table...: there's a dear.'

After tea they all continued to chat for about an hour with Emily's eyes darting from one to another. As time passed, Rita quickly realising Rachael was full of compassion; deeply involved in her brother's calling and having no designs on her man.

'Are you a church goer?' she asked Rita. Although the question was lightly asked, Rita sensed a deeper interest. She glanced at Ernest, who looked away. The small boy in him still angry at the harsh treatment he'd received from the vicar all those years before.

'Ernest and I were brought up at the same church school in the town.' She hoped that this might leave alone the need for any further questioning.

'St. Alkmunds?' Rachael's face lit up.

Rita nodded.

'St Anne's is its mother church.' She was obviously pleased.

Rita nodded again. Ernest was looking at his watch.

'I guess we ought to go Rachael, it's been a long day and Rita leaves tomorrow.'

Rita was getting tired and, although she had enjoyed Emily, she realised Rachael had unsettled her leaving her slightly exhausted. It had been a long day and was more than thankful to say her goodbyes. Ernest too was tired and a headache was developing from trying too hard to make the day perfect.

They were both grateful for the quiet evening that followed; the conversation compatible and easy. The evening wore on until Rita got up to retire.

Ernest touched his temples; a slight throbbing still remaining. He made for the kitchen to get a glass of water and an aspirin. The bottle on the kitchen table caught his eye.

Rita must have needed an aspirin too, he thought, seeing a small bottle with the lid off. Ernest shook out two tablets into his palm and was about to lift them to his mouth just as a voice shouted behind him,

'Stop'!

He froze. Rita was standing in the doorway her face ashen and limbs trembling.

'Ernest, they are not aspirin, they're my Digoxin tablets.'

Ernest stared at the two small pills in his hand and, as he focussed more, realized he hadn't looked properly at what he was taking.

'God,' he said staring at her.

Tears were streaming down her cheeks half crying, half laughing as she replaced the top on the bottle.

'Ernest, I now remember everything about the night my Aunt Ada died.'

Ernest felt the loud pumping of his heart in his chest, thinking she was getting hysterical. It was something that always alarmed him.

Rita was quick to see the alarm spread across his face and she forced herself to remain calm. She pulled up a chair to the kitchen table and beckoned him to sit down too. Spreading her hands on the tabletop, she took a deep breath watching his eyes still riveted on the Digoxin bottle.

She willed him to look at her. Slowly he raised his head to hear what she had to say.

'Remember that fateful day. The day Cousin Charlie had taken Aunt Ada out for lunch,' she paused taking yet another deep breath before continuing. 'I was relaxing after cleaning through the house and was going to pour a glass of whisky for myself when I remembered it was time for my tablets. I took out my tablets from the bottle just as the phone rang. Charlie was in a state as Aunt Ada had drunk too much again. Living alone for so long I often left the top off my tablet bottles, whilst I fetched a drink of water or something. But that night my tablets with the top off were lying by the whisky bottle. Ada came home and we rowed. She was very drunk, complaining of a headache and couldn't find her dammed aspirins. This wasn't surprising, as I had gone through her medicines whilst she was out, throwing away out-dated ones and putting the rest upstairs in the bathroom cabinet. So I went to fetch them.'

Rita slowed down, her inner mind now re-living every moment clearly. She continued on.

'Ada had poured herself a glass of whisky and must have thought my tablets were Aspirin tablets and had taken a number of them. In her state she wouldn't have known the difference; she'd be only concerned with getting rid of the headache. She had a habit of taking more than she needed. That is one of the reasons I had sorted out her medications that day.'

Ernest looked at the bottle on the table and, picking it up, he replaced the top and pushed the bottle towards her.

'You are not going to blame yourself for leaving the top off are you Rita?' He was hoping beyond hope that she could now put an end to it all.

Rita sighed.

'No Ernest, it's over now. I want to start afresh from today.'

She took his hand. 'Let's go to bed.'

Chapter 15

Rita's visit ended far too soon for both of them. As Ernest returned to his car after dropping her off at the Moore he noticed the air hung heavy with the scent of bluebells. A carpet of budding bluebells had sprung up on a grassy patch by the side of the car park. He stopped and breathed in the heady perfume; it was spring and the new beginning gave him a hope of renewal in his own life as the buds opened to the sun. Ernest opened his car window a little wider and inhaled again deeply before driving away.

In the near future he hoped he would never have to make this journey again as Rita would be coming back with him hopefully for good. Thank God she had chosen to keep her British nationality and passport and could stay in the country instead of having to return to Canada. The previous night had been long, with little sleep as they talked the hours away and the memory of her warm body pressed closely to his still lingered. He remembered plainly how they had lain together, hands entwined, talking softly about so many things, past and future.

Now Ernest felt on a high and wondered if this was what it felt like to take drugs. For the first time he came a little nearer to an understanding of the young druggies he had brought in to the station over the years. Humming a little tune, he sped back towards the motorway. The morning traffic at this time posed no problems and the sun appeared set for the day. The usual stress of driving lessened, as the traffic was light providing plenty of road space around him.

Ernest's mind, not used to being devoid of constructive thoughts for too long, followed its natural course and began dwelling on the pieces of information he had picked up about the second death in the village.

Half an hour later he turned into a transport café. Picking up a copy of the morning paper, he selected a quiet table by a window. Sipping coffee and inhaling one of his self-forbidden cigarettes his heart missed a beat as he unfolded the paper.

The discovery of the barmaid's body was splashed all over the front page. . In bold black letters the headlines read;

A KILLER LOOSE IN GELSBY.

The report was obviously evoking sensationalism, no doubt to promote sales. There was a photo taken in front of the school of the teacher who had reported the finding of the body by two young pupils. As usual the article by Geoff Leigh gave little information, simply posing many more questions.

Was the barmaid's death a mistake? This question alone forging a totally unsubstantiated link with the earlier murder of the teenager in the village by suggesting the murderer thought the prey much younger. The latest victim was quite small in stature and would have been easily mistaken for a younger girl in the darkness, the time of death having been established in the late evening of the previous night. Not content with stirring up fear, the reporter even posed questions like; "Are our children safe and what are the police doing about it?"

Irritation and anger swept over Ernest. He hated the press publishing alarmism. Now there would be an outcry from parents, which would put additional pressure on the police in no small way.

He reached for another cigarette; oblivious to the fact he had only just stubbed out the last one. The waiter brought a clean ashtray taking the filled and lingering smoky one away. By the way he held it before him and the look of disgust, the waiter obviously didn't agree with the habit.

'Fools,' muttered Ernest to himself putting the paper down. He leaned back and watched the increasing stream of traffic through the window. His mind twisted this way and that, constantly storing and rejecting the bits of information that buzzed around in his head. He just couldn't accept these as random killings. There must be something else. Ernest was convinced that the killer knew both the victims; knew their habits and he guessed they would have had no reason to fear their assassin initially

Not knowing exactly why, Ernest's thoughts kept coming back to the spot of wax on Gina's clothing. Now he was becoming obsessed as to why the barmaid was covered in stones. Whoever did it; it wasn't to hide her body.

The moment the last thought entered he head he sat up straight.

'That's it.' The stones had been placed to bring attention to the body. Ernest was experiencing the rush of adrenaline that always came with any new perspective during a homicide investigation.

'Someone had covered her body for a purpose, so if not to hide it, what?'

Ernest played around with different scenarios, taking motives from past cases, but couldn't come up with anything that made any sense.

He found he needed to get nearer the crime scene and more particularly to call in that favour he'd done for Lisa the day before. He got up, picking up a piece of cardboard-looking apple pie at the cash out for his dinner as he left.

Lisa's car was parked at the front of her cottage as he turned into the village. Ernest was now intent in getting questions resolved by talking to her. If he hadn't stopped at the transport café, he might have had his wish, but Lisa had only popped home to pick up her cell phone.

Spotting Ernest, she waved a book at him and shouted something about nipping up to the Rectory and she was in a hurry. He groaned disappointedly.

Lisa arrived at the Rectory out of breath with the cookery book in hand she'd promised. Rachael opened the door wider and invited a reluctant Lisa in.

'Come on Lisa, a cup of tea won't hurt you, ' she coaxed the harassed policewoman, 'just sit down for a few minutes.'

Lisa followed her into the kitchen trying not to think of all the piles of paperwork awaiting her at the station. 'Why should she bother?' she asked herself, Edgeworth always took much longer over lunch than anyone else.

'Robin seems to be quite taken by you.' Rachael was looking over her mug, her eyes searching for Lisa's reaction. The statement posed took Lisa completely by surprise.

'Does he?' It was all she could think of saying; the blood rushing to her face and a nervous tickle starting in her throat. She quickly lifted her mug and gulped down the warm tea to ease it before adding,

'He's very nice.' Lisa didn't quite know why, but she found just talking about Robin gave her a warm feeling and she began to relax. It was nice to have another woman she could confide in, thought Lisa, and Rachael certainly fitted that need.

Putting down her mug she blurted out, 'let's just say I'd jump at the chance if he asked me out.'

There followed a pregnant silence and Lisa thought maybe she'd overstepped the mark and was being too forward, after all these were people of the cloth.

Then in a quiet and composed voice, Rachael replied, 'it's not easy having a relationship with a man of God. Not easy at all.'

Her look was far away as if contemplating future events.

'Think very hard Lisa. It's better to stop a relationship early than regret it later.'

Lisa couldn't contain her cough this time. The conversation was becoming serious and she wasn't ready to move ahead with a relationship that hadn't even begun. So the only way out was to make a joke of it.

'Rachael, can you really see me as a rector's wife?' she said, adjusting her police badge. 'Somehow I don't think it would be a good match at all.'

To her surprise, Rachael gave a relieved laugh. Soon the two of them were laughing till both of them had tears running down their cheeks, each imagining a policewoman in a uniform and a vicar in his vestments walking down the aisle. Lisa added that any children from such a marriage would always be in conflict. They would never know whether anything they did wrong would leave them forgiven or punished.

It was all seemed so light-hearted now, any hint of the seriousness in their earlier conversation being smoothed over. Yet Lisa, after opening her car door to leave, just sat for a few moments and wanted to cry. She didn't quite know why but the feeling was strong, and starting on the way back to the station she kept asking herself over and over again, 'what was wrong with a rector or vicar marrying a policewoman anyway? What did it matter what you did as long as you loved each other.' She thought of Ernest and Rita, and these feelings deepened.

Her cell phone rang. It was the Station Sergeant.

'Lisa, there's a message from the Gov. You are to caution Gerry Platt and bring him in for questioning.'

'What?' Lisa almost shouted down the phone; 'Gerry under suspicion of murder.'

'Seems like it. Better do as the boss wants lass.'

The phone went dead.

Confused and angry, she turned on the ignition and the car sprang into life, only to be pulling up seconds later in the parking lot of the Horseshoe Inn.

Seeing the full parking lot and the presence of Geoff Leigh leaning against his car, his notebook ready in hand, she knew immediately her job was not going to be easy. He shouted something and made a move towards her. Lisa backed him off by raising the flat of her hand and shaking her head. Nevertheless he followed her into the pub.

All eyes turned towards her as she entered the bar room. She was in uniform and that told them her business was official.

Gerry looked up from pulling a draught. His colour, not good at the best of times, had taken on a sunken look. Dark hollows under his eyes gave a clue to a sleepless night. There was a long scratch mark down his cheek. His wife, further down the bar, was serving a meal to a regular. She also looked withdrawn and nervous, her eye twitching uncontrollably.

Lisa nodded to Gerry and indicated the door to his living quarters, his wife watching anxiously as Gerry and the policewoman disappeared through it.

Breakfast dishes were still on the table and it looked as if little had been eaten, cold toast remaining on the plate and cereal dishes still clean.

They stood for a moment avoiding eye contact till P.C. Smyth arrived; indicating to Lisa he had the warrant in his pocket.

Gerry's head was spinning as he looked from one to the other. God what a mess he'd got himself in and just for a bit of skirt. He'd no doubt the police would discover Sharon's pregnancy and who the father of the baby was; what with all that DNA stuff. He saw no point in denying it or that he was one of the last people to see her alive. Although Gerry would bend the rules with the best of adulterers, he had great respect for British justice. 'Better tell the truth than let the powers that be find you out in a lie,' he thought.

He had seen the disgust and disbelief in his wife's eyes earlier and felt the panic inside himself, as he realised she was thinking the worst; he being responsible for Sharon's death. He tried to talk to her but she always moved away, uncomfortable in his presence and with uncertainty in her eyes.

Donna had been questioning herself all day to find a reason why her husband hadn't come to bed until the early hours of the morning.

It was Lisa that broke the silence of the awkward moment, her voice high pitched and a little forced.

'Gerry Platt, I am arresting you on suspicion of the murder of Sharon Harrison. You do not have to say anything, but it may harm your defence if you fail to mention when questioned something that you later rely on in court. Anything you say will be taken down and given in evidence.'

Entering the room at that very moment Donna Platt's face went pale and she crumbled to the floor. Her husband saw her fall but his body was somewhere else, watching and hearing from a distance. Not until he felt the handcuffs being put on his wrists and his body pushed forward did he come to the realisation of his arrest.

Moving through the bar, faces were looking at him, flat and void of expression. Someone with a flashing camera asked him if he'd anything to say.

He hadn't, words seemed choked up in his throat. The policewoman Lisa was holding his arm steadying his movements. In a daze, Gerry could not comprehend what was happening. It was the worst possible of all nightmares. He clung firmly to the only thought that gave him strength. He firmly believed in the police and their thoroughness in situations like this.

He would have been devastated if he could have read Lisa Pharies' mind; who at that moment hadn't his faith in the system. She had a horrible feeling something was already terribly wrong. Even if the DNA proved to belong to Gerry, she didn't like the way Edgeworth was proceeding with the case. He was making too many assumptions without supporting evidence and was hinting he had the killer of both homicides.

But it had been Lisa who had been the one to interview the Platts the night of Gina's murder. Gina must have passed the pub around about closing time and no one had been drunk or rowdy that night. Neither Gerry nor his wife had stated seeing any lights in the graveyard, which could have been seen from their bedroom window. Both seemed genuinely surprised by the murder and in no way had they given any hint of guilt.

Husband and wife were each other's alibi and so was Sharon Harrison, who had stayed late that night to help cleanup. She couldn't think they would all be lying unless; she had to admit there was a slight chance of blackmail being involved. Lisa began to feel a little inadequate and yet her instincts still led her to believe in his innocence.

What would Ernest have done? She tried to think but her coughing started again. P.C. Smyth handed her a cough sweet.

Chapter 16

'Cheeky devils' muttered Ernest.

He was standing by the front window, the net curtain pulled slightly back as he watched the stream of cars making for the small parking area at the church and any space that seemed available including the front of his cottage.

'Takes a bloody murder to get people to church these days,' he let the net drop back and sighed. He was missing Rita already and felt quite at odds with himself.

'Adrift in a ruddy tin boat,' the old saying came to mind and having said it, he immediately began to feel sorrier for himself.

Plonking himself down in his favourite chair he pushed off his shoes and raised his feet, crossing his ankles on a worn tuffet.

Leaning back he scoured the ceiling as was his habit when at a lose end. He began to follow the lines of beams to the wall for a while and then dropped his gaze to stare at the unlit fire.

The church bells rang out forcing whatever grey matter was active in his head to follow the set pattern it produced. In this pensive mood he allowed his imagination to dwell on the spiritual needs most people have and the church's role over the centuries.

For a moment he felt he had missed out on something all these years, yet recalling his childhood experiences kept him from dwelling on it further.

Ernest shifted his position; turned his head and gazed at the window. He had however met a lot of nice people when he attended the church here in the village.

Deciding that sitting alone was not doing him any good and what he really needed was companionship. He rubbed his chin against the natural growth of his hair musing that a shave could be put off, as there was not too much evidence of morning shadow. A quick wash and a change of shirt prepared him for his venture. He closed the front door to his cottage behind him. A glance down to number seven told him that the occupants had already left and a brisk walk got him to the church door just as the bells stopped ringing.

Once inside the church, the large doors swung closed. Something akin to panic fluttered within Ernest's chest as all eyes seemed to turn towards him, although in truth it was an illusion of his own making. He quickly sorted out where Lisa was sitting as he could see her mother's wheelchair by the wall.

He made a move forward but a rather obese lady, who had followed him in, had already squeezed past him taking the last seat. Lisa caught his eye and pointed down the aisle, Ernest followed her gaze to an almost empty pew near the front. There was nothing he could do, the doors were closed behind him and now all eyes were waiting for him to make his move.

Feeling as if he had become the centre of attraction, he coloured and pulled at his shirt collar that all at once had become rather tight. He took a deep breath and marched stiffly down the centre aisle. Two young men sitting together in the pew turned and smiled at him, one patting the seat beside him indicating a place.

Ernest didn't dwell on the reason why this particular pew was not filled like the others, thinking instead that he would now have to take communion if he didn't want everyone looking at him again. Why was the shirt feeling so tight? He gave the collar another tug.

Kneeling down to pray gave him a chance to pull himself together and Ernest found himself actually asking the powers that be to watch over Rita. She would like that he told himself.

The blast from the organ brought him quickly to his feet as Robin came down the aisle. Ernest glanced at Robin's feet as he passed. New shiny black shoes had replaced the usual sandals and Ernest wondered if there had been other influences behind Robin's change of footwear.

The service passed quickly as Ernest listened intently to Robin's sermon on forgiveness. He found he couldn't agree on all aspects, being a policeman, although the gist of what he was saying had merit. There was a special prayer for Sharon's family and surprisingly for Gerry Platt.

As the turn came for him to take communion followed by the two young men, he wasn't aware of the reluctant and very slow movement forward of the people in the next row of pews. It wasn't until Ernest had returned to his seat and saw his companions holding hands that he realised why the pew they were in was almost empty.

'Well I'll be damned,' Ernest half smiled. 'Robin has just given communion to a couple of queers,' he said to himself without thinking. Like many others of his age, he hadn't yet gotten out of the habit of using that offending word.

He was now beginning to enjoy himself at last and when they all stood for the final and up-lifting hymn "All things bright and beautiful," he smiled cheerfully, putting a special emphasis on the "The Lord God made them all."

He felt proud of his effort in attending the service and gave a generous offering for the collection or "tip-time" as his Dad used to say on those very rare occasions they attended church. The last time being his grandmother's funeral he recalled.

Being one of the last to leave Ernest didn't have to hurry so took time to look around and admire the vaulted roof.

'Quite something isn't it.' A tall thin grey-haired gentleman with a cultured voice stood beside him. 'Our family has been coming here for over two hundred years.' He offered Ernest his hand and introduced himself. 'Frank Butterworth.'

'Ernest Heath.' They shook hands as if completing some contract, and then both went back to admiring the church's special features.

'Used to be Roman Catholic before the Reformation,' volunteered Frank. 'We have always been Protestant.' Ernest gathered he was referring to his family. Having nothing to keep the conversation going, Ernest turned to seek out Lisa and her mother. Bad cooking or not, she always attempted a traditional Sunday dinner. He was ready to make his getaway excuse until the next bit of information was offered.

'Our rector used to be a Roman Catholic.'

Ernest stared in disbelief at the man before him, but Frank was used to it and always got some secret pleasure when seeing the inevitable look of surprise.

'Robin, a Roman Catholic'!

A look of bewilderment turning to annoyance crossed the man's face.

'Of course not, I'm talking about our real rector.' He almost stuttered in his eagerness to correct Ernest's misguided thinking. His lips thinned as his surprise statement had obviously lost its impact on the newcomer.

"Our own rector is the Rev. Richards. That young man who gave the sermon today is only a curate here.'

"Ah', said Ernest, giving his full attention to his narrator who was now more determined than ever on getting the desired response he expected.

'The parents of our rector and his sister Miss Rachael were staunch Roman Catholics you know.' He laboured on the next bit of information, giving a little time before coming in with his final assault, 'and their uncle was even a Roman Catholic priest.' Having said it he stood back to watch the effect on Ernest's face.

'Ah', said Ernest for the second time. However his informant hadn't finished yet.

'Yes, our rector changed his religion.'

Now at last Ernest was giving Frank that totally surprised look he had been waiting for, and then came the question that always followed.

'So what happened then?'

At this point it became obvious that truth and imagination were taking separate paths. Because Frank had told the tale so many times now, he could no longer distinguish between the two.

'Seems he had a vision where an angel appeared and told him to stay clear of the Pope.'

Ernest put his hand up to cover the chuckle that tried to escape, before putting on a look of amazement.

But Frank wouldn't stop, now that he'd got someone to listen to him.

'Rachael changed too. Like as not she'd seen the light as well,' he stated. Suddenly Frank shuddered as a high-pitched laugh came from near by. His nostrils flared a little and a look of condemnation spread over his face.

He turned back to Ernest and nodded in the direction of the two men that had shared Ernest's pew.

'See that pair,' Frank said. 'Did you know they are___'

'Gay.' Ernest finished the sentence for him leaving Frank open-mouthed.

'I saw you___'

Again Ernest broke in, 'sitting with them you mean. Yes and why not, I have a lot of good friends that are gay.'

Ernest was at his best when justice was at stake.

'I think it's just wonderful that people are far more liberated from prejudice these days.'

Frank's mouth dropped open and nothing seemed able to come out. He nodded weakly as Ernest picked up his limp hand and gave it a manly shake.

'Good to talk to you Frank, maybe we could have a drink together some time.'

Hurrying away he tried to find Lisa but was too late, she'd already gone home. 'There goes a possible Sunday dinner,' he muttered.

Chapter 17

Monday morning brought the forecasted fine drizzle, which was supposed to last only a short time. However the dismal grey skies seemed deemed to stay much longer. Everywhere there hung a mantle of grey mist. Any artist bent on painting landscapes would have brushed on his or her canvass a large amount of Payne's grey.

Yet all the depressive drizzle didn't deter the local postman who diligently protected his precious mail until it was safely delivered. A few yards behind the postman came the paperboy; not so dedicated with his cargo.

Ernest heard the familiar rattle of the letterbox and a faint thud on the mat. He shuffled along the hallway in his oversized slippers to pick up what had been deposited. Three letters lay there and by their prepaid stamps recognised them as bills. Anger crept over his face as he saw half a newspaper protruding from the letterbox, knowing from bitter experience the other half would be wet. Giving the newspaper a sharp tug, it came away exactly as he had anticipated, damp with one side torn. Mumbling aloud, he bent down to pick up the bills, stopping abruptly in that position as a twinge caught his lower back muscles. He straightened up cautiously allowing the pain to pass. Throwing the unopened letters on the kitchen table he moved to the sink. Pulling a stained cup out of the unwashed dishes, he gave it a quick rinse under the tap before setting it down beside a pot of tea. A few days without Jeanne or Rita, he was back to his usual chaos he admitted; feeling a little sorry for himself.

Pushing the bills and the teapot and cup to one side, he unfolded the newspaper spreading it out before him to dry off a little. As he did so some of the headlines caught his attention. 'Margaret Thatcher in the limelight again I see', he murmured to himself; beside it yet another column grabbed his interest. "Canada in the market to buy nuclear submarines to patrol its Arctic waters." Ernest shook his head. The world seemed to be changing too fast for him at times. He turned the damp page over carefully.

'Man. United lost again, too bad.' He'd followed them from being a lad and always checked their progress in the League. There was little other news of any importance,___ only talk of the interest rate going up again. He was thankful he didn't have a mortgage. He reached for the teapot and was about to pour, when his eye caught a single paragraph on a part of the paper newly dried by the hot teapot it was leaning against.

Local Murders: Will DNA evidence confirm the publican arrested in Gelsby murder investigation fathered the baby the barmaid was carrying?

Ernest knew from experience it wasn't the Divisional Police that had leaked out that snippet of information. More likely it had come from one of Geoff Lewis's informants. How much had they been paid he wondered. Ernest reread the article. 'So she was pregnant' he mused.

Looking his watch, he was surprised to see it was already ten thirty. He had slept in later than usual after having a restless night suffering from the effects of his late fatty sausage and lumpy potatoes dinner.

A feeling of helplessness overwhelmed him. He couldn't always pretend he was happy to be away from the work he loved. The excitement and challenge of solving a crime stimulated him. He had tried to tell himself it wouldn't be so bad if he thought his replacement was up to doing a good job. He needed to get out; take some deep breaths, walk it off. He glanced out of the window at the rain and told himself sternly that if every Englishman avoided rain they would never go outside.

Ernest strolled through the village at his usual steady pace, a large umbrella held just touching the top of his head. He strolled along the sidewalk of a wider road with flat green fields edged in hawthorn, a car passed, spraying a fine mist adding to the dampness of his clothes. His face grim, mind blank, he maintained his steady walking pace, turning to enter a lane that meandered around the village.

Now facing a cold breeze, he shivered and would have welcomed a stiff whisky and a warm fire at the Horseshoe, but no doubt with all these tragic events it would now be closed and sadly would probably remain so for some time. Ernest tried to think of another country pub within walking distance, but nothing came to mind. Some people said if you needed a drink badly enough trust your legs to take you there. It had never happened to him. Thinking back, it was the town drunk who had said that. Ernest gave a faint smile, remembering old Sam. Maybe there was some truth in ending up where you needed to be. Ernest found himself opposite the house where the first murdered girl had lived.

'Gina Breasley.' Ernest said the name silently to himself and stopped under a large oak opposite the house. It looked as if he was sheltering, the umbrella pulled down over his head and upper face, but appearances can be deceiving, for his two piercing eyes were trained on the window opposite.

Something had arrested Ernest's attention; a sudden movement had caught the net curtain of the window and had pulled it aside.

It was a man's hand raised. Arching, it swung down across the face of someone Ernest had difficulty in identifying, as the other person was in shadow; a moment later Stan Breasley's face appeared at the window. He looked searchingly across the road but all he saw was a man with a large umbrella pulled well down against the rain.

When Ernest looked again, the net curtain was firmly drawn. He moved, keeping on the same footpath and away from the house.

He felt his blood pressure rising; his adrenaline surging and his knuckles white from clutching the umbrella handle tightly.

He'd wanted to kick the door down and put his own fist into Breasley's face smashing the nose and if needs be taking out a few teeth in the process. But he knew from long experience that it would do no good. Muriel Breasley would deny everything. Some excuse would be presented for her bruises and he himself would end up with a charge of unlawful assault. Ernest hated bullies, his own father being one of the worst.

'Why don't the victims stand up for themselves, ask for help, let the world know how they are abused.' Ernest had raised the point so many times but knew the reality of another sort of suffering. The victim feels they would lose their home and all means of support. They already had little or no self-esteem. He'd seen it all before; the brutality followed by remorse and the asking for forgiveness.

His step increased and his breathing eventually calmed as his mind ticked over. Breasley had an airtight alibi for the night Gina was murdered. Ernest couldn't get around that, but had Stan Breasley abused his daughter too. It was certainly food for thought.

His mind began to travel down a forbidden 'What if?' path. His thinking got no further however as he rounded the corner of the Horseshoe Inn. The side door of the pub was slightly ajar with an "OPEN" sign hanging on the handle. Ernest stopped dead in his tracks trying to assess whether it was a mistake; the open sign having been accidentally turned around or had been forgotten about under the present circumstances. But the light from the bar could be seen through the half opened door welcoming the weary home. Ernest didn't actually feel weary but did feel a little like a survivor of a shipwreck. He couldn't have been more chilled and damp.

Two cars were in the parking ground, one was a police car. Getting out of the other were the two men Ernest had shared a pew with. A mini pulled in. Ernest's shoulders went up and his umbrella came down as he reckoned by now the pub was well and truly open.

Leaving his folded wet brolly and his mackintosh piled on the bench in the entrance, he entered. Everything appeared to be as normal. It was quite difficult to believe the landlord had been arrested on suspicion of murder and was helping police with their investigations.

A stranger was serving behind the bar, Ernest had never seen him before but his features looked familiar. Then came the recognition as he ordered a pint and a whisky chaser.

'Donna's brother, the resemblance was too close for him to be mistaken,' he noted mentally. Turning his head, he saw that the barmaid serving tables bore no resemblance to Sharon at all. Overweight, plain and tight-mouthed, she hadn't been chosen to titillate the cliental.

Ernest heard his name called and looked around questioningly. It was PC Smyth sitting at a far table guarding two pint glasses of beer. Ernest picked up his drinks and walked over. He saw Lisa's handbag pushed up in the corner of the window seat. PC Smyth saw his glance and explained.

'Gone for a pee'; he was never the one to mince words. Ernest grinned and sat down. Taking a long sip of his amber liquid, he asked idly.

'Business as usual;' the tone of his voice was more a question than statement.

'Seems Platt's wife is not letting the beggar ruin the business and has got her family in.'

'Aye,' said Ernest, his eyes raking the room, 'business looks good.'

One of the young men that had come in raised his glass to him and, pushing back his fair silky hair with his other hand, displaying a large gold earring.

Not one to interfere with the way people lived if not breaking the law, Ernest responded. The next minute Lisa had entered the room and as she passed the blonde haired guy, she ruffled his hair. He caught her hand and kissed the inside of it. Lisa bent down and whispered something. They both laughed.

Lisa came forward, looked at Ernest for a moment as if awaiting instructions, then quickly returned to the present.

'Shove over,' she said in a strong county dialect.

'What's new?' Ernest asked in the same old way he'd always obtained updates to an ongoing investigation.

Lisa frowned and glanced at PC Smyth, but he was all too busy investigating the metrics of a mini-skirted blonde who had just entered the room. Lisa was about to say something when the last person they all wanted to see walked in the pub.

Lisa coughed.

'Bloody hell,' she said, startling PC Smyth out of his daydreaming. He muttered something and got up sideling out among the people standing by.

'On duty,' Ernest nodded his head toward the retreating figure.

Lisa shrugged her shoulders and looked uneasy as they spotted Edgeworth making his way towards them.

'Your not____,' Ernest started before being abruptly interrupted.

'No, I'm bloody well not on duty,' growled Lisa.

The Detective Inspector took the freshly vacated seat; clicked his fingers at the barmaid, ordered a whisky on ice, and turned his attention towards Lisa. Ernest felt for a moment he wasn't there.

'How's the report coming along?' he retorted testily, his expression maintaining an air of superiority.

'It just needs a bit more time sir,' she said, looking down at the puddle of spilt beer from her glass.

'No time like the present.' He cracked a smile suggesting it was more of an order than advice.

'Off duty sir.' Lisa replied, finding the effort of keeping his tactlessness out of her voice difficult.

Ernest broke in. He felt as though he would explode if he didn't.

'How's the investigation going___ any more on finding Gina's murderer?'

Edgeworth rounded on him, his eyes beginning to pop. 'Everything is going nicely, thank you very much, and we have got the person we want in custody. It will not be long before we get a confession out of him.' He didn't have to say Gerry Platt's name.

Ernest responded slowly, 'but it can't be easy trying to connect him to the Breasley girl's murder too. After all, there were too many witnesses to say where he was that night.'

Ernest knew full well he'd hit the Achilles heel. He watched as Edgeworth's hand tightened around his glass and then stoking the fire a little more, added with a silky voice,

'Seems Platt has a cast iron alibi for that one, looks like the village is still unsafe for women with another killer still running lose.'

Lisa's head shot up as Edgeworth's fist hit the table.

'Damn it man, nobody cares what you think. You're gone, out of it. It's my turf and I don't want any interference from the likes of you.'

He glared at Lisa, 'and if I hear you discussing the investigation, I'll have you off the case.'

The whole room was silent and all eyes were on the figure that was now pushing everyone aside in an effort to leave quickly.

Ernest and Lisa looked at each other. Ernest wanted to laugh and banter like they did in the old days, but Lisa looked shaken, her hands trembled as she reached for her handbag.

'Goodbye Ernest,' she said quickly. He heard her cough several times as she departed.

'Well,' thought Ernest. 'There's a turn up for the books. The bugger doesn't even know which end he's pulling on.'

He finished his pint quickly followed by the whisky chaser.

Chapter 18

Rita stood by the window of the lounge in the Moore Hospital. Although her gaze was directed across the open landscape in front of her, her thoughts were private and elsewhere.

In another room of the hospital, a group of professionals were discussing her fate as to whether her release from the hospital was to be permanent or not. The other patients including the staff left her alone, but not without furtive glances in her direction.

Rita herself was not really worried about the outcome, as she had already been reassured by her own doctor, but the process of release had to be made official.

So anyone trying to guess her thoughts would have been totally wrong, for they were not at all confined by her present location, but were some 3000 miles away. As she gazed out on the sombre moors before her, she was visualising a Canadian landscape.

The land there would be emerging from the icy grip of winter that always lasted long past the English spring. She mourned a little as she gazed over the drab moors, her thoughts recalling the deep pristine snowfall with heavily laden trees. Driving through blizzard conditions with frozen creeks and ice-covered lakes and huddling under layers of clothes as the temperatures dropped well below zero. She had thought then she would never get used to it, but its beauty and her very survival in that great land had taken possession of a small part of her.

One day she would take Ernest to Canada and let him experience a real Christmas scene. She visualised them taking a sleigh ride, the horses snorting at the cold air and rushing them through the snow laden trees, their brass harness bells ringing.

Someone called her name; she turned, as did other heads. The nurse had a smile on her face.

Beyond the distant hills at the end of the Pennine Chain, the land spread into the Cheshire plains. Here the Rev. John Richards was pulling his hand knit red shawl closer across his shoulders, as he moved away from the fire and feeling it becoming cooler.

He walked over to his desk and looked down at a much-used copy of the Latin Vulgate. Its beautifully scripted lettering looked back mockingly at him. Scattered around the book were a number of pencilled scribbled pieces of paper, some of them with thick lines scratched out.

John placed his large hand across one of the pages over the writing. Spreading out his fingers, he tightened them and crinkled the paper into a tight ball; holding it imprisoned for a second before throwing it into the waste paper basket by the desk.

He swivelled the chair around and sat down drawing his feet underneath. Pulling himself forward over the desk, he put his head in his hands.

'Am I becoming obsessive?' he thought, staring at the polished wood. His feet felt like ice and he rubbed them together to stimulate the circulation.

Bending to one side he unlocked the top drawer of his desk, pulling out a small black book. He opened it slowly; the text was again in Latin. After a while staring at it he lay it flat beside a fresh pad of paper, pulled the Latin Vulgate closer and began to write again.

His scribbled translation began with the words "The Lord spoke." On one level of understanding, he knew what he was translating but had to be sure. He got no further for a hand slapped down and closed the heavy book.

Rachael stood there, anxiety and weariness in her eyes.

'Enough John, you are torturing yourself.'

He didn't speak for a while then raised his head to look at his sister. 'What does the Lord want of me Rachael? What more can I give?'

His sister moved over to the fire, bent over to give it a poke, then stood with her back to it.

'One thing is for sure, you cannot be much use to others if you are ill.'

She rolled her head around her shoulders easing out the mounting tension. The heat of the fire warmed her back. She stepped aside.

'We need to think of getting some more heat in the old tower for Kane.' She changed the subject knowingly.

'He shouldn't be living there,' John said stiffly and with conviction. 'It is no place for anyone to live.'

'And where should he go?' Rachael's head rose defiantly. 'Here?' she added with a touch of sarcasm.

John sighed. This argument was doomed as it always had been since Kane arrived. Rachael had taken Kane under her wing like a lame duck and nobody was going to change her.

'He needs proper care', said John wearily. 'One day he's going to have an accident. He's not safe Rachael, and he scares the life out of visitors around the church.'

Rachael's face reddened, heightening the colour of her eyes, but her voice held firm with a tone of unyielding steel.

'He's not going anywhere John as long as I have breath in me,' she stared at him with defiance. But then added, her voice becoming softer and edged with compassion, 'I'll look after him.'

John took a deep breath. 'You win Rachael,' gracefully acknowledging she always did. Yet his own conviction that Kane would someday leave the church unlocked or leave a candle burning in the wrong place never left him. He'd seen how Rachael had had to draw heavy black rings around messages or reminders to Kane. He closed his eyes, his head falling back against the chair. Rachael watched him, a slight frown creasing her forehead.

Where had all the enthusiastic convictions of his early ministering days gone? Following the path of God was harder than he'd ever visualised. Remembering those times and recalling the great adoring love he'd always had for Jesus Christ who'd suffered so much.

John and his sister had had their share of suffering, as they had watched their mother slowly dying following her long battle with cancer when they were young. Their father, turning away from their emotional needs becoming a strict disciplinarian in the process. Together with his brother, a priest, they had moulded the sensitive children into God fearing souls.

Mrs Slater the housekeeper had done her best but was unable to enter into the children's world, their close relationship with each other leaving others floundering on the outside. Isolated by country living and educated at home by dominating males, they became inseparable.

But their world became too small and they grew up quickly when things went dreadfully wrong. Out of the structured life they had been used to, something happened that even their father was unable to cope with and died as a result of a heart attack. The terrible scenes with their uncle, sent John looking for solace elsewhere and he found it in the Church of England. Rachael followed him as John took up the Ministry and she became his constant companion.

It all seemed a long time ago but they both carried their many childhood scars.

John opened his eyes again and found Rachael gone.

'Rachael always digs in her heels whenever Kane is mentioned' he mused and smiled to himself, as he heard the front door close.

Rachael just had to get out of the house. She felt stifled and still angry. John had no right to ridicule Kane, no right at all.

'The Lord's my Sheppard,' she repeated over and over again to herself, 'and I am his handmaiden,' she added crossing the road and making her way to number seven.

Lisa welcomed her as she always did with a big smile and a hug.

'Emily well?' asked Rachael stiffening a little at Lisa's display of affection for her. But Lisa didn't notice the slight withdrawal and cheerfully called to her mother.

'Rachael's here mum,' she said leading her guest forward, but before they could enter the room, the front door bell sounded again.

'I'm popular,' laughed Lisa, turning around to answer it.

'Robin,' she said almost shouting, 'well this must be my morning after all.'

He looked at her quizzically.

'Two of my favourite people calling on me at the same time,' she answered in response to his dilemma.

'Ernest?' he queried.

'Rachael,' she stated but failed to see the slight disappointment cross his features.

'I'm not stopping Lisa.' He seemed at a loss for words and clearing his throat he added quickly. 'Would you like to come with me to hear Handel's Messiah at the Town Hall on Saturday?' There he said it, all in one breath too, his heart still pounding.

'Yes,' she answered far too quickly, never thinking of whether she may be on duty, or acknowledging the fact that classical music bored her silly. Pulling at the sleeve of his sweater, she added; 'don't go without saying hello to Mum.'

'Mum, its Robin the Rev.____.' She took him over to Emily.

Emily stared up at Robin, whilst all the time Rachael was watching the expression on the invalid's face. Neither gave anything away of their inner thoughts and no-one saw Rachael's hand clench as Lisa added,

'Robin has asked me out.'

The room went very quiet before Robin interjected. 'It's the Handel's Messiah___,' he stumbled before becoming lost for words.

Nobody said anything, leaving Robin looking somewhat embarrassed.

Rachael stirred, tapping Emily on the shoulder.

'I'll pop round again but I have to see Ernest now,' her voice a little high and tense as she added, 'Robin you promised to answer the Bishop's letter this morning.'

Robin, who had already decided it was time to leave, picked up her tone of annoyance quickly.

Rachael and Robin walked a few yards together, nothing more being said apart from a polite goodbye as Rachael opened Ernest's gate. She stood for a moment watching the tall figure striding back towards the Rectory.

Rachael was surprised at the warm welcome that Ernest extended to her. His mood was usually hard to read. But today was different. He was stimulated and talkative from the moment she entered. It wasn't until the teapot was filled and the cups placed on different non-matching saucers that he offered an explanation.

'Rita has been given a full discharge from hospital,' he waited for a smile from his visitor before adding, 'she's coming back here for good this time.'

'Wonderful, that's wonderful news,' exclaimed Rachael giving him a hug. She was truly pleased for she liked them both, Ernest with in his down to earth honest ways and Rita's naturally compassionate nature. She hoped it wouldn't be too long before they were married. Rachael had a hard time with anyone living in sin, even if these two were probably too old anyway to sin in that way.

'I never really knew why she was hospitalised Ernest, but if you want to talk about it, maybe I too can help her grow strong again.' Rachael leaned forward, her dark hair falling over half her face. She pushed it back, unaware that it was her attractiveness that had opened Ernest's heart in talking to her of Rita's past.

'Rita and I grew up together, she was my first love.' He spoke quietly and slowly as he recalled the memories of their past together, 'but I think I've mentioned that before to you.' She nodded and let him continue.

'Did you ever read about the World War II skeleton of an American soldier found in the old sand quarry near here?'

Nodding again, she gave him her full attention. Ernest told her the whole story of what had happened to Rita, beginning with the fact that she had witnessed the soldier's death as a child and believed it was her own mother who had been the instigator of his demise. Later her mother had committed suicide and Rita, being orphaned, had a miserable teenage life living with her aunt.

'For a time I thought Rita and I were very close. But she couldn't handle it and emigrated to Canada. I married and was later widowed before I ever saw her again. Imagine my surprise nearly thirty years later when we met. She'd flown over for an old friend's funeral. We knew instantly our feelings for each other had not changed and everything was going perfectly until Rita discovered that it was not her mother but her aunt who had caused the death of the American. Rita and her aunt were arguing on the staircase when her aunt fell and died. Rita collapsed mentally from the shock of that day, thinking she was the cause of her aunt's fall. It wasn't until later that she understood that her aunt had taken her Digoxin tablets instead of aspirin and had died as a result.'

'Digoxin?' Rachael raised her eyebrows.

'Ah, yes,' said Ernest. 'Rita suffers from arrhythmia.

'I'm sorry.' Rachael reached out for the teapot and Ernest nodded to his cup.

'It's all over now, her treatment helped her come to terms with it and I will be there for her.'

'She's lucky,' replied Rachael.

Ernest looked surprised at the sadness in Rachael's voice.

'It's the victims that suffer over and over again,' she went on, sipping her tea, her big brown eyes shining with a hint of tears in them.

'You sound as though you know from personal experience.'

Ernest kept his voice quiet; encouraging conversation whenever he sensed some new revelation was in the offing. Rachael intrigued him.

'We all need love,' she confessed. 'But sometimes the love of another human being isn't enough. Only the undying love of God can heal and strengthen us permanently.' She stood up.

'Thanks for listening,' Ernest said, as he got up rather carefully, his right knee feeling stiff.

'I'll tell you what Ernest,' said Rachael before departing, 'bring Rita over for dinner. It would be good for John to have some other company around.'

Chapter 19

One morning Ernest received an excited phone call, and it didn't take Rita long to establish her residency in his cottage. The two cases she'd brought over from Canada nearly a year before had already been unpacked.

Neat piles of clothes, toiletries and a few unwrapped presents lay on the top of the bed. The presents she had originally intended to take back to Canada for her friends had been bought with care a long time ago. Looking at them now lying in front of her, Rita knew they would never leave England and thought of giving them to Lisa.

Not wishing to take the initiative and select cupboard space for her small wardrobe, she went over to the bedroom window. Ernest was bringing in a few groceries they had picked up on their way back, or at least Ernest had, while she'd waited contentedly in the car.

Looking down from the window she saw him talking to Lisa. From their stance and quizzical expressions they seemed to be haggling over some difference of opinion between them. Then Lisa, turning her back on him, marched away. Ernest called something out to her. She didn't respond and just kept on walking.

'I wonder what that was all about,' mused Rita watching Ernest's shoulders slump as they always did when he was troubled.

Rita left the window and went downstairs, entering the kitchen just as Ernest came in. Whatever had been the cause of the incident,

Ernest had left it outside for his face broke into a happy smile as her looked at her.

'Welcome home darling,' he said cheerfully with a bright smile, relieving any lingering unease she'd felt previously.

'Tired?' asked Ernest. Throwing the car keys on the table he looked at her, anxiously scouting her face for any signs of strain.

'For goodness sake Ernest,' Rita moved over towards the kettle. She shook it to satisfy herself it had water in it, and then plugging it in, she switched it on. With her back towards him she continued chastising him.

'For the very last time, don't wrap me in cotton wool. I'm one hundred percent fit now.' Then turning to him with a slight twinkle in her eyes, she continued, 'mentally that is.' She patted her hips, 'the old body isn't what it used to be.'

'Like me?' Ernest responded in sympathy glancing at the first signs of his ever-expanding stomach then looking at her mischievously, added,

'Cross my heart Rita, from now on I'll only look after your bodily needs.'

Rita stared at him for a second; blushing a little and cleared her throat. Seeing her momentary embarrassment, Ernest took a one hundred and eighty degree turnaround in the conversation.

'We are going to the Rectory for dinner tonight.'

As soon as the words left his mouth, a cold shiver swept over him. How many times had his instant decision-making, without asking others first, led to arguments in the past? Images of his late wife's angry face flashed before him. Stumbling over his words, Ernest attempted to compensate for his lack of tact.

'That of course depends on you, I just thought it would save you cooking.' Another mistake; his breathing quickened then calmed, as Rita appeared quite unfazed as she replied.

'How thoughtful of Rachael,' there was a slight trace of irritation as she stopped to find the right words. 'I will like that.' Yet deep inside a niggling feeling pulled at her heartstrings and she recognised a twinge of jealousy at play. Insignificant and really not worth another thought, it nevertheless had manifested itself before on her last visit when Ernest had looked admiringly at the rector's sister and had commented,

'How could a good-looking woman like Rachael manage to remain unmarried all these years I'll never know?'

The moment passed as Ernest's strong arms encircled Rita and as he brought her to him she felt the rhythmic beating of his heart steadying her own arrhythmic one. Never the less the jealousy she'd experienced was as old as time itself and took time to fade.

Precisely at seven o'clock, Ernest and Rita stood on the worn stone step of the black and white Rectory. The bell was still activated by a pulley system that sent clanging echoes around the house. Honeysuckle clung tightly to a flaking wall where a few bees were still bent on gathering nectar as the flowers were closing up for the evening.

Rachael opened the thick oak door, which had been painted black along with its hinges. She greeted them warmly and assisted Rita in removing her coat. The sight of her hostess made Rita feel her age, especially as she compared her tweed skirt and somewhat out dated top against Rachael's plain but well tailored black dress and the elegance of her hairstyle pulled up into a twisted crown on her high forehead. Rita's eyes sought the natural colour of Rachael's hair under the hall light but couldn't detect the slightest hint of any grey, unlike her own. A quick memo flashed through Rita's mind that she should get her own hair coloured later on in the week. She really must brave herself for a shopping spree once she had gained more self-confidence.

The Rev. Richards came into the hallway dressed in a worn sweater and well-used slippers. Rita warmed to him at once. Although his illness had taken its toll, he was nevertheless still attractive. But unlike Rachael, his hair was totally white.

Led into a surprisingly large room, Rita and Ernest stood entranced. The room was spacious, serving both as lounge and study. The ceiling was low, one missing beam in the centre being the only indication of two smaller rooms becoming one. To the left of the room, two quaint mullion windows framed with pretty chintz curtains stood out against a black beamed and white plastered wall

It was always the large fireplace that brought the gasp of admiration from visitors. It stood exactly the same as the day it was built, sometime in the sixteen century. It was generously adorned with genuine horse brasses. A large court cabinet heavily carved was at least a couple of hundred years old, as was the magnificent oak desk with its swan brass handles and leather top. A settee and two arm chairs could not be so well dated as they had been covered with the same material as the curtains.

After taking in the charm of the room, Rita's eyes landed on an old framed embroidered sampler hanging on the wall.

She gave an exited gasp. 'My grandmother had one just like that.'

She walked over to get a better view of it with John following. He took it off the wall and gently handed it to her, adding, 'my grandmother did this one. See; her name and date of birth are stitched into her work,' he stopped for a moment as if recalling another place and time. 'It's the only thing Rachael and I have of our mother's. I remember how she used to tell us this is the way they learnt each different type of stitch.'

'I guess a lot is lost to machines now,' said Rita shaking her head sympathetically.

Feeling in the presence of a kindred soul, John went over to another wall and came back with a small oil painting framed in wood. He handed it to Rita.

'This was discovered in the old priest's chamber in the church. It is of a Roman Catholic priest as you can see by his vestments and was obviously hidden during the time of the Reformation, and was only recently discovered when repair work was needed to make the room suitable for Kane.'

'Really,' remarked Rita fascinated. 'Tell me about Kane. How did he come to take up residence in the church?'

A quick look darted between John and his sister Rachael.

'It was all my sister's doing,' he explained. Rita noticed the tendency in his voice somewhere between admiration and regret. 'Let a sparrow be found with a broken wing and she would have it bandaged; never one for logical common sense when one of God's creatures pulls at her heart strings, eh Rachael!'

Obviously John thought his sister's decisions not always wise, yet couldn't help admiring her dedication.

Rachael chipped in. 'Nobody wanted Kane as a lodger, so my solution was the old Priest's Chamber, and Kane loves it. It's the first time he's had room of his own, as he was brought up in care you know; an orphan'.

Ernest had been listening quietly in the background and now asked, 'Doesn't it bother him living in a church?' Aware of the surprised look of his hosts he added, 'at night I mean. It's a bit spooky isn't it?'

Rachael stared at him, a lack of understanding clearly written all over her face as she answered,

'It's a house of God. How can it be spooky?'

Changing the subject, their conversation progressed to books, and it quickly became obvious Rita and John shared a common interest in mythology.

'John's quite knowledgeable when it comes to myths. He is also interested in the Greek and Latin language of the time.' Rachael's remark provoked sharp and somewhat annoying glances from John.

'I'd better see to the dinner,' she said. 'Do have another drink,' indicating to John to fill the glasses.

It proved to be an excellent meal, well cooked and the Welsh lamb so tender. The roast potatoes were done to perfection and the pastry of the apple pie would have placed first at any church bazaar

'Port?' suggested John at the end of the meal. Knowing it would be taken along with coffee, back in the lounge-cum-study, Rita took the opportunity to enquire the whereabouts of the washroom. All heads turned towards her. John and Rachael looked blank.

Ernest laughed. 'She means the lavatory,' he chuckled, 'washroom is a Canadian term. It seems she needs re-educating to be an English woman again.'

Rita got up and gave his arm a sharp slap as she passed him and followed Rachael's directions up the shiny wooden stairs and along a narrow corridor.

The door on the left Rachael had said, being aware the oak-planked doors with latches all looked the same. One door was slightly ajar. Rita pushed it open and stepped in. She stopped short, her mind had visualised a toilet but instead she was in someone's bedroom. The room was quite tiny and the large beams slanted across making it difficult to walk upright. It was obvious she was in the older portion of the house.

A small leaded window was draped tastefully with the same chintz pattern as downstairs. A single bed was pushed up against one wall. In one corner of the room, a rail was fixed to the wall hiding the clothes that hung behind it. A kidney-shaped dressing table stood opposite the bed.

The dressing table with its three mirrors was just like the one she'd had as a child. Rita moved over to it, running a finger over the top sentimentally. Then she picked up a small photograph in a plain black frame standing on it.

The photograph looked as though it had been taken in the sixties. Rita recognised the style of the dress the young woman in it was wearing. She was pretty and vaguely familiar. The baby she held was very young; wrapped in a large shawl with one tiny hand showing. Behind the mother and child was an old grey stone building.

Beside the photograph, a Bible lay open. A dedication to Robin Ashton was written on the first page. Reading his name alerted Rita to the fact she was trespassing and she quickly left, finding the necessary smaller room adjacent to it.

Downstairs the next hour proved relaxing and pleasant. Nobody mentioned that Rita's last residence had been a psychiatric hospital and she was grateful for their consideration. In fact as the evening wore on Rita began to admire Rachael more and more for her unselfish devotion to John's needs and the village as a whole. She seemed to know everyone by their first name whatever their religious preference.

Glancing at the clock and being aware John was tiring, Rita placed her cup on the tray of the remaining dirty crockery and picked it up.

'I'll just pop these in the kitchen, and then we'd better be going'

As she put the tray down in the kitchen, Rita picked up a church magazine that was lying on the floor. She stood for a moment looking at a page with a thick black ring circling an event with the date and time highlighted.

Rachael came in behind her and said quickly, 'I have to tell Kane about what he's to do almost on a daily basis,' and took the magazine from her.

Goodbyes were said with a promise to do it again sometime.

Walking back to the cottage hand in hand Rita said approvingly, 'Rachael's quite nice isn't she?'

'One in a thousand,' Ernest added, tucking her hand under the fold of his arm. Rita glanced at him sideways.

'I wouldn't go quite that far,' she thought to herself.

Chapter 20

About mid-morning Rita felt a sudden urge to go for a walk. The trouble was that she had expressed a desire to go on her own as she felt it was something she needed to do.

Immediately Ernest had protested and it resulted in a clash of wills. They faced each other across the kitchen table. Rita resolute in her decision and Ernest fearing the sight of police cars and gossip would not be in Rita's best interests, although he couldn't say that. Instead told her she would be better in his company as she hadn't been out alone before.

They stared at each other, a past vision of a stubborn twelve-year-old girl refusing to jump across an overflowing brook crossed Ernest's mind momentarily. He tried another tack.

'I thought we could go for a run, have a nice lunch somewhere.' His voice was almost pleading, the facial expression emulating that of a small boy.

'Really Ernest, I'm only taking a short stroll, ten minutes is not going to make any difference to our day,' her reply adamant, expressing there was no chance of her changing her mind.

'Then let's go together, I need a breath of fresh air too,' he stood up, his face relaxing a little then changing to frustration as Rita sighed and added.

'I am going out of that door,' she indicated, her forehead wrinkled and her eyes trained along the passageway to the front door. 'Alone,' she added with a tone that ended any further discussion.

Then, relenting a little, her voice softened.

'Ernest, have you any idea what it's like to make no decisions, not to go through a door without someone enquiring where you are going?'

He knew she was right, but found himself in turmoil of his own making. He'd tried so hard to make Rita's return to normal living perfect and had never once mentioned the murders to her, even going to the extent of cancelling the newspaper delivery and saying the TV needed repair.

Now he felt a real fear of not being honest with her and found himself in a situation of his own making he didn't know how to handle. What was up with him? 'Oh what a tangled web I weave,' he muttered to himself under his breath, at the same time branding himself as one of the world's greatest idiots. Should he tell Rita now and watch her go back into her protective shell again. But not able to bring himself to do it, he compromised by finding another solution

'All right, I understand. I suggest you go down to the bottom of the road, walk a little way by the main road, you can then turn left and come up around the back. It's a pleasant fifteen minutes stroll. I do it quite often,' he added as if that sealed the deal.

'Sounds perfect darling'! Rita got up, giving his hair a little rub and patting him on the shoulder as she passed him. 'You get out the maps for our trip later and I'll be back before you know it.'

Ernest watched as the front door closed behind her. But never in his wildest dreams would he have thought she would turn in the opposite direction to the way he'd suggested.

'Gosh it's good to be in the real world again,' the words almost spoken out loud as Rita passed the cottages by the village green. Two bottles of full cream milk stood by the door of the cottage that had no garden, its front doorstep being part of the pavement.

'Late risers,' she smiled, remembering her gran, who could tell a lot about the family inside from the number of bottles, colour of the bottle tops and when they were taken in off the step.

Ahead was the Church of St. Anne's, projecting the changing ecclesiastical styles of its architecture over the centuries. Rita, like so many before her, stood before its magnificence and was overwhelmed by its splendour. Dominating the cottages and the village green by its elevated position, no one could fail to recognise the importance of the Christian faith to past generations.

Almost compelled by its presence, Rita climbed the stone steps to it and passed through the fifteenth century lynch-gate. Nearly a thousand years of internments flanked the flat worn stone path that led through the churchyard.

Rita stopped to read some of the inscriptions on the gravestones. Some were tragic; reminders of whole families being wiped out by plague or virus. One was humorous, defying death by poking fun at the Grand Reaper. Ahead a lovely old canopied tomb, placed there in the fourteenth century according to the dating carved on it in Roman figures. She gazed up at the church again, following the gargoyles with her eyes. They ran along the roofline, some acting as water spouts. The Rev. Swindells, the vicar she and Ernest had known as schoolchildren, had told them about St. Anne's, as it was also the Mother Church to the surrounding communities. Thinking back, she recalled that there had been an earlier church on the same site, a Saxon one, which had been mentioned in the Doomsday book.

She scanned the graveyard again. Over to her right was a squared off area denoted by yellow tape. Rita made her way over towards it noting the word "POLICE" written in black lettering along it.

In the middle of the area was an ancient tree; so old some of its branches were propped up by a man-made wooden support structure.

'Someone's got badly hurt,' maybe an old branch had fallen and injured someone. Ernest would know. She would ask him who it was, hoping it wasn't any child.

Satisfied with her explanation and ready to complete her walk, she turned the corner of the church only to be confronted by a partially open door. Norman arched, it wasn't very big. It's thick wooden door displaying huge iron bolts, the round iron handle encircling the oversized keyhole.

The curiosity that draws most people towards antiquities pulled Rita like a magnet. She just allowed her feet to move without her conscious intervention. Finding herself in a small room brightened by the light from the open door she had entered by, she quickly realised she was not alone. Standing facing the south wall away from her was a tall figure. Even from the back view, Rita knew immediately it was the Rev. Richards. She tried to retreat, but her legs wouldn't move. Half closing her eyes for a clearer vision, Rita could just make out some lettering on the wall in front of him that was not obscured by his body.

He was reading something on the wall and she didn't like to disturb the object of his undivided attention. Rita gazed around her. There was a small table by the door. On it was an open book, a pencil on a length of string and a candleholder with a half used candle. Black vestments hung from hooks and a long legged stool supported a few old hymnbooks whose covers needed attention. Her eyes flicked across to a heavy curtain used to separate the room from the main body of the church.

'What are you doing here?' Rita jumped. The voice was brusque, with an unmistakeable tinge of annoyance in it. She thought quickly through a variety of excuses before deciding to tell the truth. After all, she was faced with a man of the cloth.

'The door was open, and I guess I was so impressed by St. Anne's that I wanted to see inside.' She waited for her explanation to be accepted, aware of how drawn John's face had become. Not a well man, she'd assessed from her medical training.

'Sorry that I disturbed you.' She half turned to make a hasty exit, but John stepped forward and took her arm urging her through the open doorway into the main part of the church; his manner now quite friendly.

'The best view for an overall appreciation of the architecture of the place is from the west side of the nave.' He steered her through the aisles.

Rita had to admit he was right. Her head thrown back, she explored the beautifully carved ceiling, then slowly lowering her eyes to observe the delicate fan tracery of the rood screen. They walked over to the lectern and pulpit, which John told her dated from Tudor times. So engrossed in the history of the place Rita had totally forgotten her promise of a ten-minute walk and when John asked her if she would like to pray, Rita found herself saying__. Yes.

'Good,' her answer obviously pleased him. 'Then I think you will like the Lady Chapel.' She followed and was delighted with the carvings on the ceiling and the stained glass window depicting the saints. Its beauty reflecting the work of many hands; skilled at their craft and devoted to God.

John offered a candle for her to light. There was a moment of reverence in the act and, as he tilted it towards her, a tiny drop of wax dripped settling on her sleeve. John then left her alone.

Rita knelt before the altar, her heart was full but no words would come. It didn't matter, nothing mattered but the realization that God had brought her full circle and at last she and Ernest were together again.

The very thought of Ernest brought her sharply out of her meditation. She almost panicked. He would be wondering where she was. Getting up quickly, she extinguished the candle and made her way back to the vestry. John was once again standing by the wall. This time Rita could see plainly the writing that was on it. The writing in gold, red and green, although peeling off in places, was nevertheless beautifully depicted in its Latin script.

Rita moved closer to the wall, her curiosity aroused by the ancient writing was getting the better of her and Rita asked innocently,

'What does it all say?'

'Say,' he was stumbling for words, obviously not wishing to be caught in this position.

'The writing'! She pointed to the wall, 'Latin isn't it?'

Rita's experience with Latin consisted of interpreting the doctor's prescriptions she had to learn as a young nurse and a few other odd words. She did recognise the word "mother", but little else.

John appeared confused as he wiped the back of his hand over his forehead.

'I don't know, it's probably just a verse out of the bible. Probably one of the Ten Commandments, the old churches did it a lot, the Ten Commandments I mean, writing that is.'

Rita looked at him searchingly.

John looked at his watch. Rita gave a start remembering again the length of time she'd been out.

'Must go___, I told Ernest I'd be back in ten minutes.' She hurried away, leaving John gazing after her.

As she passed under the arch of the lynch gate she could see Ernest. He was standing by the gate of the cottage looking across the village green to the main road.

Rita was almost upon him when he turned around and saw her coming from the church, part relief and part horror registering on his face. The familiar frown that Rita knew so well suggesting all was not well.

'Where the ___.' he stopped short from saying, 'hell have you been'.

Rita, reading his mind, took his hand and led him indoors closing the front door behind them. She was never one to broadcast her business.

'I'm sorry love, I went to look at the church,' failing to see Ernest pale before her, she went on, 'and met John there, I sort of lost all track of time.'

She chatted away describing the church as if Ernest had never set foot in the place. Ernest's agitation lessened, convincing himself she'd not become aware of the murders. Then out of the blue, she asked.

'What is the police tape for, did someone have an accident?'

The question was asked innocently enough, but Ernest found himself in a trap that left him no choice but to explain in the best way he could about the recent homicides.

'Sit down Rita,' he said, his voice grim. 'I have to explain something to you and I don't want you to get upset.'

She sat mute, waiting for what was coming next.

'There's been a murder in the village and the spot you saw taped off was where the body was found.' He cleared his throat. 'Actually there are two victims__.' He left off awaiting the shock to sink in, but to his amazement Rita seemed to come alive and surprised him by saying

'Thank God.'

'What?' Ernest's eyes opened wide, half afraid the shock had been too much.

'Gosh Ernest, calm down a little,' said Rita, now getting a little concerned at his pallid colour. 'I know all about the investigations; did you think I don't read the newspapers. I'm just more thankful you've started to talk about it.'

For a second Ernest himself was truly in shock. He just sat down and stared at her.

'You never said,' he snapped

'Well you didn't either,' she retorted. 'I thought you were probably put out that someone else was in charge of the investigations.'

They sat looking at one another, each trying to comprehend the other's motives. Rita was the first to break the silence.

'Tell me Ernest,' she said slyly. 'Confess, aren't you the slightest bit put out?'

For the first time all morning, he gave that old boyish grin that always pulled at Rita's heartstrings.

'Lisa has been warned away from me,' he shrugged.

Rita stroked her cheek, and then cupped her chin in her hand. Her eyes narrowed.

'Nobody has warned Lisa away from me,' she said.

The look of understanding between them was clear.

'A drive in the country then,' suggested Ernest. Rising to lift her up from the chair, he picked at a white spot on her sleeve.

'What's that?' he said. She looked down at it.

'I lit a candle in the church; some of the wax must have spilt on me.'

The memory of another spot of candle wax played on Ernest's mind for the rest of the day, but he disguised it well.

Chapter 21

When Rita remarked that there was not much space in his bedroom for her clothes, it took Ernest by surprise. He gazed around in dismay at all the clutter he had accumulated. All at once there didn't seem enough space to swing a cat around, and must have acknowledged it out loud. Straightaway Rita began to explain where the phrase "swinging a cat around" had its origins.

It was a naval term, she said, referring to there not being enough room aboard to swing a cat-o-nine-tails to lash some unfortunate sailor as a punishment. Rita was full of surprises and seemed to have an answer for everything. Especially when she pointed out it wasn't so much the size of the room, just the amount of furniture he'd stuffed into it.

'What do you need four chairs for anyway?' she asked, sitting down in one and looking questioningly at the other three.

He was about to explain that they had been his mother-in-law's and his late wife had treasured them, but quickly retreated from voicing it.

'Shall I get rid of them?' he uttered. In this situation it seemed the wisest thing to say, before she probed further into his former marriage. But she had already made that decision for him from the very moment Rachael had mentioned Kane needed more furniture. Her eyes roamed the room, mentally rearranging it.

'That table under the window, it's really in the way there.' she said.

'In the way of what' Ernest wondered, but refrained from saying so. Instead he went on to say, 'I've had that all my life; bought it from the Co-op with my first wages.' He walked over touching it affectionately.

It wobbled.

Rita sniffed and gave it a sharp push and it wobbled again, rattling the bits and pieces sitting on top.

He threw up his hands in surrender and caught her around the waist. A little half-hearted struggle on Rita's part before they both landed on the bed, laughing.

Half an hour later Rita raised herself up on one elbow and prodded his chest.

'Off you go then,' she declared, having won her case that Kane really needed a few extra pieces of furniture.

'Goodness Rita.' He pretended he was being hen-pecked. 'You don't give a chap a chance. I used to lead a quiet life.'

'When did you ever live a quiet life Ernest? It would have killed you.' She laughed. 'You know what they say about idle hands.'

She helped him down the narrow stairs with a couple of chairs and the small table. He was about to argue however when she brought down Jean's favourite stain glass bedside light, but seeing the determined look on her face, thought the better of it. After all, wasn't this a new beginning for them both?

It wasn't until he was lugging two chairs from his car boot outside the church; that the thought occurred to him. Perhaps he should have phoned Rachael first.

'Who are they for?'

The question came out of the blue and Ernest nearly bumped his head on the boot lid. He wished people wouldn't creep up on him so quickly like that.

It was Kane standing behind him looking suspiciously at the furniture.

'I thought you could use these for your room.' Ernest offered warily.

Kane stared at him in disbelief, a tiny glistening spot forming at the edge of his thick lips. Tilting his large head on his shoulders, he studied Ernest for a second, and then turned his attention to the chairs.

'Present.' It was more of a statement than a question.

'Yes, yes.' Ernest answered quickly. 'I guess you can say that.'

'A table too?' Kane was pointing at the open boot and Ernest nodded, feeling a sudden pleasure in his morning's work.

Moving at a speed at odds with his body, Kane retrieved the table and banged the boot lid down with such force that Ernest cringed.

Carrying their cargo, the two of them made their way around the south side of the church, stopping by a Norman door. Kane pushed it open with his large boot and to Ernest's dismay, he found himself facing a very narrow spiral stone staircase.

'God Almighty,' he sighed.

Kane nodded in agreement leaving Ernest not sure whether they were on the same wavelength.

'Never again,' thought Ernest, gasping for breath as he parked himself wearily down on one of the chairs on reaching Kane's room. It was bad enough bringing the stuff down his stairs, without having to face these. Rita could go on bullying him all day, but he never intended to carry anything else up these damned stairs. Spiral stairs and furniture were not designed to work together.

After he helped Kane to rearrange the furniture, he sank down wearily on one of the chairs again. Kane sat on the other chair appraising him. For whatever reason, Ernest began to feel he hadn't come up to Kane's standards. However he couldn't have been more wrong as Kane saw him as his new friend and couldn't take his eyes off him.

Trying to void Kane's obsession with him, Ernest scanned the room. It spoke of centuries long ago; the musty smell still lingering in its stone walls.

The priest's chamber was square, with one long narrow window bringing in natural light. Ernest noted the glass leaded pane had black mildew along its edges and in one corner of it a spider had spun its web.

The plastered ceiling had several beams running across it. The plaster was coming off in places, leaving patches and white flakes on the stone floor.

A solitary light bulb hung down in the centre of the room, supplied by an electric cable that travelled across a beam and down one wall to the switch. An electric fire stood in a corner, it was quite new, but a fireguard had been put around it.

A single bed, surprisingly neatly made, was pushed against another wall with a three-legged stool by it. An old bench with woodworm holes in it stood underneath the window. It reminded him of an old church pew.

Then an odd thought occurred to him.

'Where do you wash?' Actually Ernest was really wondering about how he dealt with nature's calls.

'There's a lavatory and basin downstairs,' Kane answered, surprised at the question.

Ernest spotted the handle of a chamber pot under the bed. Kane followed his gaze and unabashed said,

'I've never spilt any.' There was pride in his voice.

'You are lucky.' Ernest chuckled 'I didn't always make it down the stairs without spilling a drop.' He recalled the long cold trips he had made as a child to the lavatory at the bottom of their garden

Then to his great astonishment, Kane bent down on all fours and reached under the bed.

'Damn, now I'm to have a demonstration on the correct way to hold a jerry pot,' he mused, but this vision quickly dissolved as Kane brought out a couple of tins of Coca-Cola. He offered one to Ernest who warily wiped the top with his handkerchief before pulling the tab. Sitting quite still, Kane continued watching his visitor's every movement and began to hum some familiar hymn that Ernest couldn't quite place.

Ernest looked around again, wondering what it must have been like for the old priests. He remembered what Rachael had said about the finding of ecclesiastical relics hidden behind these walls at the time of the Reformation.

He stared at a wall that looked as if it had had new plaster put on it and wondered if more hidden treasures were stacked away elsewhere.

His gaze rested on the thick floorboards and then travelled up to the old bench under the window. There was no mistaking its pew-like appearance. A lone photograph lay atop in a cheap plastic frame.

Kane was watching his friend, pleased he was taking such an interest. Getting up awkwardly he moved to the object of Ernest's attention. Lifting the photograph up, he wiped the dust off it on his sleeve and, pointing to himself, triumphantly handed it over to him.

The photo had been taken some thirty years ago. It was of a small boy with two mournful eyes peering out of a large head. The boy's torso was solid but revealed a slight deformity around the shoulders. The legs thin, looking as if the weight of the body would be too much for them.

The child was standing in a doorway and, as Ernest inspected the photograph closer, a figure of a nun could be seen in the passageway behind the open door. There was a cross carved above the door.

Ernest pieced two and two together quickly. Kane had been brought up in an orphanage run by nuns. The only piece that didn't quite fit was that most religious institutions run by nuns were Catholic and judging by the nun's habit, it was an old order. He looked over at Kane, weighing him up. There was a lot he didn't know about Kane. Although he had a child's mind, there was no doubt he was a fully-grown man.

Then it just popped out. He hadn't meant it to but after years of leading investigations, his questioning was habitual.

'Do you like girls Kane?'

Ernest looked directly at him. Kane appeared a little baffled and took his time before answering.

'I like Rachael,' he said innocently, then returned to thinking about the question.

'Mrs Cliffe is nice too, she makes biscuits for me,' frowning he continued, 'sorry I can't give you one, I got hungry.'

He suddenly got up and went over to the peg on the wall pulling off it a long red scarf. He stroked it before handing it to Ernest to do the same.

'She knitted this for me too,' he said proudly. 'I like her almost as much as Rachael.'

'Very nice.'! Ernest fingered the scarf, thrown a little by Kane's response to his question. It was a possibility that Kane was impotent and didn't view women in the same way as most young men. Anyone under fifty was young to Ernest.

Kane surprised him once again.

'Lisa likes Robin.'

'Really,' replied Ernest, careful with the tone of his reply and wondering whether this would reveal some other more sexual understanding.

'She lent him her own book,' he said it as if anything owned was very precious.

Ernest had the odd feeling his usual line of questioning wasn't going to work on Kane as each turn sent him further afield. He was beginning to have more and more respect for the police psychologists as time passed.

Strange as it seemed, Ernest had enjoyed his time spent in the priest's chamber with Kane, and really meant it when he said he was sorry to go.

Whistling cheerfully he took his leave and drove his car around to the rear of his cottage. Finding the place empty, he felt a sense of disappointment at not finding Rita awaiting him. However there was a note from her to say she'd gone to visit Emily. The disappointment changed immediately to anticipation.

He needed to patch things up with Lisa. The same thought had already occurred to Rita.

On entering number seven, Rita nearly fell over a pile of washing at the bottom of the stairs.

Lisa apologised. 'I was going to do the washing before Jeanne comes, I don't want to lose her by expecting too much from her for the money I pay.' She shrugged her shoulders indicating there wasn't much she could do about increasing the payments.

'Look Lisa, I'm not here to hinder you.' Rita placed her hand on Lisa's arm, 'I came to see Emily really. I thought it would free you up a little.'

The grateful look on Lisa's face made Rita promise herself next time she came, it would be without the need of an alternative motive.

'Get on with what you were doing and I will chat to Emily,' she opened the kitchen door for Lisa to pass through with her load of washing.

Emily lifted her good hand acknowledging her pleasure at seeing Rita. Being as practical as ever; Rita began tucking the fallen shawl around the invalid's shoulders.

'Damp again,' Rita sighed, and struck up a one-sided conversation about Emily's past with little questions like, 'Did you remember when___?'

Emily's eyes reflected she certainly did and requested her album by pointing to it. Lisa popped her head around the door.

'Both alright in there'!

Lisa didn't need an answer as she saw the two of them looking at the old photographs, with Rita making comments.

One page held Rita's attention as she gazed down in shock on the same face she'd seen in Robin's room. It was an identical photograph of the woman holding a child.

Suddenly Emily's good hand gripped Rita, and then moved to the photograph, placing two fingers across it. Rita felt instinctively that something important needed to be understood. She looked at Emily's face and saw the depth of that need in her eyes.

Rita didn't know whether she was doing the right thing, but her compassion drove her on.

'Emily I know you are trying to tell me something about the photograph and it's very important for me to understand, isn't it?'

She could actually feel Emily relax and see relief flooding her face.

'The baby, it isn't Lisa is it?' she asked, almost certain of the answer to come.

Emily shook her head. In a moment of flashback, Rita remembered Emily refusing to let Robin look at the album.

'Why?' she asked herself, then a fantastic thought struck her. Was Emily also the mother of Robin as well as Lisa? The implications were just too dreadful to comprehend as that would make them brother and sister.

Stunned at the prospect Rita felt cold; her mind refusing to go any further. Then, as the initial shock passed, she forced herself to think.

Robin was a year older than Lisa, and Lisa had been born soon after her parents were married. 'Could Emily have had a child before she was married?' she wondered.

Rita raised herself from her chair by the now sleeping Emily and went into the kitchen. Lisa had just finished pulling out a load of dried clothes from a small built-in dryer.

'Ready for a cuppa?' she asked.

Rita nodded and fetched two mugs from the cupboard.

'Emily's asleep,' she said, her back turned away from Lisa, before asking the question she really wanted to explore further.

'Did your mother and father go out together long before they married?'

Lisa turned around in surprise.

'Oh no, Dad left home at sixteen, but came back to work on a farm here and it was love at first sight. They were married within two months.'

Rita could have bitten off her tongue thinking she was going too far but Lisa didn't seem to notice; instead she seemed pleased someone was taking an interest in her mother's life.

'I think someone else from the village rather fancied her also, but left her for another woman.'

Lisa put down the last item she was folding from the dryer and gave Rita a serious look.

'That's why I like Robin. He's different from the other men around here.'

Rita felt a cold chill pass through her.

Chapter 22

Glen Bradford slipped his hand over the still warm spot beside him. He pulled a pillow towards his head and buried his face in it, drinking in the fresh clean smell of his lover's scent.

The morning light blinded him for a moment as he released the pillow. Even with his lids closed, the light seemed to penetrate through them as a bright red glow. He squeezed his eyes tightly as he tried to hold on to the memory of his partner Tim lying beside him, but the brightness of the sunlight finally destroyed any further dreaming and the momentary illusion was gone. With the duvet flung aside beside him, the indentation in the mattress was quickly becoming cold and empty.

Glen turned over with a sigh. Pushing away the rest of the pale green duvet, he swung his legs over the edge of the bed and felt the icy fingers of cold air creep over him. Shivering, he found his dressing gown and moved to the window. Placing his slender hands on the paint cracked sill, he inhaled deeply before letting the air out slowly.

The fact that the window remained shut was not an impediment to the feeling of being refreshed. Just looking over the flat fields and the gradual rise of the land towards the hills of the Pennine Chain in the distance accomplished all.

Glen loved it. He'd been born and raised in the old farm house, nursed and buried both his parents there and still stayed, never wanting to be anywhere else. Fortunately he had independent means. Not large, he would be the first to admit that his ancestors had far more when the farmhouse had been the manor house of the village. His great, great grandfather had seen the opportunity in growing corn and raising milking herds of Holsteins that were grazed on the acres of the good land surrounding the village. However none of his ancestor's offsprings had found the hard work involved all that inspiring, and little by little the land was sold off and some of the farm cottages of the estate leased.

It suited Glen just fine, for he was able to indulge in his passion for old books. It was a search for a first edition of the King James Bible that had brought him to a bookshop in Manchester that was owned by a Tim Simmons. Ever since their first meeting, they both agreed it was love at first sight.

Yet there is always something that mars that ultimate happiness and for Glen and Tim it was that they both loved the places where they resided. For Glen it was his old ancestral manor home in the village and Tim, his flat above the old bookshop in Manchester. Yet for now their relationship seemed to be working. They were indeed committed to each other.

Glen made for the bathroom and emerged some time later fully dressed and awake to enjoy a satisfying breakfast of hot buttered toast, strawberry jam and two cups of freshly brewed coffee.

Tim had left him a note. Glen picked it up, read it, gave it a kiss and placed it inside the cover of a book he was reading. For a number of years now a routine had been set. Glen would spend a few days in Manchester and Tim would spend most of his weekends in Gelsby.

It was only last Sunday they had kneeled side by side at St. Anne's, where they had taken communion together in the ancient church. Unlike a city, a village congregation always took much longer to accept change, and attitudes to any open display of other sexual preferences in their community were no exception. But it helped that a few of the cottages were still owned by the Bradford's and Glen Bradford still represented "The Lord of the Manor" to them. As a result the majority of the villagers chose to wear blinkers in his case, but there was always some twittering whenever he took Tim to the pub.

Glen's father was never aware of his sexual orientation, but his mother was, and although at first confused, she was not going to let anyone hurt her only child. Glen's relationship with his mother had been good and he never failed to take flowers to her grave regularly. This Monday morning was no exception. Glen picked up the flowers that he'd bought on the previous Saturday. They were potted chrysanthemums, ideal for the time of the year and also his mother's favourite colour of yellow.

He closed the door behind him making his way to the rear of the church via the path worn over the centuries across his property to the old graveyard. Normally anyone dying over the past seventy years would have been interned outside the existing church wall, where a number of extra acres had been purchased for a new graveyard. This graveyard was a flat field, edged by hawthorn and oak trees. The square white marble and grey granite headstones became the resting place for artificial flowers rather than fresh ones as people's lives got busier, leaving no dead flowers to gather every week and noticeably less visits to the newer graveyard.

But Glen was not heading for the new graveyard. Instead he made for the older one. Although Glen's parents had died within the last five years, it was deemed by the council that their final resting place should be beside their illustrious ancestors and, taking into account that Glen would be the last of the Bradford line, it would be fitting for the "Lords of the Old Manor" so to speak, to remain together in death.

Next to an older lopsided tombstone covered by lichen and inscribed with the Bradford name, a plain squared area had been prepared. It was covered with crushed white marble pebbles and surrounded by a stone curbing. At its centre a plain marble slab was inscribed with the names of Glen's parents.

No artificial flowers adorned this grave. A bunch of fresh flowers that had been placed there earlier were now wilting.

Glen stood at the side of the family grave, a solitary tear escaping to slither down his cheek. He wished his mother had met Tim. She would have liked him.

No thoughts about of his father crossed his mind, they never did. The tall stiff man he remembered seemed aloof and Glen always harboured the feeling he was a great disappointment to this distant man.

As he bent down to remove the dead flowers; he sensed someone watching him causing a ripple of apprehension to move through his body. Glen's body stiffened. It was the same uncomfortable feeling he'd sensed earlier when he and Tim were taking Holy Communion. He thought this is what an animal might feel like when being stalked and he felt himself freezing to the spot unable to move.

A sharp crack; someone had stepped on a twig behind him. Making a gigantic effort he swung around only to find himself relaxing from head to toe in relief.

'Hello,' he said acknowledging his companion. Looking down at the flowers he had taken from the grave, he remarked sadly. 'They don't last long in this weather do they?'

'Nothing lasts if it goes against the way the Lord intended.' The voice was cold.

Glen shifted uneasily and started towards the pile of compost that was heaped up in the corner. By the side of it stood a cold water tap and a pitchfork that was used for turning the decaying vegetation.

'God's laws are not to be treated lightly,' the voice continued in a slightly higher vein.

'Oh Tim,' Glen reflected, 'why did I insist you attend my church? This is no place for us.'

He knew from past experience it was no use getting angry or trying to explain, it never got anywhere. It was just unfortunate that he happened to be living in this age at the cusp of great changes taking place in society for people like him.

But accuser was not going to give up

'Thou shalt___,' the words hung in the air as Glen's restraining willpower suddenly snapped.

'For Christ's sake'! He watched triumphantly as the face before him paled. 'Take a good long look at nature,' he retorted testily, 'there is no such thing as black or white. Nature just is and the good Lord made all. Unfortunately the persons responsible for writing down the "Thou Shall Nots" forgot they were written by a human hand and not the Lord's.'

He made to walk away but had to step aside as his antagonizer pushed past him. Something hit his back with great force, the intensity of the pain that followed travelled through his chest.

'A heart attack__,' the thought crossing his mind or was it something outside of him. As he fell forward his fading sight settled on a long red prong that was protruding from his chest.

He never felt his arms being stretched and tugged as his body was dragged over to the rotting compost pile. A long heavy pitchfork wavered as death met decay.

As if to wash away the sin of the moment, the sky darkened and a distant rumble was heard, the clouds releasing a torrent of tears over the hapless body of the last Bradshaw.

In a bookshop in the centre of Manchester, a man was serving a customer. For a brief moment his body felt weak and cold. It took him a second or two for the feeling to pass. He needed his coffee break he reasoned. Glen was always on to him to eat breakfast. He smiled, 'what would his life be without Glen?' he mused.

The rain outside hit the shop window and rattled against the panes.

Chapter 23

Lisa drove slowly down the lane behind number seven, and Rita looked up from pegging out some clothes as she passed.

Lisa got out of her car slamming the door shut with a bang. A quick glance over the fences she caught Rita waving to her, she waved back half-heartedly. She felt depressed and her throat raw; like sandpaper.

Lisa had been annoyed but then relieved at Detective Inspector Edgeworth's insistence she went home. But he didn't need to treat her like some plague victim, recalling how quickly he'd stepped back when she sneezed. A perfectly white laundered handkerchief had been pulled out to cover his nose and mouth and with a muffled voice had muttered.

'Go home, its no use you spreading your germs around the station.'

He was treating her as if she was some big fat microbe just waiting to explode. When she hesitated he went red and irritability crept into his voice.

'For crying out loud woman; go.' Still holding a handkerchief to his face, he indicated her exit towards the door with the back of his other hand

'I've a report to finish,' she stammered which brought on a coughing bout.

'Get out,' the response was now an angry command. 'What makes you think you are so important to this investigation, I've got it tied up, no big deal__. Police work at the station is not going to stop if you're not here,' were his last words as she departed.

Dislike, frustration and anger welled up inside Lisa. She decided hatred for him could easily be accepted under her circumstances. How Edgeworth had ever got to his position defeated her reasoning. Degree or no degree, he wasn't a patch on her previous Gov. and she missed the old days with Ernest leading the pack. He was always open to any ideas in an investigation and encouraged others to look into every detail, no matter how insignificant it might appear.

Now looking over at Rita pegging out the washing, she felt a sudden need to talk to Ernest, even if it was only to express some ideas that kept running through her mind.

'Damn it,' she uttered. The decision made, Lisa turned and instead of going towards her cottage, made her way back up to lane to number eleven. Rita took one look at her visitor and put down the empty laundry basket after dropping the peg bag in it.

'You poor dear, you look awful.'

Feeling a great cloud of depression enveloping her, Lisa followed the health advisor into the kitchen. It took approximately two minutes before a thermometer was pushed under Lisa's tongue and two fingers tracking her pulse.

Lisa gazed at her friend's face for any sign of alarm; there was none. Rita's features remained indifferent. The thought occurred to Lisa that all doctors and nurses were trained to think of a patient as their property, and patients had no right to understand what was wrong with them.

'Well!' growled Lisa as the thermometer was pulled out, looked at and taken over to the kitchen sink. Here it was shaken and placed under a cold water tap.

Rita didn't even turn her head, instead directed her attention through the window to the figure walking towards the cottage.

'Oh, you'll live.'

'Thanks a lot,' muttered Lisa, 'and what sort of an answer is that?'

Ernest walked in, and looking at Lisa's flushed face remarked, 'You look awful.'

'My God; is that all anyone can say to me today.' She stared at Ernest. 'What about asking me how I feel?'

Ernest hung his coat behind the back door, pushed off his unlaced shoes with his toes and joined her at the table.

He placed one big hand over her smaller one and pushed his face forward searching his former colleague's eyes.

'Okay Lisa, lets have it. I know you have a cold and are probably feeling really rotten, but I know you.' He sat back drawing away his hands.

'It's the investigation isn't it?' he stated, 'and there's no help coming from that long streak of bacon is there?'

For the first time for ages, Lisa felt a quiet release from her tension. So much so, she wanted to laugh and cry at the same time. Ernest was always good at hitting the nail on the head with his descriptions.

Rita handed her a hot lemon and honey drink and placed two aspirins on the table in front of her.

'Thanks Rita.' Gratefully Lisa sipped the beverage.

'You're welcome;' came the response.

Ernest and Lisa exchanged glances, both affectionately picking up on that bit of Canadian in Rita. That expression and "have a nice day" often amused them both.

Lisa turned her attention back to Ernest.

'I have a strong feeling that Gina and Sharon's deaths are connected.' She paused as if searching the inner depths of her grey cells. 'I just can't get my head around it.' She looked at Ernest for some understanding.

'Is it just me? Is it that I am opposing Edgeworth's lines of reasoning because I just don't like him, or is it that I'm picking up on something that hasn't brought all the facts together? Whatever it is, something's not right. It's too much of a coincidence to have two homicides in a village of this size within a short time of one another.'

'It happens. Not usually I grant you that, but it is possible.' Ernest's reply had a distinct lack of any commitment one way or the other.

Lisa waited a few minutes, but seeing that Ernest was not offering anything further, she plunged in.

'Hell Ernest, you know there's something more going on.' She stopped, taking a deep breath. 'I know I told you to butt out, but I was only trying to follow police procedure and was fed up with Edgeworth warning me about passing on any information to you.'

'And now,' Ernest's eyes had taken on a glint of interest, his body moved forward. Rita stopped stirring the teapot.

There was an air of anticipation.

'Hell Ernest, I need your help.' Lisa declared suddenly.

The room came to life.

'Paper and pencil pet.' Ernest beckoned with his finger at Rita, who straightway produced the articles.

'Right,' Ernest said. The years seemed to fall away from him as he felt the old thrill of the chase cruising through his veins.

'Suspects,' he demanded, pencil raised.

'Edgeworth's or ours,' asked Lisa, playing the game that had once suited them both so well.

'Ours'

Lisa cupped her chin in her hands, elbows on the table and thought.

'Stan Breasley, Gerry Platt and __'. She stopped for a moment before adding 'Kane.'

Ernest wrote down the names, one under the other then returned to the first name.

Lisa continued, 'Breasley has a watertight alibi; he was halfway to Scotland up the M6 when Gina was killed. It was confirmed by the radio contact he kept with his firm and the stuff he was carrying was delivered in Glasgow. He couldn't have killed her.'

Ernest nodded in agreement, considering the fact that although Breasley might be abusive, it didn't make him a killer.

'What do we know of him?' Ernest asked frowning.

'Likes his drink; boasts a lot about being the man in his own house, and not one for women's lib. or equal rights.'

Ernest broke in. 'Could it be possible Gina was involved with someone and dare not tell her parents? You told me the inquest had concluded she wasn't a virgin.'

'It was also noted that intercourse was not normal; she was more raped than consenting, lots of bruising inside and out,' said Lisa, now fully ready to share all her knowledge.

'Incest,' Ernest queried.

'Possibly,' Lisa acknowledged quietly, 'cannot be proved, no DNA and her mother's as tight as a drum when it comes to her talking about Stan.'

Ernest tapped the pencil on the table. 'Maybe___ just maybe Gina had threatened to tell someone. Now that would put the wind up her father.'

He left it there for Lisa to take in.

'Meaning, Stan could have got someone to take care of his problem?' Lisa's eyes widened.

Ernest shrugged. 'She must have been meeting someone, I can't see a girl of her age taking a stroll in a graveyard at night, it would give most people the heebie-jeebies.'

'Ok, lets leave that one there for the moment, what do we know of Gerry Platt?' asked Ernest. 'He could have been seeing Gina to hopefully get a leg over and when she wasn't willing, he just topped her.'

'Not so,' answered Lisa wearily. 'Too many people to give him an alibi, as they had a lock-in at the pub that night.'

'Lock-in,' they both looked up, suddenly becoming aware of Rita's presence in the room with them, her question left momentarily hanging in the air.

'Friends staying behind to drink privately after the pub's closing,' explained Lisa.

'Oh,' commented Rita.

'Lock-in or not, he hadn't an alibi for Sharon's murder,' stated Lisa, stretching her head and rolling it around her neck.

I guess he'd a motive though, and a very good one at that, but___.' Ernest's voice trailed off.

'But?' prompted Lisa and adding, 'why cover her body under stones?'

Ernest passed a hand over his forehead, stroking his ageing lines.

'The stones could have been some sort of statement.' He closed his eyes.

'For what; what did the murderer wish to impart to the public?'

'Adultery,' the voice in the background chipped in again.

Both Ernest and Lisa gazed at Rita as if some code of conduct had been broken, but not quite sure how or why.

'They used to stone adulteresses.' Rita explained calmly, taking out biscuits from a packet and placing them on a plate.

She brought the plate to the table.

'In the bible, they stoned adulteresses,' she repeated letting the information sink in.

'Right,' Lisa sat straight up as if the penny had at last dropped. 'Sharon's murder could have been premeditated by someone and not a crime of passion after all; almost as an example to those who don't follow God's laws.'

An eerie silence pervaded the room as each began to focus on the next name on the list.

'Kane had an alibi.' Lisa pointed out.

'It's only Rachael's word,' suggested Rita pulling up a chair beside them.

Ernest took a biscuit, breaking it in two before asking,

'What do you mean?'

Lisa sighed, 'remember it was Rachael who gave him an alibi. She said in her statement he was watching TV in the rectory that night.'

More silence, then Rita broke in again.

'That's not to say what Rachael said was true.'

They both looked at her aghast.

'Rachael, lying;' there was absolute disbelief in Lisa's voice.

Rita was about to say she had thought the marked rings on the TV programme were worth further investigation, but changed her mind when she saw the look on their faces.

'Just a thought,' she said limply, wondering how Rachael had managed to cultivate such an angelic status in the community over the years.

'Wax,' said Lisa with a thoughtful look on her face.

'What?' asked Ernest, looking at her as if she was losing it?

'There was wax on Gina's sleeve,' she announced.

Something clicked in Ernest's mind. He remembered the wax on Rita's sleeve after she'd been in the church. Was there a connection? Everything appeared to be homing in on the church and its doctrine. He didn't get to state his thoughts out loud for Lisa's mobile rang.

She picked it up. She listened intently, her face paling.

Ernest waited, a knowing fear started in the pit of his stomach.

'There's been another homicide at the church,' she said turning off the phone.

'Glen Bradford has been found with a pitchfork through him.'

She looked very tired and strained, the next words coming out part in belief, part in denial.

'Kane's been arrested' she said, 'seems it could have been him after all, doesn't it.'

Ernest nodded, but deep down he was very disturbed.

Rita sat like a statue, too stunned to think.

Chapter 24

The door slammed shut behind Lisa as she left, leaving her companions dumbstruck. Ernest was the first to break the silence by thumping the table. It wobbled causing hot tea to spill over Rita's hand. She flinched but made no sound.

'What the hell does the fool think he's playing at?' The question was directed at his successor Detective Inspector Edgeworth; the latter becoming an irritation that Ernest found difficult to rid himself of.

'Did he think once he'd arrested someone he'd finished the job?' fumed Ernest out loud. 'Maybe the police colleges nowadays taught procedures that would lead to an early arrest first, followed by a search for the bits of evidence that fitted; rather than finding the pieces of evidence and allowing them to lead the investigation to the right arrest. It sure isn't some bloody game taught from a textbook. It takes teamwork; hours of working over every detail, even if it means sleepless nights and long days dedicated to a thorough investigation of all the facts.'

Rita listened patiently; she knew his frustration was better out than in.

Teamwork had been the foundation of Ernest's successful career and he always made sure the praise was shared equally. Never once had a wrong person been arrested, although he would be the first to admit there had been times when it had been touch and go.

Rita sipped her tea, eyeing him over the rim of her cup. She'd seen that look on his face before and once on track, he would behave like a bloodhound sniffing out every piece of evidence he could find. She knew instinctively that Ernest couldn't come to terms with Kane being a killer.

'Oh my God,' she almost spit out the warm liquid from her mouth as Rachael's face came to mind. It suddenly dawned on her that only a moment ago she was questioning Rachael's truthfulness. With Kane's arrest, compassion now took over. One thing was for sure; Rachael had done more than most for that mentally and physically challenged man.

Rita stood up. She and Ernest stared at each other across the table. Rita was first to find her voice and there was a hint of authority in it.

'Don't stop me Ernest; I'm popping across to the Rectory.' Then, as if the explanation wasn't enough she continued, 'Rachael must be devastated.'

Ernest nodded absentmindedly and stared through her; his gaze moving to the white ceiling as he leaned back, his head cupped in his hands. He found the blank surface easier to gather his thoughts together, like a great painter preparing to put the first touches of paint on a blank canvass.

Outside police cars littered the triangle of the village green. Rita stopped, stepping back as an ambulance raced passed her, coming to a stop by the lynch gate of the church. From where she stood she could clearly see the yellow police tape marking the public exclusion area. A feeling of anxiety welled up inside her followed by a sudden release of adrenaline, making her body tremble.

Taking a deep breath and remembering the hours she'd spent with her physiologist, she gained control of herself. A group of villagers were staring at her, and Rita suddenly became aware she was not one of them and felt herself almost being viewed with suspicion. She recalled what Lisa had once said to her about life in the village and of it taking a lifetime to be totally accepted by the community. Lisa had laughed as she added, "you have to be born and die here."

It had sounded funny at the time, but passing those very reserved village residents Rita realised there was some truth in it.

Crossing over to the Rectory, she caught a glimpse of the open ambulance doors and a stretcher being lifted in. The body was zipped up in a green bag; no need to wonder whose it was. She always felt anger towards the Almighty whenever she witnessed a young healthy life cut short. It was that same despair within when, as a child, she had come face to face with death after finding her mother had taken her own life.

The clicking of cameras caught her attention. Detective Inspector Edgeworth was standing on the church steps giving an interview to the local press. A noisy much heavier vehicle was moving behind her. She turned to see a TV newscast van edging its way in and very quickly becoming the main focus of attention.

A young constable freshly assigned to police duty stood in front of the Rectory and by his stance, looked as if he were guarding the crown jewels themselves.

He raised a hand as Rita approached, the tender skin on his face reddening.

'Sorry Ma'am,' he seemed slightly uncomfortable, seeing the woman's face before him so full of determination.

Rita was feeling rather embarrassed and stupid, and could feel the villagers' eyes giving that all-knowing look; their faces portraying an unspoken "and who the hell does she think she is?" sentiment. She pulled herself together. Rita knew exactly who she was, or more to the point, who she had been. She summed up all her courage.

'I'm a nurse and the rector is in need of my services.' She held the eye contact.

'Medicines young man__, medicines.' She could see he was struggling with his orders, but like his mother, she was not one to be challenged. As his thoughts were flying, his eyes were searching for a senior officer, but they were all preoccupied. He had to make a decision.

'All right Ma'am,' he said and stepped aside.

Rita raised the knocker and gave a couple of taps. No one answered.

She tried again, this time louder and had started to wonder if she was doing the right thing when the door half opened.

Rita had expected Rachael to be under some strain, but was taken aback at the drawn white face peering back at her. The door opened wider and Rachael stepped back allowing Rita to enter. Usually it would have been Rita's first impulse of support to wrap her arms around the sufferer and mumble a few comforting words. Instead she followed the tense figure into the kitchen.

Rachael turned her back on the visitor and stared out of the kitchen window. Rita waited awkwardly for a moment, then spied an open brandy bottle and took the initiative to pour a little into a couple of glasses.

Rachael didn't move, her hands still clutching the sink for support as Rita walked over and stood next to her, handing her a glass without saying a word.

Rachael looked at the brandy then raised her tear-filled eyes to Rita. A loud sob broke out from deep within, shaking her whole body. Rita steadied the trembling glass, holding it to Rachael's mouth as she gulped it down.

The shaking stopped and she let Rita lead her over to a chair. Rita pulled up another in front of her and took both her hands into her own.

'I'm so sorry Rachael,' she said gently. Time seemed to stop for a moment, and then Rachael took a deep breath.

'Kane is innocent,' she stated as if defying anyone to oppose her. She looked like a cornered animal.

Rita lowered her eyes, keeping her voice gentle and reassuring.

'Rachael, we don't know anything yet, the police have only just started their investigation.'

Rachael's hands tightened and her face took on a look of desperation.

'Kane is innocent I tell you, he's one of God's innocents.' She stood up, clutching at the table for support as she swayed, then went over to stare out of the kitchen window again.

Rita could see that Rachael had taken the news badly and was probably feeling she'd let her dependant down in some way.

'Then if he's innocent, he'll be released.' It wasn't much by way of compensation, but it was all Rita could think of at that moment.

Rachael turned slowly, her posture seemingly more relaxed. She sighed.

Rita tried to keep her voice controlled although her body and mind rebelled. She wished she had brought her tablets with her, the mild tranquillisers her doctor had given her in case she felt her emotions getting out of control.

With a tremendous effort she willed herself to focus, after all it was Rachael that was in this dreadful situation not her.

'Rachael you can't blame yourself'. She cajoled her slowly.' What do you know of Kane anyway? What was his background before he came here to work for you, do you know?'

Rachael stared at her; her lips parted slightly then glued shut, her eyes shifting to the brandy bottle.

'Another?' Rita asked.

'Yes' replied Rachael holding out her glass before adding, 'and there was something else I wanted to talk to you about.' She leaned back against the sink, as she seemed to be considering her next words.

'Let's have a cuppa then,' Rita suggested. 'Coffee or tea' she asked; getting up and putting the kettle on.

For a second Rachael appeared confused, then she straightened up.

'Coffee,' she answered.

A door creaked and the sound of footsteps faded along the hall. Rachael looked at Rita and shrugged her shoulders.

'John,' she said.

Rita poured the milk into the steaming brown liquid. The milk separated and curdled, forming tiny white blobs on the surface. Not wanting to delay their conversation further, she gave it a quick stir and kept quiet about the milk being off. Rachael didn't appear to notice.

'So what do you want to talk to me about?'

'It's silly really.' There was hesitation in Rachael's voice.

'Oh come on, don't leave me dangling,' said Rita impatiently.

'Alright then,' came the response. 'I'm concerned about just where Lisa and Robins' relationship is heading.'

For a moment Rita felt lost, sensing somehow the expected topic of conversation had gone off on a tangent.

'Crikey Rachael, you've no need to concern yourself on their behalf. They seem to be very fond of each other,' Rita's earlier thoughts on that relationship being overlooked in her concern for Rachael.

'That's just it.' The words came quick.

Rita stared at Rachael.

'What do you mean?'

Rachael placed her hands on the table, the gesture resembling a card player about to lay down his dummy hand at bridge.

'I'm worried for Robin; he's a good curate. A little new to his responsibilities but time and God are on his side and I think he's very dedicated.'

'Well,' butted in Rita, agreeing on that point, but failing to see where the conversation was leading unless Rachael was about to come out with some other revelation.

Rachael rolled her shoulders forward.

'Come on Rita, you know as well as I that it would be very difficult for Robin to remain a curate.'

'Why?'

'Lisa isn't a true believer you know, she only comes to church because of her mother.'

For a moment Rita was speechless. She opened her mouth to say something, but couldn't think of anything to add.

Rachael was quick to pick up on the expression on Rita's face.

'So you do understand.'

Rita nodded; still a little confused inside between emotion and logic and on being drawn along a path she didn't want to go down.

'Maybe,' she protested feebly. 'But maybe she has her own ideas about God.'

Rachael smiled weakly.

'I don't think she would change that much,' adding, 'and returning to God just to please someone else is not a good start to a relationship or the parish.'

On that Rita had to agree, and before getting up to leave, promised she'd talk to Lisa about the importance of Robin's vocation.

On the way out she passed John in the hallway.

'Sorry about everything John, it must be a dreadful shock.' She held out her hand, which to her surprise was ignored.

'Just leave us alone,' he growled and turned away.

She stood for a moment hardly believing his rudeness. She could understand him being upset, but he had no need to speak to her like that.

Rachael rushed to the rescue.

'He's not himself. It's all taking the toll on him and honestly he didn't mean it.'

Rita accepted the explanation and left the Rectory feeling as if it was herself that needed support and a friendly face. Tiredness began to overtake her, the skipping beat of her arrhythmic heart sounding loud in her ears.

'Home,' she thought; 'home and Ernest.' Her legs carrying her drained mind and tired body back to number eleven to where she knew both could be found.

Chapter 25

There was no need for Rita to tell Ernest that something had upset her. She bore that certain look that he was familiar with. Alarm bells began to ring in his head. Were the murders in the village too much for her? He blamed himself for being so stupid and insensitive to bring her here.

He watched anxiously as she hung her coat over the peg in the hall. She walked past him, dropping herself into the armchair without saying a word.

'Rita,' he began tentatively, almost afraid to break the silence. For the first time in his life he felt out of control. Even the terrible time when he'd witnessed Rita's breakdown after her aunt's death had not affected him like he felt now. He hadn't placed the blame on himself the last time. Now he did.

What could he do? He couldn't pack up and leave; the last thought lingering before changing into another.

'Perhaps they just could leave the cottage for a while after all___, why not' he mused to himself. 'A holiday in the hills and seaside of North Wales perhaps; or even abroad, Spain maybe.' The latter vision shocked him a little as he wasn't one to travel and had never stepped a foot outside Britain.

Two blue eyes, rimmed with black were watching him as he struggled to come to terms with himself.

'Rita,' he began again, but before he could voice his plans, she stepped in.

'Honestly Ernest, the man didn't have to be so rude.' She twisted herself into a more comfortable position.

'What?' All the images going through his mind at that moment crumbled. He wanted to shake his head to clear it and understand what Rita's statement was all about. He momentarily thought he'd lost the point of some earlier discussion he must have been party to.

She sat up straight by pulling on one of the chair arms.

'John was extremely rude as I was leaving.' She went on to tell Ernest all about her morning, finishing off with John's remark as she was departing.

Ernest listened, half relieved Rita was just behaving normally, the other half wanting to go around to the Rectory and confront the Rev. John Richards. Ill or not, he had no right to speak to Rita that way, but in the end all he said was,

'Ah love, I'm sorry'. Leaning forward, he covered her cold hands with his.

'Do you think he's alright?' asked Rita questioningly.

'Who'

'John.'

'I don't know,' confessed Ernest, never very good as assessing illness. 'What do you think?'

Rita sat with a frown on her face, wondering whether to mention her other encounter with John in the church. That incident related to her finding him absorbed in some scripture written on a wall in the church. His comments at the time had niggled at her ever since.

'Do you remember Rachael saying that John was good at languages, including Latin?'

Ernest had a vague memory of the conversation and gazed at Rita with a puzzled look, not quite understanding where it was all leading to.

She told him that when she had found John in the room with the wall scriptures, John had said he didn't understand it at all.

'Some old English can be extremely hard to read,' Ernest pointed out, remembering the trouble he had had with his Shakespeare. 'We get used to our way of spelling and the way they spelt then was quite different,' he said, before offering another thought. 'Maybe he could read it, but was still struggling with parts of the text that were a little illegible and he just needed more time.' Ernest's effort for a rational explanation was flattened by her next remark.

'But it wasn't in Old English,' she declared with conviction. 'It was written in Latin.'

'How an earth do you know that?' He could have bitten off his tongue there and then, for in truth he knew little of Rita's life in Canada and for all he knew, she could have studied the language. The thought also occurred to him that a lot of medical terminology used to be in Latin and maybe she'd done a course as part of her nursing training.

Rita broke in,' I don't understand Latin as such, but some words were familiar.'

'Such as what'! Ernest found himself getting drawn into Rita's little mystery.

'Pater for father and mater for mother and I think soror means sister,' she stopped; then added, 'I just know he was lying.'

Ernest bent his head to one side, picking at his front tooth with his thumbnail while he thought.

'What else did you see?' he eventually asked. He knew from experience the more one visualised a scene, the more something else came to mind.

'The writing you mean?' Rita asked.

Ernest nodded and studied Rita's face as she closed her eyes.

'The letters LEV come to mind,' she said.

'Go on,' urged Ernest.

Rita closed her eyes again, the seconds ticked loudly from the clock on the mantelshelf, and then she blinked with annoyance and said flatly,

'LEV___ then some more large letters following, I think indicating Roman numerals. There, it was Latin, and I even remember some of those Roman numerals. There was an X, a V and three III's, giving the Latin equivalent for eighteen.'

Ernest gave a deep breath and let her continue.

'There's another thing Ernest.'

He gave her his full attention and listened intently as she went on to tell him about the photograph that Emily and Robin had.

After she'd finished she waited for some comment and finding nothing forthcoming added,

'I swear it is the same person in both the photographs.'

'Rita, you cannot be sure, those old black and white pictures don't pick out hair colour and other things. Hairstyles were fairly much the same and clothing was usually in the fashion of the time. It could be some similarity between them that you saw.'

Rita wasn't one to be told her eyesight wasn't to be trusted and from the tone in her voice, Ernest picked up a little resentment.'

'Well the building behind was most certainly the same,' she retorted.

'How on earth can you verify that?' Ernest was impressed by her recollections and couldn't help admiring her.

'I just know it was the same building.' she continued, and looking him straight in the eye she added, 'would that be also in style at that time too?'

Ernest relented and felt a secret pleasure in Rita's company. Hints of their childhood years spent together were being rekindled once again. She was always a little nearer to the finishing post than he was.

'I saw Lisa drive in half an hour ago,' Ernest stated nonchalantly and folded his hands behind his head, eyes scanning the white ceiling above.

'Might as well see how she is,' proclaimed Rita rising from her chair.

There was no answer as Ernest tried to appear disinterested.

The back door of number seven was half open, so Rita popped her head around it calling,

'Coo-ee, it's only me.'

One thing Rita hated most in the world was people phoning her and she having to guess who they were, but calling on people without announcing herself properly was never given another thought.

'Mother's asleep,' Lisa confided, quietly confirming the need to let things be in that department.

'I didn't really come to see Emily,' Rita confessed, 'just wanted to know how you were feeling.'

'A little better,' answered Lisa, sniffing and giving a small dry cough.

Rita smiled in sympathy. 'I always say that a virus has three lifetimes.

'What?' quizzed Lisa; looking mystified.

Rita held up three fingers,

'One week incubation, one week full cold and one week recovery.'

'Sounds reasonable,' agreed Lisa, wondering why the formula never seemed to work for her.

'How's Kane bearing up?' Rita came straight out with it; never one to beat about the bush when there was something she wanted to know, 'what evidence have you got?'

Lisa rubbed her arm and bit her bottom lip showing some degree of discomfort.

'You know full well I can't tell you everything. Don't think I don't know who sent you. It was Ernest wasn't it?'___. Lisa was now wondering if she'd already gone too far as it was.

'Ah,' said Rita, the sound conveying a realisation that she had been found out.

The opening of back door broke the awkward silence that followed and Jeanne came in. She looked surprised at seeing Rita but gave her a nod of recognition. Rita wondered if Jeanne was put out by the fact that Ernest no longer needed her services.

She and Lisa sat at the small kitchen table watching; as Jeanne bent down to get the cleaning materials from under the sink.

'Don't mind me.' muttered Jeanne as she stood up and started to clean the top of the stove.

Lisa took no notice of the hint to move. She wasn't going into the lounge to disturb her mum for no one.

'Seen anything of Robin?' Rita's inquiry was casual.

Lisa's grin lit up her face. 'Yes, we are going out on the moors this evening and Sue from work is coming to see to mother.'

A plate crashed to the floor sending pieces scattering around. Jeanne stood looking at it, her hand trembling.

'It's Ok Jeanne,' Lisa said quietly, 'it's an odd one anyway.'

Lisa turned back to Rita, her statement taking another turn that brought Rita up with a jerk.

'He's adopted you know.'

Seeing the look of surprise on her friend's face she added, 'his mother gave him up for adoption soon after he was born.'

'Father?' inquired Rita.

'Unmarried I guess.'

'Did Robin ever try to find out who his real mother was?'

A cup fell into the sink clattering among the steel rings taken from the stove for cleaning.

'You really do have butter fingers today Jeanne,' Lisa looked over to where Jeanne stood. 'If I didn't know you better I would think you'd been into the sauce.'

Jeanne snorted and began scraping the stove with renewed vigour.

'Did he ever inquire about his real parents?' asked Rita getting back to Robin again.

'He hasn't as yet,' Lisa confided, 'but he does have a photograph of her, which his mother wanted him to have.'

'Golly' was all Rita could say.

Lisa went on, 'his adopted father died when he was four, poor little sod; and his adopted mother died two years ago.'

Lisa turned to Jeanne. 'Put the kettle on, there's a luv.'

Sitting up and stretching her arms behind her head, she looked back at Rita.

'He's going to make some inquires about his real family pretty soon,' he told me last night; heavens knows what he might find out.'

The plug of the kettle was yanked out forcefully.

Chapter 26

Lisa's previous evening with Robin had been strained; all he'd wanted to do was talk about the effect Kane's arrest was having on Rachael.

Now Sue, her police buddy at the station, was telling her she was looking tired and hardly eating enough to keep a gnat alive. Sue had insisted on coming over to see Lisa later that evening to spend some time with her, during which their conversation was mostly directed at men and their insensitive natures. It was now getting late and as Lisa had the next day off and Sue the next morning, Lisa asked her to stay overnight.

Accepting her request, Sue advised her friend to go and have a good long soak in the tub. 'A bit of time spent on yourself never goes amiss__, like my old dad used to say, look after the horse and the job's as good as done.'

Sue gave Lisa a comforting pat on her shoulder and pushed her towards the bathroom door. Not one to argue with a good suggestion, Lisa did as she was told. Tears welled up in her eyes at the comforting concern of Sue. Lisa knew she wasn't working at her full potential. Her cough remained, even though her cold had cleared up. The irritation in her throat had disturbed her sleep and once awake, found that other irritation she harboured towards Detective Inspector Edgeworth, the worst of the two. Always pouncing around like he was the only one on the investigation, his motto for each day was the usual ___ "Keep it Simple."

Lisa began to suspect he was probably top of his class academically but in practice totally useless as far as she was concerned.

'Look at the way he fraternizes with that idiot of a newspaper reporter, Geoff Lewis. There was a creep if ever there was one.' she told herself.

The only thing she could find in Edgeworth's favour was that he opposed the use of the traditional title of Gov, and Lisa was only too happy to oblige. Ernest and his title Gov were too well established in her mind to confuse him with that idiot.

The bath filled. Lisa found an old packet of bath salts and emptied it in, watching as the water turned green. It seemed like an eternity that she lay immersed, occasionally using her big toe to turn on more hot water as the bathwater cooled. She thought of Robin, and consciously pushed away any vision of the dog collar. It was the Robin, in jeans and a sweater, striding out across the Derbyshire moors, who was at her side, her own face turned to the wind and her hair flowing free. She was so relaxed she didn't hear the first knock on the door.

The second one was louder. Lisa sat up displacing the water from around her.

'Yes,' she yelled, her ear trained for a reply and her body automatically tensing for action.

'It's the phone luv,' yelled back Sue.

'Hell,' thought Lisa under her breath and sat up. Then the thought of the horse came to mind and she slid back under the water.

'Tell them I'm out.'

Half an hour later she emerged wrapped in a dressing gown that had seen better days and wearing an unlaced pair of sneakers.

She plastered down her wet hair with a comb causing it to highlight the shape and contours of her skull.

'Who was it?' she asked, glancing towards the phone whilst stuffing a piece of freshly buttered toast into her mouth. Sue cut another piece of bread and shook her head.

'Don't know, the caller never said,' she passed the jam over to Lisa, 'sounded a long way off,' she added.

Lisa's forehead wrinkled as her mind raced through a list of potential long distance callers, then gave up.

'Asked when you'd be in though,' Sue remembered suddenly.

'Reckon whoever it was will phone again then.' Lisa remarked, dismissing the incident and suddenly feeling she could eat another round spread with jam.

The phone did ring again after Sue had left the next morning.

'Hello,' said Lisa, picking it up.

There was a moment of silence, and then a muffled voice came through.

'Is that Lisa Pharies?' it said.

Lisa put the phone closer to her ear, her trained mind recognising someone trying to keep the voice disguised. Instantly all her energies were focussed.

'Yes,' she replied, giving nothing away but leaving the communication open.

'I have some information for you about the recent deaths.'

'Right,' replied Lisa, wishing she could get hold of someone to trace the phone caller's location, but there wasn't and she knew she'd have to get as much information as possible.

'Who are you and where are you phoning from?' she asked quietly.

There was a laugh.

'Nice try, but my information is for you only.'

'Ok,' responded Lisa.

Silence, and Lisa wondered if she had blown it.

The voice started again. Lisa knew it was speaking into a cloth or something to disguise it.

'Meet me tonight at eleven. Be on the road towards Belton.'

Lisa was just about to say something when the voice cut in again.

'Do as I say if you want my information. I'll find you and I'll know if you are alone.' The phone clicked as the caller rang off.

Lisa walked back into the room where her mother was sleeping. Sitting down, her arms folded, she relived the details of the dialogue she had just had.

There was no identification to sex, although she was convinced the voice was muffled by something. A local call she guessed, probably from a phone box. There were only two in the village, one at the petrol station and the other located on a corner at the other end of the village. The click was certainly that of an ordinary phone, not one from a cell.

Common police procedure would have been to inform her superior and have surveillance available while meeting with her caller. Instinctively she knew something would go wrong if she did that and considered her best bet was to not go by the book, but go it alone.

Who ever it was only wanted to pass on information, probably someone who doesn't want to have any involvement with the police, she reasoned. It often happens within families when a member sees odd behaviour in another, but feels ashamed at inflicting the other family members to police interrogations and the inevitable humiliation.

Lisa had a bout of coughing and Emily woke up. They looked at each other, each wishing they could communicate. Lisa rose, bent over and kissed the white head, then phoned Rita.

Although it was a strange time to ask anyone to come round for an hour, Rita accepted willingly and didn't ask any questions.

Ernest fidgeted with the tassels on the chair's arm covering.

'Something up Rita?' he asked, after she'd told him she would be slipping out later that evening to look after Emily for a while.

'Wonder where she is going at eleven o'clock at night? mused Rita, her lips presenting a thin line. 'Maybe she and Robin have something planned.'

Ernest smirked.

'At that time of night girl, don't be daft.'

'How the dickens would I know then,' she said flatly, 'maybe he had a sermon to finish and needed Lisa's help.'

Ernest didn't rise to the sarcasm. He still thought it odd, surely the two could talk over the phone, forgetting his own past needs to see Rita between work periods even if only for ten minutes or so.

The daylight dimmed bringing its own shades of grey as the countryside settled down to its own rhythm. Rita had catnapped while reading a book on medieval history that left her interest lacking, being written by an American.

At fifteen minutes to the hour, she shouted 'bye' to Ernest, who had already promised to keep their bed warm for her return.

From the upstairs window he watched as Rita passed below. Five minutes later Lisa hurried by, her anorak hood pulled up and hands pushed deep into her pockets. There wasn't much he could do but wait until they both returned.

Lisa hastened her step, and pulling out her hands from her pockets, she pressed the little knob on the side of her watch. The face of the watch lit up showing five minutes to eleven.

Passing the pub gate and the narrow path that went alongside the field to the school, the sidewalk petered out leaving a small grass strip between the narrow road and the hawthorn hedge. The road swung off to the right, twisting its way behind the village to end up some miles later at the hamlet of Belton.

Lisa checked her watch again. It showed eleven.

She stopped and looked around, suddenly feeling extremely vulnerable. It was almost too dark to see and her nerves were at the peak of their sensitivity.

Suddenly everything was happening. A bright light beamed down on her and she heard someone shout.

'It's going to hit you___, move.'

She sprang, hurling herself into the hawthorn; the thorns scratching her face and hands as she did so. A car roared past.

A small soft light was moving towards her and she heard the clicking of a bicycle wheel. Preparing to defend herself, she tried to stand up but to her horror found her hand wouldn't take her weight.

'Are you alright luv?' A man's voice came out from the darkness behind the light.

He laid his bike down and helped her up, noticing she was holding her wrist tentatively with her other hand.

'You were lucky there.' Her rescuer picked up his cycle again. 'Some mad fool and full of drink I suppose. Reckon he didn't see you.'

Lisa nodded, strangely thinking, 'why a "he" and not a "she"?' She shook her head to clear it.

Slowly however it dawned on her; whoever the person was who drove at her had seen her all right. The person on the phone wanted her dead. She shivered.

'From the village?' the man enquired.

'Yes, I am,' replied Lisa.

'Come on then, I'll walk thee home.' His accent was thick broad Cheshire and its familiar sound helped Lisa gather herself together.

'Thou's not hurt too bad then,' he said, focusing his attention on her limp hand as Lisa managed to move her fingers.

She walked slowly back the way she had come, listening to the chatter of the man pushing his bike beside her.

'I'm Ted Green by the way.' He held out his hand when they got to number seven; then withdrew it, seeing she was reluctant to offer hers, as she was still holding her injured wrist.

'My name is Lisa,' she offered instead; finding herself taken aback as the porch light beam fell across her knight errant.

Why had she assumed he was just a country bumpkin? He appeared quite presentable as she quickly placed him within her own age group. A lock of ginger curly hair fell across his forehead and his eyes held a permanent twinkle.

'I've a farm up yonder,' he said looking back the way they'd come. 'Just finished milking the cows.'

He seemed a little reluctant to go, but Lisa thanked him again and put the key in her door.

The remnants of a slight but distinct smell of manure entered with her.

'What on earth has happened to you?' Rita gasped in alarm seeing the scratches on Lisa's face and the grass streaks in her hair.

Her first thoughts were of rape and Lisa recognised the assumption and quickly set the record straight.

'I nearly got knocked down,' she admitted, 'no point in telling any lies to you is there? I wasn't looking where I was walking and a car came along a little too fast.'

Rita forced herself to remain calm and appeared to accept Lisa's version, but inwardly she had grave doubts that it was an accident.

So instead of tackling Lisa on what really happened, she led the shaken woman in to the kitchen and proceeded to wash her facial scratches with disinfectant.

When Lisa refused to hold out her hands, Rita turned on her professionalism and took command, forcing Lisa to show them to her. Not saying a word Rita inspected the injured wrist. Coming to the conclusion it was a bad sprain, she proceeded to show her skill with a bandage and, to round it off picked up a clean tea towel to form a makeshift sling.

She stepped back to admire her handiwork. 'I think that calls for a stiff brandy,' she remarked.

At precisely one am, Rita left. At three am the same morning, Rita and Ernest were still talking, the empty cups scattered around, indicating a number of pots of tea had been made and the nearly empty tin of chocolate digestives had provided some nourishment.

Ernest lay back in his chair, his legs crossed over on a tuffet facing the fire.

Rita sat on the floor, her back resting against the side of another armchair. On her knee was a large version of the King James Bible.

It was opened at page one hundred and sixty of the Old Testament, the heading at the top of the page was LEVITICUS and the corner of the page was folded over at chapter eighteen.

Chapter 27

Badly shaken and torn between duty and keeping quiet made it a difficult workday to get through. Lisa stewed all day long about what had happened to her the previous night without coming to any decision on whether to tell her superior.

Detective Inspector Edgeworth himself was in foul mood after being called into the Superintendent's office. No one in his or her right mind would have put more coal on the fire that day. It just wasn't the right timing Lisa decided, with a feeling of relief.

She reasoned it was her own stupid fault she had nearly been killed and would from now on be on her guard. But the bantering of her colleagues didn't help.

As soon as they saw the scratches, the comments began.

"Thought you'd be past having it off in a field," and "get him to cut his nails next time," while growling and clawing their hands at her. Nobody really believed she'd missed her footing and fell into a hawthorn hedge, and even if they did, it was still too good an opportunity to let pass without some inane comment or other.

As the day passed her mood darkened and by the time she'd arrived home, was more than ready to vent her frustration.

It was the big grey tabby from next door that got it. It's purring around Lisa's legs would normally have received a scratch around the ears for its trouble. Today a foot lifted the tabby in the air and it went flying into the hedge. It shrieked, snarled and sank back into the foliage, its yellow eyes glinting.

'Lisa.'

She turned; one hand on the door latch.

'Christ Ernest, not now,' she cursed, as she saw Rita standing behind him.

'I'm bushed and don't need to be interrogated by you two just now.'

She turned her back on them, but he slipped by her, pushing the door open and hustling her inside.

'This can't wait, we need to talk.' There was a desperate urgency in Ernest's voice.

She sighed in resignation. It was little use arguing with her old Gov. when he had a bee in his bonnet.

'Oh, what the fuck,' she stopped short, conscious of Ernest's dislike for her wider vocabulary. Then her eyes narrowed as she caught sight of a book Rita was hugging to her chest.

It was a Bible. This was all she needed.

Jeanne pushed by the small knot of people without so much as a by your leave. She just muttered her goodbyes, but no one paid any attention to her.

Ernest took Lisa's elbow and steered her into the kitchen, nodding to Rita to close the door. He didn't want Emily to overhear what he was about to say. He waited for Lisa to sit down then stood before her, his posture indicating he was deadly serious.

He came straight to the point.

'It was no accident the other night. Whoever was driving that car wanted you dead.'

Lisa paled and coughed.

'Are you sure?' She was not usually one to question Ernest's conclusions. Her voice was already wavering and fear was clearly showing in her eyes.

'I'm ninety-nine per cent sure, although no real evidence.' He was frowning; some of his past confidence visibly missing. He hated having a piece that didn't quite fit, although some far-fetched murder scenario was obviously taking root in his mind.

'I also believe that Gina was actually killed in the church and not outside it.' He awaited the response before continuing, but her expression never changed.

'The thought struck me after seeing the spot of wax on Rita's sleeve after she lit a candle in the church.'

Not a muscle moved on Lisa's face.

'It was Rita that came up with the motive behind all the deaths, and I'll back my reputation on it. His voice was edged with unmistakable pride as he took the Bible out of Rita's grasp. Laying it down in the middle of the table, he thumped it with the flat of his hand.

Lisa jumped, confusion now written all over her pale white face.

'It's all here,' he said thumping the book again.

'Any hard stuff around?' he asked; leaving the previous words hanging in the air.

Lisa pointed to the cupboard. She appeared numbed and responding automatically, got up and poured out three brandies.

Ernest downed his in one; the other two were left still toying with their glasses.

Then as he began to tell Lisa about the writings on the wall inside the church, she tipped her brandy back and let the warm glow loosen her stiff frame. She listened intently to what he had to say.

'In a small room at the church there is a wall with some old writing on it.' Lisa wondered where all this was leading but remained quiet.

'Rita saw the writing and thought it was in Latin, but then John had confused her by saying he was unable to read it.' Ernest paused.

'It was that very denial that made Rita curious because Robin had said that both Rachael and John could understand Latin.' Ernest scratched one side of his nose, his other hand playing with a piece of paper stuck between the pages of the Bible.

Lisa sat staring at him in bewilderment.

Ernest went on. 'Rita dug out my grandmother's old Bible.'

Rita chimed in. 'At first I checked the New Testament and was about to put it down when just for something else to do, I decided to look through the pages of the Old Testament as well, and___.' Rita was by now looking quite excited and added, 'I came across the book of LEVITICUS and recalled seeing the letters LEV on the wall. She stopped, catching her breath before continuing.

'Reading the book on Leviticus in the Bible, I thought it was nothing more than another record of the Lord's instructions to Moses in the Ten Commandments. I read some verses from the first part about the Lord telling Moses to keep his ordinances and statues, of the ways of good living, of sacrifices and clean and unclean foods. At this point I was getting bored; all that old stuff we used to get rammed down our throats when we were kids at school.' She glanced at Ernest, with a slight smirk on her face.

'But as I continued reading on, I remembered seeing the Roman numerals XVIII on the wall also, and realised they were referring to the chapter eighteen. Here I began to be interested because it spoke of forbidden sexual relationships.'

Pulling the Bible towards her and tilting it to the window for better light she started to read. 'None of you shall approach anyone near of kin to uncover nakedness; I am the Lord.'

She continued, 'uncovering of nakedness; strange words I thought, but quickly grasped their meaning.' Rita then spaced her words as she slowly read other verses from the same chapter.

'Thou shalt not uncover the nakedness of thy father, which is the nakedness of your mother. She is your mother and you shall not uncover her nakedness.'

Rita looked up to see if they were following the repetition and then added 'It goes on and on about every member of a family.'

She put the Bible down and brushed her hair back with her hand before delivering another one of the abominations, taking a breath before continuing.

'Thou shalt not lie with mankind as with womankind, it is an abomination.'

As Rita put the book down, an insight began to dawn on Lisa. Ernest had long suspected the young girl Gina had somehow been involved in incest, Sharon was an out and out adulteress and Glen and Tim's behaviour spoke for itself. Now like Ernest, she was thinking along the same the lines, that some religious fanatic had been responsible for all three murders.

Frowning, she turned to Ernest

'You said I was an intended victim but I have not broken any of those laws. She looked from one to the other for an answer. Both started talking at the same time, which made her feel like a spectator at a tennis match. She held up her hand.

'One at a time, please.'

Ernest took the lead leaving Rita tracing an imaginary ring with her finger on the table. He chose his words carefully.

'That's the fly in the ointment.'

'So there you are,' Lisa said dismissing the theory.

Ernest looked awkward, looking over to Rita for help.

Rita gazed back at him for a moment, then having made a decision, she told Lisa bluntly.

'There's a real possibility of Robin and yourself being closely related.'

Lisa gasped in horror. She didn't know whether to laugh or get angry, but long police training made her wait for a full explanation.

She listened while Rita told her about the photograph of the woman in Robin's room, which was identical to the one in her mother's album.

She coughed, her voice noticeably showing signs of stress.

'Are you __', she coughed again. 'Are you suggesting my mother had a child before she was married?' Her words were choked as she spat out, 'and Robin's my brother?'

The tinkle of Emily's bell broke the silence. All three of them looked uncomfortable and somewhat distraught. Suddenly Lisa jumped up. 'Well' she said with a distinct matter-of-fact intonation in her voice, 'my mother is the only one to ask about that, isn't she?'

'Oh God,' moaned Rita, inwardly wandering if they had overstepped the mark. She looked at Ernest for help, but all he did was shrug his shoulders and stand up. Together they followed Lisa. They found Emily a little distressed. A coal had fallen to the front of the grate and the smoke clearly was an irritant. Lisa picked it up with the fire tongues, placing it well back before adding another one. Without a word she picked up the photograph album up and handed it to her mother, opening at the page where a pretty young woman was standing holding a baby. Lisa's nose wrinkled as she pointed to the woman asking?

'Mother, is that your Auntie May?'

Emily held her daughter's gaze for a moment, looked down and placed two fingers over the photograph.

Lisa let out a long sigh of relief.

'Auntie May.'

There was no other sound in the room apart from the crackling of the fire. Ernest and Rita's faces held blank expressions. Lisa spoke again to her mother. The tone was gentle and caressing,

'Mum is that Auntie May's baby?'

A tear formed in Emily's eye. Lisa wiped it away tenderly.

'A boy?' she asked. Her mother nodded and tried hard to speak but no words came forth.

A pained look spread over Emily's face, telling Lisa all she wanted to know.

'It's okay Mum,' squeezing her mother's hand. There's nothing to worry about, it's just that it's important and we had to know. After tucking her mother's shawl closer around her shoulders, she stood up.

'I'll get you a nice cuppa Mum.'

In the kitchen she explained to Ernest that her Mother and Auntie May were twin sisters. All she knew about May was that she had died young.

Ernest had been quietly listening to every word and realised his first assumption was correct.

'Somebody thinks Robin is Emily's child, which would make him your brother.' It took only a second for it to dawn on Lisa what Ernest was getting at.

'You mean I really am an intended victim,' she said, her eyes showing alarm.

Ernest nodded.

'I'm afraid so, you'll have to watch your step lass.'

'Easier said than done,' mused Lisa, squaring her shoulders as anger crept over her. She didn't intend being some sorry religious maniac's victim.

Ernest picked up the tray of tea, taking it to where Rita was talking gently to Emily. Lisa hung back for a few minutes, thinking about how she was going to tell Robin. The thought made her somewhat uneasy.

'What did she know of Robin anyway?' he seemed to enjoy her company and she certainly did his, but he had never actually made any advances, and why did John pretend he couldn't read the writing on the wall.

Now she was determined to be nobody's victim and would follow correct police procedure by telling Edgeworth about her near escape.

Chapter 28

There was an unmistakable air of general discontent during the morning meeting at the Police Headquarters. The mumblings came to an abrupt stop as Detective Inspector Edgeworth entered the room.

A coin could have been heard dropping as Edgeworth announced stiffly that Kane Oakland had been charged with first-degree murder on all three counts, and Gerry Platt released.

The announcement was greeted by a stony silence and just as Detective Inspector Edgeworth was about to leave, a hand went up at the back of the room. All eyes turned on the youngest police constable whose face at this point had turned noticeably scarlet as he stood up.

'What is it constable?' Edgeworth's voice was clipped.

'Miers sir, Constable Miers,' the young man replied with an uneasy articulation.

'I didn't ask your name. What is your question?' The detective inspector raised his voice, irritability creeping in.

Miers asked the question that most of his colleagues themselves were thinking.

'What about his alibi for the first homicide sir?'

The murmuring started again around the room with a nodding of heads. The detective inspector growled, then focussed on his underling as if he was the most stupid of men. Constable Miers felt his forehead becoming damp as he broke out in a cold sweat.

'He doesn't have an alibi.' Edgeworth gave a short wave of his backhand suggesting that was the end of the matter.

The police constable would have been given full marks for persistence. His hand went up again.

Someone giggled.

'But the rector's sister gave him one,' this time his voice sounded stronger as his confidence grew.

Lisa smiled to herself. Her old gov. would have already earmarked him for showing such promise, while at the same time wishing she herself had been more assertive. Still she kept her silence, preferring instead to watch the slight twitching on her superior's face. Detective Inspector Edgeworth met her gaze with an unflinching stare, his voice now lowered into an icy cold monotone as he began his explanation of the facts of the case.

'There is significant evidence to suggest that Miss Richards___.' He paused, placing a special emphasis on "Miss Richards," 'was not there at the time Kane Oakland was supposed to be watching TV.' Then, as if to put a stop once and for all to any further challenge to his conclusions added, 'the said information was given in a statement by the Reverend Richards himself.'

Constable Miers sat down, a bead of sweat now running down his forehead.

Lisa raised her hand.

'Can you elaborate on the rector's statement sir?'

Pure dislike etched itself across the inspector's facial features.

'Because Miss Rachael was helping him in his library at the time,' he said, shouting as if she was deaf.

'What time would that be?' Lisa was trying to recall the details of Rachael's statement; she herself had taken down.

Detective Inspector Edgeworth threw up his hands.

'I suggest you read your own report.' The door swung to with a bang as he left the room.

Someone patted Lisa on her shoulder; the others sidled off to their various duties. Lisa walked over to the coffee percolator, her heart racing with exasperation and resentment.

'Not like the old days eh.' P.C. Buzzard passed her a packet of dried milk, 'miss him, do you?'

She nodded and took the plastic spoon offered, stirring the coffee as she watched him leave, his familiar gait adding little comfort to her depression.

'Maybe I should quit,' she mumbled to herself. The hot liquid burnt her mouth and the taste bitter. She left the coffee sitting by the percolator and made for her office.

There was a note from Edgeworth lying on her desk.

'Sod you,' she said after reading it, angrily screwing up the note and throwing it towards the wastepaper bin. It missed.

'Sod it,' she stated again, making no move to pick it up.

Her thoughts were taken up with the prospect of seeing Rachael's face when she broke the news.

'Why me; why pick me to do his dirty work?'

She left her office, banging the door behind her, and made off for the parking lot.

Her small car sped along the motorway. There was plenty of traffic, mostly trucks and salesmen doing their routine journeys. She could always spot a salesman, driving alone in a new car, tidy hairstyle, briefcase lying in the back window and invariably a cell phone pressed against the ear.

She overtook a shabby looking Ford. Although it had seen better days, it was travelling quite fast.

She looked at her speedometer.

'Damn,' she breathed and put her foot softly on her brake. The last thing she needed was being pulled over by one of her own. Moving back into the slower lane, the Ford overtook her again.

A grinning face looked over at her. She gave it two fingers.

The sign she was looking for loomed up. She dropped her speed again and drifted into the off-lane.

Picking up a half-eaten sandwich from her passenger seat with one hand, she took a bite. It tasted a bit off, but she needed the sustenance and swallowed. Then instead of following the road straight into Gelsby, she made another left that would take her around the village towards Belton. She needed to relax, her shoulders and neck felt tight. Rolling her head from side to side she brought her speed right down and cruised slowly along the narrow winding road.

She didn't need a psychoanalyst to tell her that most of her anger was directed at herself. If she had been an intended victim, then Kane couldn't possibly have been the murderer.

Kane couldn't drive.

Bile arose in her oesophagus leaving a burning sensation. She couldn't be sure whether it was the ham in her sandwich or the ensuing panic that caused it.

She'd really blown it this time trying to go it alone. She'd withheld vital evidence and maybe the wrong person would be going to trial.

The thought of quitting loomed up again, but she couldn't uproot her mother and take her to a place full of strangers, but the bigger problem was; how would she earn the money to keep them both. Self-pity took hold; hot tears forming, and through them she caught sight of a sign that read Green's Farm. A tall figure was walking across the field driving a herd of cows.

She couldn't be certain about the man's identity, but it brought to mind her knight-in-shining-armour, as Ernest would have called him.

'Nice chap,' she thought recalling his laughing eyes.

'Blue,' as she recalled.

She passed the spot where she had nearly been killed the night before and, after negotiating a multi-point turn on the narrow road, she headed back to Gelsby. There didn't seem any reason in delaying her mission anymore.

She lifted her mobile, pressed the number of the Police Headquarters and gave her position.

She was tempted to nip home for decent coffee but the thought that Jeanne might think she was being checked on, she made straight for the Rectory instead.

She was a little taken aback when Robin opened the door to her knock. His face broke into a huge smile.

'Come on in,' he took her coat although she hadn't intended to take it off. Now she felt uncertain how to proceed and she found herself being directed into the library.

The fire was lit and scattered around on the floor and armchairs were sheets of discarded writing paper.

'Sermon,' he said with a hint of laughter. 'It always gets to me.'

She picked a couple of scribbled on sheets and read them out aloud. 'He who speaks the truth declares righteousness.' Her legs felt weak as she read on. 'The wicked are overthrown and are no more.'

'Crickey,' she said, handing them to Robin who had by now picked up the rest.

He took them over to the large desk where the Latin Vulgate lay open. Turning quickly, he nearly bumped into Lisa who had come up behind him.

'Who's the expert?' she asked.

He stared at her for a moment, and then looked over at the Vulgate.

'Both John and I are familiar with Latin, all part of the job, but it's Rachael that excels; quite good for a woman too.' As soon as he'd said it and seen the frown on Lisa's face his cheeks burned.

'Whoops.' Robin exclaimed. 'I didn't mean to be disrespectful of your sex.'

Lisa turned away.

'Golly I'm sorry,' he exclaimed taking her move as an expression of her being offended.

He stepped forward and put his arm around her; she put her head into his chest and giggled. She knew she had to tell him about their relationship to each other, and had surprised herself by liking him more as a friend than anything else.

Nothing prepared them for the outburst that followed.

'What are you doing here?' Rachael had entered the room and was standing with her fists clenched.

Lisa was quick to realise the question was directed at her as a police officer, not as a visitor. She placed her hand on Robin's arm for him to be silent.

'Best get it over with,' she thought.

'Rachael, I'm so very sorry and wish I wasn't the one to bring the news, but Kane's been charged with all three deaths.'

Rachael stumbled and clutched at the doorframe for support as she reeled backwards.

Lisa stepped forward, but Rachael held her off, her eyes piercing like a cornered animal.

'You can't,' she seemed to lose her breath then inhaled forcefully, 'he wouldn't hurt a fly.' A lock of hair dropped, she pulled it back almost tearing it out by its roots.

'He was here watching TV,' she stated, her voice dropping to a whisper.

John joined them. He looked all in, his face ashen.

'Rachael,' he said quietly. 'He didn't come here that night, and you were working with me until after ten pm.'

His sister's life energy seemed to leave her body. John moved to her side and placed an arm around her. Lisa noticed her flinch and stiffen as he did so.

'Robin, fetch a brandy.' John took command. Robin cleared his voice and quickly taking in the situation, he turned to Lisa.

'I think its best you went now.'

With her head bowed she made for the hall, detesting her job more and more. So preoccupied with her own self, she almost fell over the vacuum cleaner.

'Careful.' Jeanne reached for her arm to steady her.

Lisa stared at the apparition before her. At first she thought her mind was playing tricks, but it was Jeanne large as life facing her.

'What the heck are you doing here?' Lisa could only think of her mum alone in the house. Jeanne pulled the vacuum cleaner cord a little and let it go as it wound itself up inside the machine. She looked a little concerned at Lisa's reaction.

'I told you I had arranged for Miss Rita to sit with your mother. Remember I asked whether I could do the Rectory today instead of Saturday.'

Lisa put her hand against her forehead. Of course, now she remembered, and felt rather stupid. She had forgotten quite a few things lately. Time she relaxed.

'Are you alright Lisa?' Jeanne's voice penetrated through Lisa's fogged mind. She shook her head as if to clear it.

'Overload at work Jeanne, that's all,' she smiled as best she could.

Jeanne stood at the front door and watched as Lisa started her car and left.

Chapter 29

Sleep didn't come easily to give the much-needed rest to Lisa's over active mind. She tossed and turned until the early morning light broke through with the dawn chorus.

Even then she lay wide-awake; visions of Rachael's face floated in and out of her fogged brain. The slight ache behind her eyes and the anxious surges in her stomach took their toll. Lisa jumped out of bed, rushed to the bathroom and was sick. She stared at the remains of the ham sandwich, which obviously hadn't agreed with her; and realised she'd eaten nothing since.

Shivering she came back to her room and sat on the edge of the bed; her hands gripping the mattress and her head bowed in rhythmic pain. For half an hour she just sat there, and when at last she rose to get dressed, she had made a decision that could change her life. She had to tell Edgeworth about the caller and the attempt on her life.

Downstairs Emily looked at her curiously from her place by the fire; pain evident in her faded blue eyes as she noted her daughter's distress.

Jeanne, who was folding some laundry, also studied Lisa's pale face.

To add to Lisa's problems, she knew she was late for work and as she went to get into her car she realised Jeanne had parked too close for her to leave. She stamped back into the house; her frustration evident.

'Jeanne,' she shouted. 'Will you please move your damned car, can't you see I'm blocked in.'

Jeanne quickly picked up the irritation in the voice and in return became resentful. But obligingly she shuffled out of the kitchen and started her car, moving it in about a foot; any more it would have scraped along the fence.

Lisa said nothing; she just sat waiting before driving away, feeling very irritated with her cleaner.

Jeanne stood for a moment watching the car disappear before going back to finish her jobs.

P.C. Buzzard looked up from his paperwork and was about to open his mouth with his usual greeting, but after taking one look at Lisa's face and the direction she was heading, he closed it again. Retirement appeared better and better as the days rolled by. Two more months and he could enjoy his little piece of garden every day. He sighed at the thought.

Lisa raised her hand ready to knock on the door marked Detective Inspector Edgeworth, held it in mid air for a second, then rapped three times.

'Come,' the voice commanded from the other side of the door.

'Right,' Lisa whispered to herself. 'This is it.'

She took a deep breath and entered.

Detective Inspector Edgeworth's back was towards her, his chair facing the window. She stood stiffly, her eyes noting the absolute tidiness of his desk. A flash memory of Ernest's piles of paper on the same desk flicked through her mind.

Without turning Edgeworth's voice broke in,

'Well?'

'Sir, I have some vital evidence that might prove that Kane Oakland is not the person we want.' Her voice was steady much to her own surprise.

The chair wheeled around, accompanied by a slight squeak from a poorly maintained mechanism.

'What the hell are you talking about?' His face looked like thunder.

Lisa's legs trembled slightly, she wished she could sit down, but there wasn't going to be any invitation coming her way.

'I received a phone call,' she hesitated before adding, 'last week.' Seeing no response, she continued, 'I don't know whether it was a male or female calling as I believe the voice to be disguised.'

She waited again, but Edgeworth never said a word; only his cold eyes pinned her down.

'Well sir, the person asked to meet me later that evening; whoever it was told me they had some important information about the homicides.'

'Go on.' Edgeworth's fingers drummed on the desk.

'I know I should have reported it sir, but I thought I could handle it myself.'

Edgeworth leaned forward; his facial muscles hardening around his mouth; his lips forming a thin line.

'And___.'

Here Lisa took a few rapid breaths before taking a longer one.

'I walked along the lane toward Belton as directed, when a car came at full speed from behind me and, if it wasn't for a cyclist calling out; the car would have certainly killed me.'

Here she stopped, everything within her seemed to relax, and a great tiredness swept over her. It was done. Now she was no longer in bondage to her emotions, and at that point would have willingly accepted her suspension from further duties.

Edgeworth raised himself out of his chair; pushing it back, he strolled over to the window, his hands clasped behind his back.

Not a word was said; Lisa's heart began to pound in her ears.

Suddenly he spoke, but his voice had changed, becoming sympathetic and friendly.

'So what you are saying is that if you were an intended victim, then Kane Oakland, who doesn't drive, is off our books.'

'Yes Sir,' the relief she felt was so great she almost lost her balance as her legs became weak.

Edgeworth turned abruptly.

'Sit down,' he nodded towards a chair. 'Lisa, isn't it?'

She gave a nod and did as she was told, the weight of her body slipping into the chair gratefully. He sat down too and pulled his seat forward so he could lean over his desk. Picking up a pencil he rolled it around in his fingers whilst looking at her like some benevolent mentor.

'In my experience these things happen.' He allowed his words to sink in, emphasising his years in the department far outweighed hers.

'It happens, some plonker wanting to mess up an investigation by resorting to making stupid phone calls.'

Lisa sat stunned, her mouth opened and her words came out choked.

'But sir, someone tried to kill me.'

'Now Lisa, try to think clearly. If someone had tried to kill you they would have, you would have been a sitting duck on that road.'

'Someone called out to me.' Lisa was becoming desperate. 'If he hadn't I would have been killed.'

Silence followed. A twitch began under the inspector's left eye.

'Did you report it Pharies?' The tone had changed and so had his address.

She shook her head and looked down.

'There you see, a competent person like you would have reported it right way if you had been sure.' He put his pencil down and let his gaze travel over her head before closing the interview.

'Go home and take a few days off,' he said very paternally before adding, 'you've had a terrible shock.'

Lisa walked past P.C. Buzzard without a word. Someone shouted her name from a doorway. She ignored them both. Her tiredness was beginning to change into rage but this time not against herself, but against the man whose office she'd just left.

She sat in her car, her hands gripping the wheel tightly. Her thoughts no longer jumbled but forming little patterns. She reached across the car to a black case that held a phone directory and some road maps. Checking them, she then started the car.

After having a cup of strong coffee and a muffin at a transport café, she began to gather her thoughts. The directory and a map of Cheshire were spread before her and she began circling certain places on the map.

Two hours later, Lisa was standing before the huge iron gates of a grey stone building that supported the sign "Oakland Orphanage."

She wiped her mouth getting rid of a piece of sticky muffin and walked up the drive, leaving her car parked outside on the grass verge.

The house was typical of the turn of the century; big solid framed bay windows with overhanging eves, and a large door supporting a large brass knocker.

She looked around. The garden was well maintained. Near a copse of large oaks, a couple of swings, a slide and what looked like a sand pit.

Lisa lifted the heavy knocker and banged it down, hearing the noise echo down the hall inside; she waited. Lifting her gaze to the carved crucifix above the door, she was absolutely certain she had found what she was looking for. Ernest had described the essential details of the photo well.

The door cracked partly open and a woman in a grey headdress peered around it.

'Yes?' A strong Irish accent was unmistakable.

'My name is Lisa Pharies, and I need some help.'

The nun stepped back looking as if that request had been asked of her many times. She nodded, leading Lisa into a large hall with a black and white tiled floor that resembled marble. The nun pointed to an old monk's bench by the wall.

'Wait here,' she instructed. 'Miss Pharies did you say?'

Lisa nodded, wondering why she was being taken for a single person. She looked down at her gloved hands. The odd notion then struck her that it was probably only single women that came to visit here. For a moment she indulged in wishful thinking but didn't relish the thought of one having to leave one's offspring in this place.

Soon she was ushered into a pleasant room with large bays giving lovely views of the countryside. It had been made homely and welcoming, even with the half dozen statuettes of the Virgin Mary, some alone, some holding the Christ Child.

An older and more ample-sized woman also dressed in the same grey garb entered. She held out her plump hand. Lisa felt the warmth from it as she shook it.

'So my dear'! The nun waited for Lisa to speak.

After Lisa had made it perfectly clear she wasn't pregnant and in need of their services the elder nun's manner changed. Instead of the initial motherly approach, she became stiff and guarded.

'Well in for a penny in for a pound.' thought Lisa grimly, she had already stepped over the line with Edgeworth.

'It's about Kane Oakland.' She placed the emphasis on Oakland purposely, and then waited for the response.

Straight away there was a reaction.

'Has he had an accident?' the elderly nun said, showing signs of alarm

'No,' said Lisa but wondering if there would be any comfort in what she was about to impart.

The nun sat rigid, her hands tucked under her habit. It took a long time for everything to sink in about Kane's arrest but when the first question came, it was not expected.

'You are telling me that Kane was working at a Protestant Church?

'Well yes, I guess,' she could have shaken herself for not thinking about that before. 'Kane must have been a Roman Catholic, yes?'

The nun looked at her sourly. 'We are a Catholic order,' she said quietly.

Lisa managed a bleak smile, and got back to the subject.

'What can you tell me about him?'

A bell rang outside the room and the sound of children's voices filled the air.

'Tea, I think Miss Pharies,' said the nun getting up and ringing a small bell on the table. Almost immediately a head popped around the door; looked to see how many people there were, and disappeared.

Five minutes later she appeared with a tray of tea.

The elderly nun whose name Lisa got to know as Sister Martha began to relate what she herself knew of Kane.

'First you must understand I cannot tell you who the mother of Kane was. It was before my time and this is confidential information.'

'Single mother?' queried Lisa.

The nun waved her hand in front of her, indicating there had been enough said in that direction already.

'What I can tell you though, is that although Kane suffered a great deal of bullying and jokes at his expense, he always took it good-heartedly. He hasn't a morose bone in his poor twisted body. That's why I find it hard to think he may have harmed anyone.'

'One can change,' offered Lisa.

'Not Kane,' answered the nun with conviction. 'You are looking at the wrong person, God have mercy on the poor man.'

Lisa felt relieved by the answer and urged the nun to continue.

'There was a woman that used to come every Saturday morning and always seemed to single him out and he grew very fond of her, but like so many good doers she stopped coming after a time.'

Lisa ears perked up,

'What was she like?'

The nun stared at her for a moment before answering with a touch of annoyance.

'Goodness girl, do you ever stop to think of the many faces that pass though these doors?' she glared at Lisa before going on. 'Nobody wanted to adopt Kane, so he just stayed here helping with the odd jobs and the garden.'

'How did he come to get a job then?'

The question that Lisa asked hung in the air for a moment, before the nun answered. 'I really don't know, it was about the time I was sent back to the Mother House for contemplation.' She focussed her eyes on a statue of the Virgin Mary before continuing, 'Kane had already gone when I came back.'

'Gone?'

'Yes, some kind person had offered him a job and a home.'

She looked uncomfortable as she confessed it was a relief to them, but Lisa nodded in sympathy.

The nun folded her hands beneath her habit again and gazed searchingly at Lisa before asking.

'You did say he was employed by a Church of England priest didn't you.'

'A rector.' corrected Lisa;

'Yes of course,' the nun agreed, and then she stopped for a second with a confused look. 'I really cannot see our order permitting that.'

'But he was of age to go anywhere he wanted, wasn't he,' stated Lisa before asking, 'was he declared unfit or anything?'

The nun looked aghast. 'Heavens no, he was just slow that was all.'

It seems there was nothing else to find out, so Lisa said her goodbyes. But before she left remarked,

'There must be a lot of people with the surname of Oakland I guess.'

The nun just gave her a tired smile.

Back in the car Lisa sat awhile, the engine turned off. She gazed ahead along the road she'd come. Thinking about what had been said.

Kane had indeed been born there and taken the name of the orphanage for his surname. Because of his many handicaps, no one had wanted to adopt him so he'd grown up there, eventually working in the gardens.

Lisa felt as if she was making some progress even if it was on her own. She'd dismissed Edgeworth. She'd been honest with him and that was all she needed to do.

As for Robin, that was another matter. One she didn't want to think about just yet.

She started the car.

'Could Kane's visitor have been Rachael?' she wondered, and if so the next question would surely open a Pandora's Box.

Chapter 30

Emily watched her daughter out of the corner of her eye. She longed to reach out and touch the unruly head of hair.

Lisa looked up from the article she was reading.

'Ok Mum?' she asked.

Emily nodded and pulled her paralysed hand closer to her body, then gazed into the fire. Sometimes she wished she had never recovered from the stroke. It would have been easier on Lisa; letting her daughter get on with her normal life. Emily felt herself becoming more and more of a burden, and couldn't see any solution unless she went into a nursing home. Knowing her daughter, that would not happen. Lisa would work herself into an early grave first. Once she had thought her twin sister May lucky that she hadn't had to face the trials of aging; but after seeing Robin, she knew May would have battled with anything just to see her son grow up.

The fire blazed, sending a hot spark onto the hearth. She watched its heat cooling and dying. That's how May's life had been; full of energy one moment then fading away from cancer the next.

Emily had recognised Robin from the very first time he'd set foot in the house. He was the image of the man who had abandoned her sister, who had found herself pregnant. She hated Jamie Armstrong with a passion, and held no sympathy when he was killed in a road accident.

However the more Robin came around, the more she began to see May in him; sometimes in a certain look; the shape of his lips and his soft compassionate nature.

Lisa was standing up and looking at the clock. Leaving the room, she came back with her coat on.

The doorbell rang. It was Rita, and Emily knew she had come to sit with her. She liked Rita; it was easier to communicate with someone who had been trained to look after people in her condition.

As the front door closed behind her, Lisa's faith in her ability to tell Robin the truth faded a little. What if he was actually in love with her? Lisa sighed; whom was she kidding? Even an old maid like her knew the difference between passion and friendship. He'd never displayed any of the former, only a great deal of the latter.

Lisa walked over to the Rectory and knocked on the heavy door. John opened it, his usual pale face going paler on seeing the policewoman.

'Can I speak to Robin?' she asked; a little too quickly making her words stumble over each other.

John raised an eyebrow; looking at her for a moment before telling her Robin was in the church.

The police constable, who was guarding the off-limits area in the churchyard, touched the peak of his hat in recognition as she passed by. Lisa tried the main door of the church. It was locked. She then made her way around to the other small door on the west side of the church, which was ajar.

A musty smell mingled with lemon polish lingered in the passageway and became fainter as she entered the main building.

Robin was piling up some hymnbooks. He turned, smiling openly when he saw whom it was.

'Lisa love, what a nice surprise,' his long steps brought him quickly to her side.

She didn't meet his eyes, instead asked him to enter one of the pews with her and listen to what she had to say.

Puzzled, he obeyed.

'Robin, you may be upset by what I have to tell you, but it has to be done.'

She saw his startled look and sensed him stiffen, becoming guarded as if expecting bad news.

'Here goes,' she thought taking a deep breath.

'You have a photograph of your mother in your room Robin, don't you?' Lisa knew that she was treading on thin ice now but there was no way of avoiding it. Robin however didn't seem to consider his privacy had been invaded.

'The photograph, yes,' he brought up his hand and stroked his forehead. 'I have always treasured it; I feel she is watching over me. A bit silly isn't it?'

This was going to be harder than she had thought, Lisa realized.

She placed one hand over his and said as gently as she could. 'I've something important to tell you.' Lisa squeezed his hand and her words tumbled out.

'Your real mother was my Auntie May.'

Disbelief, astonishment and bewilderment registered on his face. He'd pulled his hand away abruptly.

'What on earth are you talking about and what makes you think that?' He looked so lost that all Lisa wanted to do was to fling her arms around him, but instinct warned her against it.

'I always knew my mother had a twin sister that died at an early age,' explained Lisa. 'We have the same identical photograph in our album at home that you have.'

Robin covered his face with his hands and bent forward.

Lisa went on. 'My mother knows who you are, I guess she could see things in you we couldn't, probably a likeness to your father as well as her sister.'

Astonishment swept his face, it was all too much and he wasn't ready to take it all in.

'I have to be on my own Lisa,' he said fiercely.

'Oh, oh yes I understand.' She stood up and was about to leave him alone, but to her surprise he pushed past her instead.

'I need to go for a walk,' his tall figure sagged a little around the head and shoulders as he strode down the aisle to the doorway. Lisa noticed he didn't bow as usual as he walked in front of the alter steps, but just kept on going as if on some private and urgent mission.

She sat where she was for a while after he'd left, feeling slightly guilty. Was he glad to know whose genes he possessed, or was he sorry? She had already come to terms with the fact he was her cousin. Would he do so as easily?

'Enough to shock you to pieces,' thought Lisa sympathetically.

A sound at the back of the church made her turn but nothing moved, only a cold draft swept against Lisa's legs from some door opening and closing.

She got up and walked down the aisle. Then, she turned into the small Norman room that Ernest and Rita had talked about. She looked at the writing on the wall. Although badly flaked by time and wear, she could still make out the golds, reds and greens of the illuminated design of the opening first letter. It was somewhat faded over time but nevertheless still painstakingly detailed in all its glory. Not one word of the writing made any sense to her. She shivered, feeling the cold damp emanating from the ancient walls.

Ernest put down the phone at number eleven after talking to Rita. She was insisting he take a pie to the Rectory and to check up on what was going on there.

He found the pie in the fridge. It smelt good and he was a little put out that it wasn't made for him. He liked apple pie.

Dutifully he placed it on the table and looked for some sort of carrier. He wasn't going to carry a pie in his hands for all to see. A brown paper bag that had held some new potatoes lay empty on the floor next to the fridge.

'Just the thing,' he contemplated and in went the pie.

Leaving number eleven and walking up the road towards the Rectory, he spotted Robin hurrying down the church steps. He called, but Robin ignored him and hastened away in the opposite direction.

On reaching the Rectory, Ernest was surprised to find himself facing John, as he had half expected Rachael to open the door.

He thrust the brown bag at John, saying quickly 'Rita thought you might like this.'

'Best come in then.' John shuffled his way back into the overly warm library.

Ernest made himself comfortable in the chair opposite to John's and assessed his host. It was clear John was in no state to be taxed with questions, for he looked frail and at his wits end. But from past experience, Ernest knew that this was good ground for gaining information when defences were weak.

'You will kill yourself if you bottle it all up John.' His voice was soothing but purposeful; learned from many years of police interrogations.

John seemed to shrink into himself, his pupils dilating and his eyes staring and unfocussed.

'You wouldn't understand.' he whispered.

'Try me.' Ernest replied.

'I am worried about Rachael, I fear she is falling apart and I don't know what to do.'

'Do you want Lisa to pop in?' suggested Ernest.

John shook his head. 'She was here a few moments ago looking for Robin and I told her he was in the church.'

'Where is Rachael?' Ernest asked, eyes crossing the room to the half open door expecting her to come in with coffee.

John smiled wistfully before answering, 'gone over to the church to tidy Kane's room'.

Realizing there was no coffee in the offing, Ernest decided he wasn't going to go home empty handed.

He leaned forward and looked directly at his host.

'Why did you tell Rita that you didn't understand the writing on the church wall John?'

A pin could have dropped as John's mouth gaped open, but before he could utter a word Ernest had jumped in again.

'It's all about LEVITICUS___, chapter eighteen wasn't it?'

For a brief moment he thought he'd overstepped the mark and John was about to have a heart attack, for John's face registered great pain as his shoulders sank forward.

It seemed an eternity before John raised his head. With a look of utter resignation, he stared back at Ernest.

'It's Rachael; she has become obsessed by the text.'

Ernest's mind jumped one step ahead of itself, as he juggled the pieces of information into some sort of pattern.

Did John think that Rachael might have killed all those people from some pious notion? Was she not at the Rectory that night after all when Gina was killed? His mind tumbled on. John would have known he was giving her an alibi; by saying she was with him.

Suddenly the image of Lisa in the church alone with Rachel flashed through his mind. He jumped up and shook John's shoulder, yelling at him as he made for the door.

'Quick John, phone the police, I think Lisa is in danger.'

John shouted after him,

'She will be all right, Jeanne is over there too.'

Something akin to a bomb exploded within Ernest's mind.

Chapter 31

Ernest flew through the front door of the Rectory into the arms of Robin.

'Steady Ernest.' Robin backed off, but within a fleeting second found his jacket grabbed and him being pulled along by it.

A villager making a trip to the post box with a handful of letters wasn't quick enough to stand aside from the onslaught that hit her. The letters scattered at her feet.

Robin bent over to retrieve them but Ernest gave him another tug.

'For God's sake Robin, Lisa is in danger,' he shouted furiously.

The woman, about to retrieve her fallen letters was again thrust aside, this time by John. The rector pushed past her without a word, one large foot trampling a white envelope into the damp grass. She stood mouth open, words failing as the three made for the steps of the church.

Must be an emergency, common sense told her. The rector would never behave like that otherwise. The worst thing she could think of was another murder and the twinge of excitement in relating this next piece of village gossip swept through her. Letters scooped up she was now more than anxious to confide in anyone who would listen.

Robin was the first to reach the massive main door of the church. He struggled to push his hand into his pocket only to bring out a set of car keys. Frustrated, he glanced over at John, who was unable to speak through his laboured breathing, but just shook his head.

Over the centuries the same old studded door with its large iron hinges and lock had barred many from entry, as it did during the Reformation and Civil War, only to lead to many deaths.

'Quick, the Norman door.' Robin loped off disappearing around the side of the church.

Ernest felt the years slipping away as his legs moved with a will of their own to catch up with him. Nobody noticed John stopping; his hand clutching his chest as he leaned against the old stone wall for support.

'Oh Lord, not now,' he whispered as the pain began to travel down his arm, but there was no great vision to comfort him, only the face of Rachael as she had been years before, black shiny hair trailing over her white shoulders. Then in the middle of the terrible pain that was now ripping him apart, Kane's face came into focus, his large mouth twisted and grinning in triumph. Then he was looking into Rachael's eyes, their blackness swallowing him up into the depths of oblivion.

'God forgive me.' The words swept out with his last breath and were picked up by a slight breeze that blew over the ancient gravestones causing a faint sound of nature's laughter as the leaves danced.

Robin turned the iron ring to open the Norman door. It creaked. He stopped, waited, and then tried again. After a few more attempts, the latch opened and he and Ernest pushed against the heavy door. It swung open slowly making a grating noise. Ernest cringed and stepped through the archway.

Nothing in the whole world could have prepared him for what he encountered. Both he and Robin stiffened in shock and disbelief.

Lisa was standing, her back against the south wall of the small room, behind her the old Latin writing, faint and peeling. Her terrified eyes moved towards them; a tiny spark of hope flared and died.

'Too late.' Jeanne stepped out of the shadows, a long solid brass candlestick raised above her head. Robin took a step forward, but

Ernest's hand restrained him; his mind working overtime. He had been convinced it was Rachael behind all the deaths until John had mentioned Jeanne. Then, for a first time in his life he realised he'd miscalculated. Jeanne had had access to everything, but what then was her motive?

Nothing added up. What reason had Jeanne to commit murder?

Humour her, play for time his instinct told him. Don't make any sudden moves; the candlestick was to close to Lisa's head.

He tried to calm his voice.

'Jeanne you don't want to hurt Lisa, do you? Think of Emily and what it would do to her.'

Jeanne's eyes narrowed, a muscle twitched in her throat. Then she spat out words filled with violent emotion; the candlestick arched backwards.

'She has to die, its God's will.'

Lisa closed her eyes. Ernest and Robin froze, and then a soft sound was heard as a figure emerged from behind the curtain that closed off the room from the main church.

'Put it down.' Rachael commanded as she stepped forward.

Jeanne glared at her. Then with her voice taking on a distinct air of misplaced authority, she replied,

'I have to. You of all people should know that, after reading God's words,' her voice now becoming almost a screech; insanity beginning to show itself.

Rachael's gaze rested on the writing on the wall.

'You must have been through my personal files.' Her voice was now steady and quiet as she added, 'you've read my translations, haven't you.'

Jeanne nodded, the candlestick wavering in the air.

'God chose you and I, Rachael. I hadn't cleaned His house for Him properly. He sent you to me Rachael with your knowledge of Latin don't you see, so I could understand fully what he wanted of me.'

Jeanne looked triumphantly at Ernest, then at Robin; willing them both to understand as well.

'Read it Rachael, read it___, so they know I have to do it.'

Rachael stepped closer, Jeanne watching every step until Rachael was facing the wall. Then she read out aloud in a clear voice, no hesitation or fear, but firm and calm.

'None of you shall approach any that are near of kin, to uncover their nakedness. I am the Lord.' Rachael, translating read on; line after line.

When she had finished, Jeanne gave an odd laugh and added,

'Brother with sister.' She looked around at Lisa wildly. 'I will cleanse God's House of this Eve for tempting him.' She threw a dark look at Robin. The atmosphere in the room became oppressive, the fear almost giving off an odour of its own. Rachael broke the impasse.

'Oh Jeanne, how innocent you are in your false belief of God's wishes. Do you not know you have been far closer to the real sinner than you could ever have imagined.'

'What?' For a brief moment the candlestick was lowered a little. Ernest waited his chance, hoping whatever Rachael had to say would distract Jeanne and give him an opening.

'When John and I were young our mother died.'

Jeanne was now getting visibly irritated,

'What's that got to do with sinning?' She breathed angrily, the weight in her hands beginning to tell.

'Patience Jeanne,' Rachael half smiled at her. 'You shall have your clean house of God after I've told you my story.'

It appeared to pacify her and she quietened as Rachael continued.

'John and I were brought up with only a father. To cut a long story short, he was our sole educator and disciplinarian. Cruel and self-opinionated, we were kept away from the day to day life of the village and only had each other for companionship.' Rachael inhaled deeply, continuing in a manner suggesting her resignation to the consequences of what she was about to say next.

'I became pregnant and was sent away. My father could not deal with the consequences. The child was taken from me at birth and when I came home my father never looked at me or talked to me again.' She stopped, her eyes now trained on the writing on the wall; her next words revealed all her pent-up and hidden anguish.

'It was my brother's child you see.'

No one was prepared for the bloody consequences that followed. Jeanne moved like lightening swinging the raised candlestick, bringing it down on Rachael's head. Rachael uttered a weak cry as her body crumpled to the stone floor.

Then, in a quick movement, Jeanne slammed down the weapon and leapt forward, disappearing into the nave of the church. Ernest and Lisa started after her, calling to Robin to stay with Rachael.

Robin knelt down beside Rachael. Through her death rattle she was still trying to say something.

'Kane,' was all she was able to utter. She died in Robin's arms as he murmured the last rites. He closed the lids over her glazed eyes. Then after standing for a moment looking at her, he followed after the others into the nave.

Everywhere was quiet; the door to the tower was ajar. Robin took the worn stone steps of the circular staircase two at a time.

He froze at the top step, sensing any sudden movement could invite danger.

Ernest was coaching Jeanne away from the tower battlements.

'Let me help you Jeanne, you are not well.' He held out his hand as an offering of support.

Lisa moved a step forward.

'Get away from me.' Jeanne's eyes were wild as she turned to Lisa. 'Fornicator, you're another Eve who destroys the Lord's servants.'

Ernest kept is voice level and friendly.

'Jeanne you have it wrong. Robin and Lisa are cousins, not brother and sister.'

For a second Jeanne released her grip on the stone behind her as she considered his statement, then tensed up again.

'Thou shalt not uncover the nakedness of thy aunt's offspring.' She stated triumphantly, unsure of the wording but sure she'd remembered the meaning.

Lisa rushed in, her voice denoting impatience and anger; all her exasperation now released.

'For God's sake woman, Robin and I didn't go to bed together.'

So startled was the response that Jeanne's watchful eyes left Ernest as she tried to refocus her remaining revulsion of Lisa.

Ernest leapt forward but not quick enough, for Jeanne had seen him move. She turned sharply and flung herself over the castellated edge of the tower.

They didn't witness her falling as they turned quickly and raced back down the same steps that had witnessed so many other tragedies in the past.

They passed Rachael's bloodstained body. Rushing outside, Robin stopped as he found John slumped against the church wall, while Ernest and Lisa discovered the crumpled and broken body of Jeanne.

A fine drizzle of rain had started, bringing with it a cold dampness and grey skies. Lisa reached for her mobile and asked for Detective Inspector Edgeworth.

Chapter 32

A ray of light distorted itself through the pane of fault glass in the window. It danced across the round dark oak table and climbed Ernest's beer mug.

He watched as it tinted the amber liquid in his glass, and then disappeared. His mood reflected the sunray's passage. He felt as if he had stepped onto a merry-go-round and had suddenly been thrown off. He wouldn't have felt too bad if it was just himself he was thinking about, but it wasn't; it was Rita. Guilt hit him hard in the stomach like a stone and he could feel the weight of it pulling him down.

Suddenly he was conscious of Rita watching him across the pub table. She had been unusually quiet all morning and, even after suggesting a drink, the silence prevailed.

All around them, the hum of tongues wagging filled the bar room with a constant drone; like bees around a hive.

The Horseshoe was unusually full for a weekday, and it seemed to Ernest that the whole village had turned out. There was no need for him to guess the topic of conversation; the shaking of heads and the eager way they leaned over the tables to listen to any gossip, told it all.

Finding out it was one of their own that was responsible for the homicides, came as a nasty shock. Yet it wasn't long before each gave their own first hand account of Jeanne's character. Most revealed that they had always thought her odd and much too religious. Then came the nodding of heads again about how dangerous it was when people took the Bible literally. Jeanne it seemed could be passed off as totally unstable, but the rector and his sister's deaths left them a little uneasy. Of these two, not much was said apart from agreeing it was a tragedy. It was the general consensus that Rachael's good deeds and her devotion to the parish would be rewarded in Heaven. Little did they know the real truth, for Rachael's and John's secret went to the grave with them. Those that witnessed Rachael's death and heard her confession had already sealed it up in their hearts, never to be told. They all agreed Rachael and John had suffered enough whilst they lived, so that they should now rest quietly in death

Not far from the table where Rita and Ernest were sitting, Geoff Lewis leaned against the bar; his hand in his pocket ready to fill anyone's glass again who showed signs of imparting any other titbits of information. He smiled at the knot of people milling around him like some great benefactor. Now and then he would cast a furtive glance over at the couple sitting silently and would have readily given a month's wages to read their minds.

Gerry Platt, once the loud joke-cracking publican, was now quite restrained; his head constantly lowered over the taps or cleaning glasses. There was no sexy flirting barmaid offering glimpses of her attributes and giving rise to lecherous flights of fancy to the young and old alike of the opposite sex.

Donna Platt was much more visible, shouting orders and rattling the till with great efficiency. A lot had changed in the village as well as the pub. It was said that terrible rows could be heard in Stan Breasley's house, since his wife had been persuaded to join the AA. It was murmured that the worm had turned since the death of her daughter.

A hand slipped over the polished table and came to rest over Ernest's large one.

'Penny for your thoughts luv'! Rita had leaned forward, looking at him intently. Ernest clasped her fingers, curling them into his own.

'Oh Rita, I feel as if I have let you down, I should never have let myself become obsessed with thinking I could do better than Edgeworth.' Rita's laugh sounded like music to Ernest's ears, his heart leapt as he caught the old sparkle in her eyes.

'Whatever am I going to do with you Ernest, you are not going to change and I don't want you to. I just want that same little boy with his shiny jersey sleeves I fell in love with a very long time ago'.

'Shiny sleeves?' Ernest went red.

'Oh you remember how you would rub your nose along your sleeve, and heaven help anyone that remarked on it.' Rita looked him straight in the eyes until he lowered his own in embarrassment. But he knew Rita was on his side, and decided to open up.

'I was convinced it was Rachael who did the killing; everything seemed to point that way. She must have recognized that the photograph in Robin's room was identical to the one Emily had. So why did she keep quiet about it? And then, why lie about Kane watching TV?' He stopped at this point to take a long swig of his beer. 'The wax on Gina's sleeve kept bringing me back to the church and I was convinced she had been murdered inside it. That led me on to consider those people who had full time access to the church. The writing on the wall, that I knew Rachael could translate better than anyone, got me thinking about those with religious fervour and who fitted the bill best. She came out number one.'

Rita broke in. 'But you told me at the last moment you realized you were wrong and it was Jeanne who was the murderer.' Ernest sat back; shadows of regret flitting over his face as he continued his explanation.

'It was when John mentioned that Jeanne cleaned both the Rectory and the church, that I remembered seeing translations of Latin to English on his desk. Jeanne could have well read them and recognised the same words on the church wall. She also saw the photographs, but like Rachael she remained quiet. I asked myself 'Why?'

He didn't get any further in his explanations. Rita had spied Lisa pushing her way towards them and gave Ernest a kick under the table to make him aware of the approaching company.

He caught the barmaid's attention by raising his hand indicating another round; a few more signals between the two and the barmaid understood exactly what he wanted.

'Hello you two,' Lisa plonked herself down, then proceeded to scan the bar ignoring Geoff Lewis's wave as she did so.

'Busy,' she commented sipping on the beer that appeared.

'Who's with Emily?' It was Rita who was quizzing Lisa, leaving Ernest wondering why he'd never bothered to think of asking.

'No wonder I need Rita to humanise me,' he thought to himself.

Lisa smiled, 'I called Social Services to see what they could offer. They were just great and a very nice lady is going to cover for me. I don't know why I had such an aversion to making use of their services before.'

'Probably because it made you feel you were not coping,' Rita chipped in, her explanation hinting at her past work experience. Holding their attention, she continued, 'it's quite common for a daughter, son or even a husband to feel they are not coping when they have to resort to the Social. It's much easier on their emotional makeup to have someone they know to sit in for them. Your mother knew Jeanne; she attended the same church and could tell her about all the goings-on in the village. It was like bringing the outside in.'

Ernest suddenly felt an overwhelming pride in Rita.

'Well I've learnt one lesson,' said Lisa looking around for someone to serve them again. 'I shall want references signed and delivered before anyone goes near my mother in future.'

Lisa coughed and cleared her throat. 'I suppose we should make a toast, but somehow I don't feel like it. I just keep thinking of poor Rachael and John.'

'The need to love and be loved is very strong,' mused Rita, quietly reflecting on her own past and Ernest's. 'John and Rachael were thrown together, probably not understanding the awakening of their sexuality. Just imagine poor Rachael when the child was born, she would be only sixteen and insisting on seeing it.' There was silence as they each reflected on how it would be for so young a mother to look upon a deformed baby. 'She must have thought she was being punished, but a child does not have to be pretty to invoke strong maternal feelings.' Rita was speaking with great understanding.

'What are you saying?' Ernest queried, 'are you implying she regretted giving her baby up, so she visited the Orphanage regularly in hopes of seeing him.' He frowned before uttering, 'but surely the nuns would know who she was.'

Lisa, picking up the thread of the conversation adding, 'it seems when John and Rachael's father died, John changed his religion and Rachael followed suit. They even changed their name from Manning to Richards. No wonder the nuns didn't connect Rachael to Kane. In some way we don't understand, John needed to devote himself to God and eventually took Holy Orders. The strain of trying to bury his past and live a sin-free life caught up with him however, and he suffered a minor heart attack. But with Rachael's support of his work, he managed to carry on. In the meantime it got more and more difficult for Rachael to catch glimpses of her son, and when their local gravedigger died, she seized on the opportunity of having Kane where she could look after him.'

'So Kane never knew of his relationship to Rachael?' enquired Rita.

'No, oh no___; neither did John,' added Lisa.

'Oh for Christ's sake,' exclaimed Rita, a little too loudly, drawing glances from the occupant's of an adjacent table.

Undaunted by Rita's outburst, Lisa continued, 'everything was going well, especially when Robin came to help. Although Rachael wasn't keen on having him, it did take the strain off John. But then something happened she could never have dreamed of.'

'Gina Breasley's murder I guess,' added Ernest. 'That would be unsettling, but it would be Sharon's murder that would really begin to frighten Rachael.'

'Why?' Rita enquired, 'Did she think Kane responsible?'

'No,' Lisa replied. 'It was John that Rachael suspected as having done it.' Both Ernest and Rita were obviously taken aback by this revelation

'What do you mean?' asked Rita looking puzzled 'are you saying they each suspected the other and both had become unhinged by the writing ___; the guilt being all too much for them.'

'Something like that; we will never know the real truth, but I think each tried to cover for the other,' added Lisa. 'Rachael had interpreted the Latin scripture written on the wall and thought it was God's way of reminding her that they had both committed a dreadful sin. The fact was she became obsessed by it.'

A new understanding came over Ernest's face; it was all now starting to add up. Rita chipped in suddenly, 'John probably pretended he couldn't read the writing on the wall because he didn't want any focus on it, thinking Rachael was becoming unhinged by the translation.'

Lisa picked up her glass and downed her remaining drink. Ernest indicated another round, but she shook her head before saying. 'But unknown to both of them someone else was influenced by the writing.'

'Jeanne?' piped up Rita.

'Yes, nobody ever thought of Jeanne.' Ernest continued. 'You know what she was like; quiet, good at her job, liked everything in its place and devoted to the church. All in all a good clean living woman with high morals. But her fundamental religious beliefs eventually destroyed the balance of her mind. She saw her job cleaning the church as the very reason for her existence. She had been given the role of keeping God's house clean and took it extremely seriously. Imagine her reaction when she found a paper in English of Rachael's translation of the writing on the wall. That was all she needed to send her over the edge.'

Lisa gave a nervous giggle. 'Good choice of words.'

Rita looked at her sourly and picked up the conversation.

'You mean she was trying to clean out anything that God had ordained sinful from the church.'

Lisa sighed, 'not just any church, but God's House. She'd probably guessed or had been given the hint by Gina's mother about what was going on in their home. Having killed her, Sharon became her next victim and Glen's murder speaks for itself.'

Rita frowned. 'But why Gina: Surely she was innocent?'

'Yes, that's what I thought,' said Lisa, 'but the police psychiatrist said Jeanne saw each of the women as Eve and without them, Adam wouldn't have been tempted.'

'Crickey,' ventured Rita sitting back, all the wind now taken out of her sails.

'So poor old Glen didn't stand a chance, after he'd brought his lover to church,' Ernest added.

Rita fiddled with her empty glass, her voice low. 'I guess you were the next Eve on her list,' her gaze directed at Lisa, who shuddered.

'Yes, her first attempt at running me over failed and I reckon she thought it pre-ordained when she discovered me alone in the church. If it hadn't been for Rachael's confession, I wouldn't be sitting here.'

'I think Rachael knew that, yes___, she saved you,' added Rita.

Lisa and Ernest's faces reflected their own thoughts on the horrific events surrounding Jeanne's final attack that day and all three sat silent for a while immersed in their own thoughts.

Robin entered the pub and spotted the three of them in the corner of the room. He sidled over to them and sat down beside Lisa. All four of them talked for a while before Robin said. 'The greatest thing one can do is to lay down one's life for another.'

'Do you think she did it on purpose Robin?' Lisa asked. He put his arm around her, giving her a hug.

'What will happen to Kane now?' Rita asked; her face full of concern.

Robin looked down at his glass, 'I honestly don't know, he is quite traumatised by everything, especially the absence of Rachael. Unfortunately he may have to be put into care, then who knows,' his shoulders dropped in resignation. He looked around and spotted somebody standing at the bar giving Lisa a slight dig with his foot, he said.

'Now my cousin, there's a very nice young man over there, hoping to catch your attention if I'm not mistaken.'

All heads at the table turned to look at the red-haired farmer standing by the bar looking their way.

Lisa coloured and looked at Robin who was now nudging her forward in that general direction.

The End.